FUN
&
GAMES

D1571179

DAVID MICHAEL SLATER

LIBRARY TALES PUBLISHING
NEW YORK, NY

FUN & GAMES

Published by:
Library Tales Publishing, Inc.
244 5th Avenue, Suite Q222
New York, NY 10001
www.LibraryTalesPublishing.com

For general information on our other products and services, please contact our Customer Care Department at 1-800-754-5016, or fax 917-463-0892. For technical support, please visit www.LibraryTalesPublishing.com

Library Tales Publishing also publishes its books in a variety of electronic formats. Every content that appears in print is available in electronic books.

ISBN-13: 978-0615774152
ISBN-10: 0615774156

PRINTED IN THE UNITED STATES OF AMERICA

You are free and that is why you are lost.

— Franz Kafka

PREFACE/DISCLAIMER

If what follows is a mess, I apologize, but as these pages will represent my life so far, it would only be appropriate. "Write what you know!" Dad always told the young writers who sought his advice. So there's that, too.

And though my father would have scorned a book prefaced by disclaimers, I feel compelled to offer a few: 1) broken hand; 2) fractured eye socket; 3) ears still ringing from concussion; 4) black and purple nose stuffed with gauze; and, last but not least, 5) crippling grief.

And now that you're feeling sorry for me, I'll tell you the real reason all of this will surely strike you as a train wreck. If I may adapt a familiar phrase: the engineer had his head up his ass for eighteen years.

Some people find train wrecks compelling. I'm counting on that. If you can imagine my face at all right now, you already know that things are going to get ugly.

PART I

❪❪ Kids, go upstairs and find something useful to do."
     This was a phrase I heard frequently in our Squirrel Hill home. The order was always issued by my mother, usually from the curtains next to the front door (through which she watched for deranged fans coming to meet or marry my father). She also said it just about every time the doorbell rang. It got to the point where the three of us simply headed up to the third floor at the sound of the chime, conditioned like Pavlov's dog.

I'm not sure 'useful' is the best word to describe the kind of things we did upstairs. Case in point: the first Friday night in June, 1983, the night before my Bar Mitzvah was supposed to have taken place.

"Rip the dude's intestines out," Jake suggested. "We'll strangle him with them." He had forty-one pennies stacked on his elbow, poised to break The Fonz's cousin's record for catching the most in a single swoop of the arm.

"Dude, that's sick," Cory replied, "and hold up. We should discuss this first. It's like Coach Lombardi said, 'Individual commitment to a *group* effort,' right? 'That's what makes a team —'"

"Shut your ass with those effing quotes!" Milo screamed from behind his manuals, charts, and graphs.

Pennies went flying in all directions. Cory dove for one like it was a pass from Terry Bradshaw. When he hit the floor, my baseball light fixture nearly fell off the ceiling.

My friends and I were in ninth grade. They were fourteen—I was a birthday behind, having skipped kindergarten. It was Jake Baker, Cory Minor, Milo Atkins, and me.

The main purpose of the evening was to continue a long-running game of *Dungeons and Dragons*. These were always fairly chaotic affairs involving the rolling of many oddly shaped dice, the consulting of cryptic manuals, and a great deal of furious debate. But two other highly complex tasks were also on tap that night. The first was an evaluation of the better-looking girls in our grade. This required the passing back and forth of a chart circulated from Health class with columns in which to mark a score for the following categories: Face, Chest, Butt, Eyes, Mouth, Hair, Clothes, Overall Body, and lastly, for tie-breaking purposes, Personality. On the back was an appendix created by Dougie Marlin to settle disputes that arose from the dissemination of earlier versions of the chart. I remember under 'Chest' it said that voting was for size and shape alone—and that points couldn't be added because a girl frequently didn't wear a bra, purposely kept extra buttons open on her tops, intentionally brushed past boys in the hall with her boobs, or pressed them into you when you hugged her.

The other activity was called "The Purity Test," which was a list of 100 questions that determined what was called one's "Purity Rating." A score of zero indicated absolute purity, while a score of one hundred signified ultimate depravity, neither of which was in the realm of possibility for any real human being, at least any we knew. The hope was for a respectably high score, which meant one checked the yes box for a fair number of questions. Anything in the low fifties was passable for a ninth-grader, though in no way impressive. Dom Lambert supposedly got an 81, which no one really believed, but no one really doubted, either.

Rumor had it he fooled around with his cousins. The point of a decent score was to signal an adventurous nature, not to be disgusting.

There were many questions that were givens, things like, "Have you ever lied to your parents?" and "Have you ever seen a naked picture of a member of the opposite sex?" Of course, "Have you ever masturbated?" could be taken for granted as well, but people (other than Milo) tended to count that one and keep going without comment. And then there was always, "Would you perform oral sex on yourself if you could?" This is why the test was typically taken in at least semi-private—but only semi because some questions we aspired to answer yes to publicly. These included the likes of, "Have you ever seen a porno?", "Have you ever gotten drunk enough to puke?", and all of the sex questions: "Have you ever had sex in a car? On an airplane? Outside? In your parents' bed?"

The seemingly innocent question, "Have you ever kissed two different girls within twenty-four hours?" was currently causing controversy because kids looking for loopholes wanted to count mother- and sister-kisses. It was later revised to "French kissed," by Dougie Marlin, who was also the facilitator for the Purity Test. I happened to be present when he was drafting a new version with this change. He looked at me after altering the term and said, "I kid you not, bro: if Olivia were my sister, I'd totally put the moves on her. I swear to God, I'd have a check in the incest box so freakin' fast."

The questions no one wanted to answer affirmatively, privately or not, were often the sort that sent us to our giant dictionary, the one that sat like a great stone slab on an old music stand in my mom's second floor office—words like *hermaphrodite*, *bestiality*, and *cunnilingus*. Earlier that same evening, we used it to confirm Jake's impressive knowledge of the expression, *menage-à-trois*. Dad stuck his head in the room while were poring over the definition. He scratched his beard and said, "I'm really impressed with you guys. Most kids your age don't even know what the word 'dictionary' means and don't know how to find out." He observed us for a moment then, no doubt wondering why we looked as if we'd been caught dragging a still twitching corpse away from the scene of a crime. He scratched his beard again. Then he left us to our own devices. We sprinted back upstairs.

Though that night began in this fairly typical manner, 'typical' doesn't remotely describe how things turned out.

In D & D, the lives of all characters are eventually placed in jeopardy. We had to know when to drop our distractions and get serious about how many "hit points" we had left, especially with Milo as "Dungeon Master" (or Dungeon Master-Bator, as he insisted on being called). Losing a character was no laughing matter. Peter Buckwalter had, only weeks earlier, lost a level nineteen wizard who'd survived for six months before being felled by a type V demon. We heard he actually cried when it happened and that he tried to pummel his DM. No one at school made fun of Peter, though. In fact, he was treated rather deferentially for a few days, as if his mother or dog had died.

Milo had introduced our characters to a soothsayer, so we were on high alert. What was going to happen was obvious: he was going to turn into a Homunculus or Shambling Mound, or some other heinous beast. Milo's parents were into palm reading, astrological signs, and the like, and they thoroughly embarrassed him. Whenever a character appeared in our games even remotely connected to the occult, an attack of some sort was imminent.

This is why Jake suggested evisceration so quickly. Cory's Dwarf Fighter had great ability scores in Strength and Constitution, so we often suggested he use brute force at the first sign of danger, regardless of what his beloved Vince Lombardi might have to say about it. Cory himself was freakishly strong. He was no dwarf, though, at already nearly six-feet and one hundred and eighty pounds.

Jake's Elf had great Charisma and Dexterity.

I was a human mage whose only useful trait was Intelligence.

"Hey, Jon," Cory said, getting up while fishing pennies out of his hair. "What about maybe just casting a paralysis spell on him?"

I was striking Conan the Barbarian poses with a four-foot wooden broadsword the three of us made at school and traded around. I chopped the air with it and said, "I know, let's hack the guy's head off and shit down his neck."

"Jesus, Schwartz," Cory gagged, "get me a barf bag. And go easy with that thing. It's all fun and games until—"

"Holy hell!" Milo suddenly cried, cutting Cory off. He leapt to his feet, staring, aghast, at the ratings chart. "What kind of back-assward bullcrap is this?" he demanded, lurching wildly across the room. "That *asswipe*, Schumacher, gave Jennifer Paris a TEN in Overall Body! The girl's a freakin' *carpenter's dream!* He gave her a THREE in Chest, so how in the—*ARRRGGHHH!*"

Milo's diatribe was abruptly terminated when he stepped on the sharp point of the infamous D & D triangular die. Some of the tiny pyramids had their points flattened, but this was a cheap one with very sharp tips. Milo instantly forgot about Jennifer Paris and began hopping around my bedroom, unleashing a torrent of colorful expletives. But then he landed with his good foot on half a broken pencil, debris from earlier pencil fighting competitions. He collapsed in a shrieking heap, then started rolling from side to side on his back, cradling his injured feet. Cory, Jake, and I all wound up in similar fetal positions trying to stop the abdominal pain induced by our cackling.

I happened to be facing the door when it opened. There appeared, impossibly, Shoshana Silver, one of Olivia's friends. She stepped into the room, smirking, with her eyes cast down at the carpet, cool and coy.

The paralysis spell was cast on us.

Our free glimpses of Olivia and her crew — they were in eleventh grade, a mix of late sixteens and early seventeens — were almost always courtesy of loosely choreographed hallway crossings. Never before had any of them actually ventured into my room.

Shoshana was nearly five foot ten, lanky, long-faced, blonde-haired, and athletic. She ran track and read the announcements over the PA system when she was in middle school with us. I looked at her and immediately understood how Sean Schumacher could give a girl a three in Chest but a ten in Body. She was lithe, electric.

"Listen, Jonson," she cooed, using my family nickname. She was wearing one of Olivia's pink sweatshirts with the collar torn out. Her hair was gathered up in an over-sized banana clip. I could feel her eyes on me, but couldn't meet them. "We need some advice," she said. "A bunch of us are trying on some new stuff we got today at the mall, and we want some male opinions. So if there are any in here, send one over in exactly one minute, okay? I'm first."

No one replied, presumably because we were all suspecting a trap, but also imagining how rewarding it might be.

"That is," Shoshana added, "unless you'd rather stay in here comparing the size of your swords."

She sauntered out of the room.

Milo put his limbs down and stood up.

"Don't do it," I warned, but he just looked at me like I was a complete and total idiot.

"You are a complete and total idiot," he said. "You know what they say, Schwartz, *When opportunity has knockers —* "

Rather than complete his aphorism, Milo smoothed down his always unruly coif, straightened up the collar on his teal Izod and said, "You chumps can fight for sloppy seconds."

Then he went to face his fate.

For the next few minutes, the three of us sat where we were, snickering about how stupid Milo was going to feel for taking the bait so easily.

"Maybe it's revenge for Tracy Taylor," Jake suggested.

Milo had nearly been suspended earlier that year when it was discovered that he'd been orchestrating some entertainment for the boys who sat with him in the back of his bus. Tracy lived up an alley only visible from the rear seats at the bus stop, so every few days Milo would call out that she wasn't coming just as she stepped out onto her porch. Consequently, Tracy would have to sprint down the alley waving her arms, which called dramatic attention to her ample chest. Not the quickest on the uptake, she didn't catch on for nearly two months. Then it took the driver weeks to figure out Milo was the culprit, which was even more absurd. Milo did things like that all the time. He was semi-legendary at school for asking every new teacher at the beginning of the year (and any new substitute who ever had any of his classes at any time) if he could do an extra-credit oral report on Lake Titicaca — not to mention for submitting "Dick Butkis" every time charades was played.

But Tracy Taylor wasn't in the same league as my sister and her friends, so when Milo failed to skulk back in forthwith, we didn't know what to think. I suggested we all sit at my door and listen for incriminating noises. Jake and I took up position, but Cory said spying was for cowards. He picked up some juggling balls and started squeezing them. He was always looking for any little thing to make him stronger. His plan was to play for the Steelers.

Jake and I spied on the hall for a while. Michael Jackson was playing, but nothing happened.

Eventually, Cory said, "You don't think they're having sex in there, do you? Maybe we're going to lose our virginity tonight.

I could use some practice before the cheerleaders start boinking me left, right, and center. Practice makes perfect, you know."

The mere suggestion that intercourse might be in the offing was laughable. Jake was the only one of us who'd ever even French kissed a girl. He probably could have done a lot more, but he dumped his girlfriends too quickly.

"Doubtful," I said. "It's not like Sarah Glickman's in there."

Cory turned white, which was exactly what I'd been aiming for. He'd been nursing a crush on Sarah for years, though he never found the courage to speak to her. She'd been in my Hebrew School class, also having skipped kindergarten, and she was the rabbi's daughter. She wasn't bad looking.

"We know she's not in there," Jake added, "because Shoshana didn't tell us to bring any money."

Now Cory's ears purpled. It was an effect we treasured.

Before Cory got the chance to pretend he was going to pound one of us, Milo, demented, fell into the room. He wobbled past the three of us, then sunk, evidently insensible, into my beanbag chair. His left eye was twitching.

Jake and I got up. We all saw the stain on the inner thigh of his plaid pajama bottoms right away.

"That cannot be what it looks like," Cory said.

"Somebody else!" Milo suddenly cried, his eyes popping out. "They want someone else — in five minutes!"

"You're full of shit, Milo," Jake said. "Tell me you didn't cream your jeans over there."

Milo took a deep breath. He was clutching at his hair, running black coils through a quivering fist. "It's like right out of a frickin' porno," he said, to nobody, really. "I swear to God." His eyes were glassy and wandering. "That was the most humiliating thing that ever happened to me in my entire goddamn life. Fuckin' A. Give me some paper — I'm writing to Forum."

"What — the — hell — *happened!*" we all demanded.

Milo took another deep breath. "Look, I go in there, right?" he panted. "The lights are all dim and music comes on, like the second I opened the door. I was looking at my watch until a minute was up. But the weird thing was it didn't look like anyone was in there. The room seemed totally empty. I was just standing there like a frickin' idiot, wondering why in hell someone would paint their entire room pink, when I hear that Shoshana girl, from behind the closet door with all the Madonna posters on it. It was open and making a kind of wall with that dresser with the big mirror attached to it, you know—"

I nodded, though I had no idea what Olivia's room looked like because I never went in there.

"So, she tells me she's gonna show me some new stuff, and can I say if guys would be into it or not. So I say sure, what the hell, thinking she'd come out in some tight sweater or something. Not that that would've sucked, mind you, but Jesus H. Christ on a popsicle stick—"

Milo mopped his brow as Cory, Jake, and I all sat down like elementary school kids at story time.

"So, get *this*," Milo continued, "she comes out in some lingerie or whatever—clips and straps and shit everywhere—and this black bra that was squeezing her tits together. I didn't know she had 'em. You can't tell, normally. Anyway, the high beams were on all over the place! I got a prize-winning woody in, like, one second."

"Where was everyone else?" Jake asked, wondering the same thing I was.

"I'm getting to that," Milo promised.

I couldn't tell whether Cory and Jake believed any of this. I didn't know what to think. Milo would never hesitate to lie for the sake of a joke, but he was obviously so excited he could barely contain himself. His hands were trembling. Curls were pasted on his forehead.

"I couldn't push my goddamn boner down in these stupid pajamas," he said, "so I started counting to ten as many times as I could to get rid of it, thinking of dead cats and my mother and shit. So then music comes on again—Dexy's Midnight Runners. I didn't even notice it went off. So she starts moving around me, and I couldn't stop looking at her. She goes, 'Are you sure this is okay? Would my boyfriend like this?' I'm nodding like a retard, and sweat was running down my fucking forehead! So finally, she says, 'Thanks,' and goes to give me a kiss, only she kisses right beside my face. Her tit, like almost rubbed my arm, the left one. Left tit, I mean, not left arm. It was my right arm. So, anyway, I can't take it any more. I had the *Big O*—like a stinkin' nuclear explosion right there."

"No," Jake muttered, mostly to himself. "There—is—no—eff-ing way."

"Wait," Milo went on. "So the music clicks off and someone else in the room yells, 'Bingo!' or some shit like that right then, and I realize all those other bitches are in the room. Your sister was the one who shouted, and she's staring at my crotch through a pair of binoculars. They were kneeling behind the bed next to the ghetto blaster—I guess the whole time—and giggling like crazy. That's when I ran the hell out of there."

Cory, Jake, and I looked at each other.

"It's almost time!" Milo cried. "Someone else go!"

Cory, Jake, and I looked at each other some more.

The next thing I knew, Jake and Cory were pushing me toward the door.

"It's your house," Jake said. "You have dibs."

"He's so full of it," Cory added. "Find out what the hell is really going on. Whatever it is, you'll know how to handle it."

I actually dug my heels into the carpet, but the door closed behind me anyway.

I raised a fist to bash my way back into the room, but the

music came on. I turned around.

Olivia's pink door beckoned me like the portal to a tantalizing but perilous alternate dimension. I looked again at my plain old regular door and knew I couldn't go back in there. The consequences of copping out were too much to even contemplate.

With no other choice, I began creeping down the hall, which now looked miles long. It felt like I was suddenly in some kind of funhouse—the kind that turns out to be a haunted house full of sexy cannibal clowns.

Halfway there I stopped. I couldn't go any further, but neither could I go back. All I could do was just stand there wondering why Jake and Cory thought that if Milo had been somehow recruited to participate in a prank on the rest of us, I'd be immune to it. Suddenly, the music cut out. Someone in Olivia's room shouted, "Goddamn it! Rewind! Where the hell are they?"

Panicking, I tried to rush forward and backward at the same time and wound up falling against the wall—which turned out not to be a wall, but a door, Nadia's door. It was black, the entrance to a black hole as far as I was concerned. I'd never been inside her room, either. She always seemed to be in there, anyway.

Suddenly, it opened. Nadia grabbed me by the arm and yanked me into her room. She was strong for someone five foot ten and barely over one hundred pounds. I was shoved into a chair, which was piled with medical books of some sort, which was no surprise. Nadia, at nearly nineteen, should've been in college but was still living at home, still without the high school diploma she was supposedly somehow working toward without actually going to high school—but she read medical and psychological textbooks like I read Spiderman comics.

"Nice job, dipshit," she said. "I didn't think you'd get on to me so fast."

"Ah—"

"What a bunch of pathetic, absurdly suggestible, weak-willed, half-wits."

"What do you mean?"

"If you must know, I saw those ditzes come home with all that lacy—"feminine"—bullshit and had a little talk with them about the upcoming Prom."

Of course Nadia was involved.

"They may appear to be sex-goddesses to you and your pre-pubescent pack of dice-heads, but they're total wannabes," Nadia ranted. "Trust me, their heads are so far up their asses, all they can see are their tits. This was almost too easy. Frankly, I'm embar-rassed."

"Nadia, what did you do?"

"I casually perused their purchases and purposely said some-thing they wouldn't understand to intimidate them."

"What did you say?"

"Well, I said to that stuck-up bitch Sandy *Suck*offski that she must be a 'No-touch goddess,' and of course she pretended to know what I was talking about. But I knew Olivia would ask because she wants to know everything about sex so badly she doesn't care how naive she looks. So I told her no junior girl sur-vives Prom without getting date-raped unless she's mastered the *No-touch.*"

I guess I looked baffled because Nadia let out an exasperated sigh and said, "To make a long story short for the mental midgets in the room: I convinced those bimbettes that everyone knows se-nior guys expect to get horizontal with their Prom dates, so unless sexual-assault was on their evening itineraries, they better be able to make the boys lose it before they get violent."

"You mean—?"

"Yep. Got 'em so scared they're practicing on you dipsticks. The most pathetic thing of all is that it sounds like it's working. I amaze myself sometimes. Wait—Oh, shit. *Shhhh* — "

Nadia focused on her intercom, which made me realize we

could hear the girls whispering in Olivia's room.

Just then, Milo's voice came through. "Where's Jon?" he asked.

"Who knows?" Olivia's voice replied. Was she in my room? Then she said, "Someone come over in sixty seconds. I'll personally make it worth your while."

Nadia had our bedroom intercoms on talk-lock.

There was profound silence for a good ten seconds, after which we heard Olivia, back in her room, say, "Done deal." Then, as if to prove her point, Jake and Cory simultaneously said, "I'm going."

The intercom then broadcast the sounds of struggle: grunting, then a body slam—after which Cory proclaimed, "As the great Chuck Noll says, 'Good things come to those who wait, but only what's left behind by those who hustle.'"

"Here we go," Nadia said. And then she suddenly left the room.

I just stood there stupidly, unsure what to do. After a minute or so, I decided to check the hall, but Nadia came back in before I got the chance. She looked annoyed.

"What's going on now?" I asked.

"Nothing—*Shhhh.*"

We could hear whispers from Olivia's room again. Then music came on: The Kinks' *Come Dancing.*

"Like the song selection?" Nadia asked. "Olivia's touch, even though Mother Dearest claims subliminal advertising doesn't work. I'm not entirely unimpressed."

I thought back. It was Michael Jackson earlier. *"Beat it?"* I said, puzzled. "Oh, you can't be serious." Nadia smiled. "But then Milo said it was Dexy's Midnight—Oh, my god." The song was *Come on Eileen,* of course.

Cory's voice came on the intercom. "Ah, anyone in here?"

Then we heard him gasp and choke and start to breathe like a psychopath. "Oh, man," he moaned.

"Spaz," Nadia declared.

"Oh, man. *Shit!*"

Heavy feet charged past the room, shaking the walls.

Wild cackling from the girls.

"Told you I wouldn't even have to change clothes!" Olivia crowed.

Nadia was looking at her watch. "Sweet Mother of God," she said, shaking her head. "The girl spends more time wiping her ass. I'm sure I just created a monster." Then she looked at me seriously. "Here," she said. "We have to hurry. Take this."

She was offering me a tiny yellow ponytail holder she'd taken from her back pocket.

"What's that for?"

"I want that skank Sandy to fail," Nadia explained. Sort of. "She's the only one left, and I want to implant a lifelong sexual inferiority complex in her tonight."

"This — this is all about Sandy Sikofski?"

Nadia shrugged.

"What do you have against her?" Sandy Sikofski had cute short brown hair, a petite nose, and a chest that garnered high marks from nearly everyone.

"Nothing, really," Nadia said, "except when we were downstairs she made that clicking noise in her throat and gave me that, 'What's your damage?' look when I first started talking to them. I guess I'm not cool enough to enter their reality space — not that there's much room in a fucking vacuum."

"But how am I supposed to make her fail?"

"Put it on real tight, and she'll lose."

"Put it on? I don't have long hair, Nadia."

"Put it on your *dick*, fuckwit!"

Nadia swore she'd ruin my life if I refused, and I knew it was no empty threat. When I was in fifth grade, she convinced my diminutive and oft-persecuted friend, Rudy Pignut, that a pattern of freckles behind his left ear foretold a certain, agonizing descent into the unspeakable horrors of testicular cancer, and that the sooner he decided between sex-change and suicide, the easier it would go for him. Rudy's freckle-spattered face transformed into a throbbing smear of red and orange, then he bolted the house and sprinted home without his dirt bike. My mother had to work overtime to placate an irate Mrs. Pignut, who phoned in a rage twenty minutes later. Nadia had also recently ruined the first time a girl ever came home with me after school, if only to complete a project. My sister was sitting on the bottom step at the far end of our entrance hallway, apparently doing nothing, when I opened the door for Melanie Baxter. Nadia lifted her wan, oval face with the slightest trace of surprise in her shadowy eyes and then shouted, without any preliminary greeting, that I had recently missed three days of school because I suffered a curvature of the penis so pronounced that I'd required surgery to stop me from urinating on myself. I had strep throat! Melanie didn't cry or run, but she performed a stupendously protracted eye-roll, then turned around and left.

And Nadia wasn't mad at me either of those times.

So, yes, I put it on.

Nadia went down to my room to make sure Jake didn't try to enter the picture at this critical juncture. I went back into the hall and approached the Pink Door. Quiet Riot was blaring behind it.

Cum on Feel the Noize.

I stood there, swaying with fantasy and fear, queasy about the fact that my own sister was involved in these shenanigans, and already in no small amount of pain. But I couldn't open the door. But I couldn't face Nadia, either. Or my friends.

Something had to give, and luckily it did.

"I'm not doing it!" someone shouted from Olivia's room. Sandy. The door swung open, hitting me squarely in the forehead.

"Oh," Sandy said, finding me standing there, dazed. "You heard then." The door slammed shut again.

A few seconds later, Nadia was in the hall looking none too pleased. But all she said was, "Darn," and went back into her room.

After recovering my wits, I made a quick trip to the bathroom to reestablish some vital circulation and to wet my pajama bottoms in the appropriate spot. Then I went back to my room and pretended it was all too awesome to talk about.

My friends were impressed by my composure and lack of need to brag, but they were distracted anyway by Cory's on-going (and shamelessly embellished) description of the sexy dance Olivia had done for him in her string bikini. They didn't even remember I'd gone AWOL for a while.

No further summons were issued from Olivia's room, but Jake claimed he wasn't going to do it anyway.

"Then why'd I have to suplex you?" Cory challenged.

"Temporary insanity," Jake replied. "Why window shop when I can get the keys to the store?"

"True," we all had to admit. He'd just dumped his girlfriend a few days earlier, but we knew he'd get another soon enough.

And so that was that. The evening was over. Unprecedented as it was, I hoped we'd all forget about it as soon as possible. It seemed we all felt similarly because it would be years before any of us ever mentioned it again.

The reason my Bar Mitzvah did not take place the following morning was that Myna, my grandmother, made a guest appearance at my Hebrew School class. That catastrophe happened a few months earlier, in December of 1982.

It all started with the annual attempt my Hebrew School teachers made to get my grandfather, Leon, to come talk about his experiences hiding from the Nazis. I only knew the general outline of the story from my mother because Leon wouldn't talk about it. He grew up in Paris and was twenty-two in 1940 when France surrendered to Hitler. Leon, his parents, and his first wife, Suzanne, I was told, managed to survive until France's liberation by hiding in a then obscure village called Le Chambon in the high mountains of south-central France. They were sheltered in a barn loft by a Protestant couple for nearly four years. Le Chambon became world famous after the war because it secretly served as a haven for upwards of five thousand Jews, protected in similar circumstances in surrounding villages and farms. We learned about it every year, which is why every year Leon got calls.

The most bitter of ironies occurred as the war concluded in early October of 1944. Though France was free and the German army fled, Leon and his family came out of hiding too soon. The truck the farmer and his wife were driving the liberated family back to Paris in hit a mine on the road. The only survivors were Leon and the baby he was cradling. This was my mother, who was born on the farm in January that year, a fact that always amazed me because I couldn't fathom normal life continuing under such arduous circumstances.

The Protestant wife who'd harbored Leon and his family had been a teacher with a good command of English. She'd offered to teach them all the language, but only Leon accepted. Without her instructions, he told my mother in one of the few conversations she ever had with him on the subject, he never would have survived their relocation.

Leon and my mother came alone to America in early 1945. He raised her alone, with apparent outrageous strictness, earning a living tailoring clothes from their two-bedroom house on Jackson Street in Pittsburgh.

Usually, Leon simply said, "No," and hung up on whoever called from the shul, but for whatever reason, this time, he told my teacher, Tziporah, that Myna had also "escaped Adolf," as she liked to put it. He passed the phone to her and within minutes a visit was arranged.

I tried to fake sick that Sunday morning, but my mother would have none of it.

Myna was late and, unfortunately, Tziporah had no filler ready. To stall, she trotted out an old reliable discussion topic: *Hannah Senesh: Jewish girl parachutes behind enemy lines!* When that failed to inspire, she upped the ante: *Mass suicide on Masadah!* But nobody was in the mood. Not even the class clowns had the energy to toy with her Israeli accent. Getting her to tell us to take out a *'piss'* or, better, a *'shit'* of paper was usually worth a little effort. But even Sarah Glickman's head was dipping and jerking in front of me.

It was risky for all of us to demonstrate indifference simultaneously, because, if all else failed, we knew Tziporah would show us a documentary about the Holocaust. Which is exactly what she did.

I don't remember which one it was, but they were all the same to me: black and white and full of inhuman creatures emaciated beyond the possible. They were depressing dispatches from an awful but expired universe, so I tuned them out. We all did—well, most of us did. Once in a while someone ran out of the room to puke.

Fortunately, whenever Tziporah put a video on, she sank into her lopsided rolling wooden desk chair and tuned us out. Never an introduction or a wrap-up from Tziporah. I'm sure she assumed the movies spoke for themselves.

As per my usual habit, I surreptitiously placed a penny on my desk to practice Penny Basketball, a game in which a penny is spun across a table toward a basket made by an opponent's interlocked fingers.

Fear of the impending catastrophe—and I knew it was going to be a catastrophe long before it actually became one—must have muddled my thinking, because I tipped the penny back and flicked it into the air the way one "kicks" a paper football. It hit Sarah smartly on the back of her neck. She yelped in pain, clutching the spot as if she'd been stung.

Tziporah, roused, rushed to her star pupil's aid. After prying Sarah's hand from her neck, she discovered the incriminating penny stuck there. Then she turned and gave me the Screw Eye, something I was not accustomed to — but just then Myna appeared in the doorway.

I was grateful, but that wouldn't last long.

Sixty seconds later, the video had been returned to its drawer, and the class was sitting up straight, staring at both Myna's blue velour running suit and the lavender scarf on her head, while Tziporah introduced her as a brave woman who had seen the kinds of things she prayed every night we would never know, but about which she had to make sure we knew, which is also why we'd been watching that awful movie.

"It is in March, 1939," Myna said with no further ado. "I come here to America with my first husband, Nathan Schwartz, from Moravia, Czechoslovakia. We leave just weeks after Hitler's armies come and call it part of their Protectorate. We have a tiny time to get away because the first 'Protector' — he tries to pretend for a while that they weren't there to murder us all good and dead."

I started clapping. I didn't mean to, but I thought it wasn't absolutely impossible that she was done. There wasn't all that much left to the story. Everyone turned and looked at me, so I stopped. But I could see from their eyes my clapping was the first interesting thing that had happened all class long.

Myna went on to tell how she and Nathan had owned and operated a small general store in Moravia for nearly ten years, then how they sold it in late 1938, even before their country lost its bordering territories (and thus all its defensive capabilities) because they could "read the letters on the wall."

"Nathan was a pessimist, thanks to God," Myna told my bored class. Then she added, "We are all of us pessimists now. Do you know why this is so?"

Receiving no response, she answered her own question.

"The pessimists went to America," my grandmother declared with a twisted grin and her finger in the air. "The optimists went to the gas chambers."

I clapped again. Only four claps this time because Tziporah gave me the Major Screw Eye. Fortunately, no one appeared to be listening.

Myna looked a bit concerned about the lack of reaction she was getting, but nevertheless proceeded to share the boring story of her flight to America, the gist of which was that after selling their store, she and Nathan applied for visas with a group of extended family members. Neither had siblings or living parents. The Nazis had by then taken over, but somehow the applications were approved anyway. Myna ascribed this amazing good luck to the chaotic nature of those first uncertain weeks. "We could have been approved for tickets to the moon!" she cried. "Such numskulls, they were! No one knew who was in charge of what or what was in charge of who! All we needed was some money for a nice Jewish bribe, and *poof!* we are coming to America. Any questions?"

She was warming up. That last remark was a bad sign. Any minute now she was going to tell a Jewish joke. The world was about to find out that my grandmother, the Holocaust survivor, told Jewish jokes. But maybe she was done. There was no way anyone was going to ask a question.

Sarah Glickman raised her hand. I wanted to chop it off. *Where was our broadsword when I needed it?*

"Did you keep in touch with everyone after you got here?" she asked.

It was my impression that a dozen or so family members made the journey, though neither names nor exact numbers were ever made clear because the entire group wound up scattered across the country. We were never in contact with any of them, and Myna never talked about her relatives except to say they didn't get along.

My grandmother shrugged. "To run for our lives — on this, we could agree, but nothing else. Once we got off the boat — What's the point? Besides, most of us got different names when we arrived to Ellis Island."

Sarah had no follow-up question, thank God. I prayed we were finally done, but someone else asked what Myna and Nathan did when they got to Pittsburgh.

Damn you all! I wanted to scream. *You don't care!*

"Some money, we still had," Myna explained. "We open a new general store in thirteen months, if you can believe! My son, Michael — he was born in 1944, but my Nathan died from cancer in the liver just a year later, so I run the business myself and raise him there. But then, many years later, I finally married to Jon's grandfather, Leon."

I stood up and clapped like crazy. Show over.

"Jonathan!" Tziporah snapped. "What is wrong with you? Sit down this instant! This is your grandmother!"

I sat down. Myna winked at me. She was having a grand time.

"Did you say you married Jon's grandfather?" someone asked.

"Yes," Myna said. "I married to his mother's father."

All at once, the entire class un-slouched.

"So, his mother's father married his father's mother? Isn't that, like, incest?"

Oh, we had buy-in now. Engaging curriculum!

"What is this word?" Myna asked. No one had the guts to define it for her.

My grandmother regarded the class with a slightly impish grin, which made the contents of my stomach churn. I thought maybe I could puke my guts out.

"Children, let me ask you a question," she said. "Show me what a smart bunch of kinderlach you are. In the desert for forty years, why did the Jewish people wander so long?"

I scanned the room. The door was blocked by too many desks. I could hurl myself through the window, though.

Myna had asked this "question" during dinner at our house a week earlier and almost made my father raise his voice. While Dad was famous for his opposition to religion, he had nothing against religious people in general, and certainly nothing against Jews in particular. He couldn't fathom why someone who'd gone through the things Myna had would ever tell such jokes. More amazing was the fact that Leon, who'd apparently tolerated nothing in the way of either rudeness or a sense-of-humor in raising my mom, never objected to these outrages.

Apparently, the night Myna met Leon (they both chaperoned the blind date my parents went on as freshmen at Pitt), she watched him puff on his cigar after picking them up in his broken down Dodge and asked him how many Jews fit in the new Mercedes Benz.

506 was the answer.

Six in the seats.

And five hundred in the ashtray.

Leon evidently didn't laugh, or even smile, but he also didn't spend the rest of the date browbeating Dad into never asking his daughter out again—something he did to every other date she'd ever had, not that he'd permitted many.

My parents were mortified from the start that night, but also falling in love.

None of my classmates responded to Myna's query about wandering Jews. This was worse than a boring story. Tests were for real school.

Tziporah surveyed us, angrily. I wondered if I should throw myself on the floor and simulate a seizure. Anything.

"Jonathan," Tziporah said. "I'm sure you can answer the question."

I couldn't, and despite years of instruction, I was willing to bet most of the rest of the class couldn't either, but that was beside the point. "But she doesn't actually want the real—" I started to protest.

"Jonathan, your grandmother has taken the time to come to our class. You've been nothing but rude. Pretending to be ignorant impresses no one."

Absolutely wrong! I wanted to shout. And I wasn't pretending!

"Oh, he knows all right," Myna said. She was smiling ear-to-ear.

The whole class was looking at me. Now I was defying my teacher and my own grandmother. Finally, I mumbled something unintelligible under my breath.

"What, Jonathan?" Tziporah asked.

Myna kindly clarified. "He said the Jews wander in the desert for forty years because someone drops a shekel!"

Everyone gaped at me. Then they all turned as one to see how Tziporah was going to react.

React she did.

My teacher rose from her chair like a column of black, smoking death. She flew at me in a fulminating rage, then dragged me to the hall by my right armpit, which I assumed was some secret Israeli army maneuver. I caught a glimpse of a genuinely surprised look on Myna's face as I was manhandled past her.

In the hall, Tziporah berated me for fifteen minutes about my blatant disrespect for my grandmother, not to mention six million murdered brothers and sisters of mine, for my clear manifestation of something called the "Self-hating Jew Syndrome," and for trading my obvious academic potential for a jester's cap. I had no choice but to tell her Myna was not actually quizzing the class on its level of biblical scholarship, but that only made her skull appear dangerously close to exploding.

A burst of laughter came from the classroom, snapping Tziporah out of her conniption. She shoved me back into the room just as Myna was thanking my classmates for their attention.

I threw myself into my seat with a huff.

"You've been wonderful children," Myna cooed. "I want you to remember just one thing—one thing only. Adolf is alive. He is hiding in every non-Jew. Scratch deep enough, and you'll find him. So don't scratch, okay? Get a good ointment and slather it all over the goyim. No one likes the rash."

The class giggled. Tziporah looked confused. She managed some polite clapping that was a signal for us to do the same. Myna bowed slightly and flashed me a wink.

Then she left.

When the door closed behind her, Amy Baumgardner said, "She's cool."

Tziporah, somewhat regrouped, asked the class to share what they'd learned.

Andy Katz said, "That Jon's lucky he doesn't have three heads and six arms."

Incredibly, unjustly, Tziporah let this pass. She just shook her head and reloaded the video machine. After hitting Play, she yanked me down the hall to the principal's office.

Mrs. Frankel called my house, but to my profound relief, wound up defending me on the phone. I gathered from her end of the conversation that my father was trying to get her to expel me. Of course, he never wanted any of us to attend Hebrew School to begin with. My mother insisted, though, that we be given the opportunity to reject our religious heritage based on some actual knowledge of it—an argument my father, the expert debater, admitted had merit. Nadia and Olivia never even went once, but I offered to try—I think so Mom wouldn't be oh-for-three. And it turned out that, at least when I was a little kid, I liked going to hear the folktales and fables we were always learning. Truth is, I never stopped liking them.

The funny thing was that after I started attending regularly, Mom seemed as disinterested in the whole subject as my father.

Though 'disinterested' isn't the best way to describe Dad's attitude about the whole thing. He tried to let me form my own opinions, but he couldn't always help himself. I remember, in third grade, telling him we'd read the story of Noah's Ark. He scratched his beard awhile, thinking. I know now he was fighting an urge. Finally, he gave in and hurried off, only to return with an armload of books. Then he made me, on the spot, read stories from what seemed like an endless number of other religions that featured similar watery cataclysms. There was the one from the Koran in which Nuh builds an ark *("Nuh?* Jonson! An *ark!")* and the Hindu story in which a holy man is warned by Vishnu of the impending flood, then rescued with the animals in a ship ("Warned! Ahead of time, Jonson! Rescued the animals! In a ship!"). There was also the Chinese tale of Nu Wa, who repaired the rent skies that had drowned the Earth. I had to read about Deucalion and Pyrrha from Ancient Greece, a Maori flood tale, and still others from Sumeria, Liberia, Vietnam, Babylon, and various Native American cultures.

To this day, I'm still not exactly sure what his point was.

When all the reading wore me out, Dad asked whether my class had gotten to the Garden of Eden or Moses' birth, because he would be happy to demonstrate parallels to those stories as well. We had, of course, but there was no way I was going to tell him so. From then on, I decided it would be best to keep my religious learning to myself.

Dad spoke with Mrs. Frankel briefly in person when he came

to get me, but he didn't share the results of the conversation until we were nearly home. Until then, he hadn't said a word. He just shook his head as he drove, which was never a good sign. I had no idea what my punishment would be, or whether I ought to be explaining myself, which would mean blaming Myna. Finally, I couldn't take it anymore.

"Am I in trouble, Dad?" I asked.

"Seems I am," was his response.

"What do you mean?"

"Seems I'll be required to justify myself to Rabbi *Pollyanna*. I'm supposed to call and make an appointment." He shook his head some more.

I asked nothing further, shocked to hear that he was being put out. Dad was very protective of his Writing Time.

I was also wondering if we were getting a new rabbi, and what that might mean for Cory if Sarah Glickman was moving.

Dad kept putting off arranging the meeting, so finally someone from the shul phoned Mom and scheduled it for after New Year's.

Once everyone was in place around the card table, the Family Meeting commenced. Mom took a deep breath, so Nadia rolled her eyes. "That's enough, Nadia," she said. "And Olivia — please." Olivia was tilting back in her chair, not even feigning interest. Her eyes were covered by two slices of cucumber held in place by a green facial mask under her feathered raven hair. She deigned to uncover one eye. "This is no big deal," Mom foolishly added. Of course it was no big deal, but Family Meetings were about what our parents *thought* were big deals. "We just have a favor to ask of you girls. The rabbi is coming over to speak with your brother and us and we —"

"What'd he do, douse the Eternal Light?" Nadia asked. Olivia peered at me questioningly with her free eye.

Dad piped in. "He's just coming over to talk, to have a *reasonable* discussion." The most popular word at Family Meetings was 'reasonable,' at least while my father held the floor. He looked upon the sessions as golden opportunities to demonstrate that Reason was all that was necessary to facilitate harmonious interpersonal relationships.

"Ah—" I said, unable to control my curiosity but worried about exposing myself as an idiot. "You said the rabbi's coming over, right?"

"Yes," my father said. He hated repeating himself. "You know very well he is."

"And, which rabbi would that be, exactly?"

My father looked at me, thinking. He scratched his beard.

"Jonathan," Mom sighed, "this is hardly the time for nonsense." Then she turned to my sisters and said, "Rabbi Glickman is coming over tonight. We'd appreciate it if you girls would remain on the third floor while he is here."

Why on Earth my parents didn't comprehend the folly of asking for something guaranteed to take place without the request was beyond me. To ask was to assure things did *not* go the way they wanted. I could only conclude that sometimes they weren't as intelligent as they seemed.

"What are we, *freaks?*" Nadia asked. She was wearing military fatigues and a surgeon's mask, having recently taken to waging war against the deadly microbes slowly consuming the rest of us from within. My father regarded her blankly for a second. The beard was scratched again.

"Well, for one thing young lady," Mom said to Olivia, "I wouldn't like Rabbi Glickman to see you parading around the house in that charming outfit." She was wearing a pair of boxer shorts with the elastic rolled down and an undershirt looped into her cleavage.

"But it'd be really neat," Nadia said, "if when he comes up the front walk, he looks up at her window and sees her posing in her underwear for the Murphy pervs across the street."

Olivia turned a red so bright it was visible right through the green layer of facial cream. The flush spread down over her neck and up to her ears. She couldn't suppress it, so she jumped up, knocking her chair to the floor behind her. "Liar!" she screamed, then fled the room.

One down, I thought to myself. *Took long enough.*

"Is she doing that?" Dad asked, looking to Mom. They both suddenly seemed terribly weary.

"Call Mrs. Murphy and ask if she's been losing twenties from her wallet lately," Nadia said.

"Anyway," Mom sighed, "the Murphys are moving to China. They'll be renting the place out in a few weeks."

Nadia raised an eyebrow at this, but then said, "So how long are we talking about here, this confinement?" It seemed negotiations were officially underway.

"An hour or so," Mom said.

"Weasel word!" I cried. "That could mean *five* hours!"

Mom worked at an ad agency. She spent most of her time handling its pro bono public service campaigns. Years earlier, she'd taught us to recognize persuasion techniques by trying to slip them past us in conversation, but it had been a long time since we'd done that. It was just that she'd panicked me. The last Monday Night Football game of the season was on in an hour and a half.

"We'd simply like some privacy during this meeting," Dad explained to Nadia. "It's a reasonable request."

"Jonson," my sister said, turning to me, "they're giving you to the priesthood. Run!"

"Nadia," Mom snapped, "we don't want to see you downstairs while the rabbi is here. Is that understood? And don't call over the intercom asking if anyone has seen your Homicidal Tendencies tape or any other questionable item you own. Keep Olivia up there—and make sure she's fully clothed. You are her big sister, and you provide her with no guidance whatsoever. You—"

"Deana," Dad interrupted, which was rare.

Mom turned to Dad. "Michael, maybe I should do the talking."

"Excuse me?" he said.

At that point, my stress quadrupled. I pulled the bill of my Stargell Star-covered Pirates cap down to my nose and slouched in my chair.

Nadia stood up and said, "Listen, this little marital meltdown, highly amusing as it is, isn't what I planned for my evening's entertainment. Call me if you need therapy." She moved toward the door, but stopped at the mirror hanging next to it, put her face right up to the glass, and said, "I'd stop the experiment right now if I were you." Then she left the room.

My parents glowered at each other. I held my breath, simultaneously horrified and fascinated by this inexplicable confrontation and afraid to see what was coming next. *One to go,* I thought.

And then the doorbell rang.

We all took seats around the marble-topped coffee table in Mom's office. She brought up a tray with four glasses of lemonade and passed them around. I eyed the rabbi while I sipped from a bendy straw. He was tall and wiry, with thinning hair and pinkish skin. He was wearing rumpled slacks and a white oxford and blazer with no tie. The only personal thing I knew about him was that his wife died giving birth to Sarah. We'd had very few interactions because he only occasionally came to talk to the Hebrew School classes, though he had met individually with each of us boys once to begin our Bar Mitzvah training.

I checked the clock. *Plenty of time.*

But then I had another panic attack because I remembered that in my meeting with the rabbi, I asked him if when I had to lift the Torah and show it to the congregation, I dropped it, whether the synagogue would reimburse my family for the lunch buffet scheduled afterward. It seemed important after I learned everyone who witnessed such a thing would have to fast for sixty days. He assumed I was joking and told me it was time to leave childish things behind. I was suddenly sure he was going to rat me out about that.

We sipped some more lemonade, and then the rabbi finally spoke. "Mr. and Mrs. Schwartz—" he said, but then lapsed into one of his notorious pauses. Rabbi Glickman talked very, very slowly and always through a big, dopey grin, and he was annoyingly optimistic about everything. Some of the older kids referred to the synagogue as "Rabbi Rogers' Neighborhood" when he wasn't around.

Eventually, he continued. "I know there was some trouble—at the religious school—concerning your son," he said, "but mostly I'm not concerned with—that. I came over just to chat—maybe—perhaps—I might ask you a few questions, or even—answer a few you might have. Is that acceptable to you?"

My father nodded ominously, but Mom said it was wonderful and that she was glad for the visit.

Rabbi Glickman smiled. "Mr. and Mrs. Schwartz," he began, "let me first say what—honor you both bring to your family with the good works you—do. Michael, despite my disagreement with the theses of your novels, I find them to be brilliant."

Dad had three novels out: *Original Sins, Chosen People,* and *Veiled Threats.* I hadn't read any of them, but I knew they'd turned him into a famous author and a hero to everyone who didn't like religion.

"And Deana," Rabbi Glickman continued, "your PSA's are well known in town. You are a pair of real mensches."

"Don't *mench-in* it," I quipped.

Before I could bask in everyone's laughter, my father said, "If you say so, Rabbi." His voice was cold. "The truth is," he added, "I'm selfish. I simply see that the only way to lead a truly safe and satisfying life requires making sure everyone else can, too."

The rabbi smiled again, or he seemed to even though he was already smiling. "If you don't mind my asking," he said, stroking his beard, "are you interested—in your son becoming a Bar Mitzvah?"

"The fact of the matter is, Rabbi," said my father, "I am *uncomfortable* with all ritual, all superstition—it's ignorance, plain and simple. Bertrand Russell averred accurately that ignorance is a chief source of cruelty. The first step to wisdom is conquering irrational attachments."

"Wisdom—this is a—slippery thing, no?" the rabbi replied. "'In truth we know nothing, for truth—lies in depth.' Democritus, I believe."

My father shook his head. "In truth, we know *some*, Rabbi," he said. "To spend a life as you do—with all due respect—is to spend a life on a subject you can't know even a small part of as truth. What you don't know about God is exactly equivalent to what you say about her."

"Perhaps so," the rabbi conceded and then fell silent. I figured he'd been vanquished, but he was only mired in a pause. "But I would say," he finally offered, "as Richard Eberhart so— eloquently put it, that 'It is what man—does not know about God that composes—the visible poem of the world.' A man of letters— such as yourself—must appreciate this, no?"

I was thrilled by the developing scene, partly because I'd never witnessed one of my father's debates, but mostly because it seemed I'd become irrelevant to the proceedings. I was thinking Monday Night Football was a cinch.

"Pubilius Syrus," intoned my father. "'Better be ignorant of a matter than half know it.'"

"Yes, I know these words," said the rabbi. The two men were

leaning toward each other suddenly, not aggressively, but intensely. "Thomas Henry Huxley has an—answer: 'If a little knowledge—is dangerous, where is the man who has—so much as to be out of—danger?'"

"None of us are out of danger," my father retorted, "partially because the high walls religious factions build between themselves aren't high enough to keep missiles out. This is the danger created by the great and visible poetry of their ignorance."

"That's—interesting," replied Rabbi Glickman. "I don't look at Judaism as a wall keeping—us apart from others. I see it—as a foundation from which we can stretch forth our hands."

"Yet the stretched-forth hands in the Middle East are all wielding Uzis, are they not?" Dad asked. "David Hume put it perfectly: 'Oppose one species of superstition to another, set them a-quarreling, while we ourselves, during their fury and contention, happily make our escape into the calm, though obscure regions of philosophy.' In my house, Rabbi, you've come into that calm."

I just barely stifled a snort at that.

"It would be my contention," Rabbi Glickman said, "that the pocket of calm—in which you repose—exists—only through the triumph of the great ethical—monotheistic religions, spearheaded by Judaism—itself."

My father leaned in further. The rabbi smiled bigger. I checked the clock.

Mom suddenly rose with an exclamation that sounded like a cross between, 'Oh!' and, 'Hey!' She walked over to her desk by the window and picked up a book lying next to the computer. "Rabbi, please pardon the interruption," she said. "I want to ask you something before I forget." She started paging through the book in search of something, but a loud clanging from outside made her stop.

It sounded as if something metal was being raked along the rails of our front fence. Mom squinted out the window, but then looked back at us and shrugged. Then she quickly approached the rabbi with the book held open.

My father's expression revealed nothing about what he thought of this development. I was furious. *Delay of game!*

Mom held the book out. "I was reading this recently," she said, "and this word here—"

"The Golem," Rabbi Glickman read. "Ah, a very interesting—thing."

"What is it?" Mom asked, sounding as if she cared about nothing else in the world. She took the book from Rabbi Glickman and returned to her seat, glancing at the window on the way.

"Golems can be Flesh, Iron, or Stone."

"What, Jonathan?" my mother asked.

"In D & D—they're created with different animate object spells, magical tomes and stuff like that. They can help, but they're kind of dangerous."

"This is a game you—play?" Rabbi Glickman asked. I nodded tentatively, fearing a trap. "I suspect you had no idea those creatures—were derived from—ancient Jewish—tradition."

I shook my head, hoping I hadn't said anything wrong.

"According to the mystics," the rabbi explained, "it is possible to animate a giant—of living clay. In the Talmud the term—means 'unformed clay,' but later, in the middle ages, it came to—represent the finest expression of a powerless people's longing—for resistance and redemption, a giant, raging, unstoppable—beast to protect the Jews! Such a creature, with its—immense powers, can only be created by a Tzaddik, a righteous man through—the secrets of the Kabbalah."

My mother's smile sank as Rabbi Glickman shared this. She could plainly see the expression of mockery forming on my father's face. I was sure she was wishing she'd actually looked that word up earlier.

The Rabbi continued with wide eyes. "According to legend,

the golem—like you say, Jonathan—is a very dangerous thing. If he is summoned by an unrighteous man—*Oy*, the damage he can cause! He is even known to become dangerous to—his own creator and his own—community as he grows. Even in the best case—he must be laid low before it is—too late. A wonderful metaphor, no? I see the golem as an expression of Jewish impatience—for the messiah, may his arrival be in our lifetime."

Dad let out an undisguised grunt of derision for both the story and the Rabbi's interpretation of it. Mom was frantically turning pages again but couldn't find whatever she was looking for in time to head off another quotation.

"Valéry," my father said. "'The folly of mistaking a paradox for a discovery, a metaphor for a proof, a torrent of verbiage for a spring of truth, and oneself for an oracle, is inborn in us.' And short of Original Sin," Dad added, "there is scarcely a more offensive religious doctrine than one that cons people into accepting their suffering because their savior is surely on the way."

"I'd love to discuss this subject further with you, Michael," the Rabbi said, "but I suppose now is not the best time. I—find you to be a—fascinating person. You could do so much for the Jewish community."

"I'd do whatever I could to integrate it into the world community."

"Let me tell you something your—mother said to me," Rabbi Glickman replied. This jarred all of us, and I looked away from the clock. The Rabbi could see we were all startled. "She called to explain her role—in what happened between Jonathan and Morah Tziporah," he explained. My mother and father looked at each other as he continued. "We were talking about life leading up to the war, and she—suddenly remembered something she'd once heard, a Bulgarian proverb—concerning the Christian conversion of Jews. It asserted that there was one thing—to keep in mind when one—baptized a Jew. This was that one must hold the Jew's head under water—for five minutes."

I perked up. This had to be his way of acknowledging that it was all Myna's fault we were there—now in serious jeopardy of missing the Vikings and Cowboys in about half an hour.

My father leaned forward to speak but held back when Rabbi Glickman added, "Your mother also told me—something about you, Michael." Dad's eyebrows lifted. "She was very anxious that Jon—not be perceived as disrespectful, and she was sorry she'd gotten carried away."

Dad beard-scratched, waiting for the Rabbi to get to the point. Meanwhile, relief washed over me. I was exonerated!

"She mentioned how difficult it was for you, Michael," Rabbi Glickman finally said, "when the young neighborhood no-good-nicks—came into her store. She said they called it the 'Jew Store,' in part because—it sat adjacent to a shoe store, and that they—frequently barged in screaming all kinds of—awful slurs."

"And she said it was difficult for me?"

Dad sounded skeptical, but alarmed, which made me wonder if he wasn't suddenly losing the debate.

"She said it was difficult for you to understand because—being Jewish meant absolutely nothing to you. It was—just a word without meaning that somehow—applied to your family."

I'd hopelessly lost the thread of the conversation, but I could see my father had been knocked off balance. He was actually flushing like Olivia had downstairs. It was something I'd never witnessed before, and I don't think my mother had ever seen anything like it either, because she was just staring at Dad, mesmerized.

"I am no longer a child, Rabbi," my father said, sharply. "And I no longer suffer from childish fears."

"Yes," replied the Rabbi. "Your mother mentioned this remarkable transformation."

"*She what?*"

"She told me about that day. She was thinking of it because of Jon's age."

"I'm sorry?"

"When you were thirteen, when the inebriated Hungarian man kicked down the door to the store yelling, "'Kill the greedy Jews! Kill the greedy Jews!' Your mother said it was the first time an adult had done such a thing—and that it gave you a terrible shock. You weren't even able to slide—to the floor behind the counter as you did when the young thugs came in every day—I apologize, I don't mean to embarrass you. You obviously know the story. I don't need to go on."

"I insist, Rabbi. Please continue. I'm interested in my mother's memory."

"Well, she said the man started—throwing handfuls of coins—pennies—into the store. Your mother—without thinking, reached into her cashbox, which sat on a shelf under the counter—and came out with a roll of quarters, which she threw—a good distance she says. By chance—she hit the man between the eyes, knocking him to his knees. He was so stunned that he could barely manage to crawl out of the store. Your mother said you— stopped crying at the sight of this. She never did such a thing before, or ever again, and—though the harassment didn't stop that day, she said, your—worrying about it did."

My father closed his eyes for a moment and seemed to disappear into himself. I don't know what about him gave me this impression, but it was distinct. It's possible the rabbi made a similar observation because he suddenly turned from my father and looked at me.

"Do you want to become a Bar Mitzvah, Jonathan?" he asked.

Panicked, I muttered the idiotic response I always ridiculed Milo for giving when he got interrogated by teachers at "regular" school, which was, "I don't know." As soon as I said it, I understood what a blissful, though temporary, refuge it was.

"Come now," the Rabbi urged, "I'm certain—you've given the subject some serious consideration. You can be a very mature boy. I don't know many who could sit through such—lengthy, adult discourse and stay so focused and calm. I'm not surprised, though. I was—sure you could handle it."

"Ah—"

"I notice you're looking to your mother."

This put the spotlight on Mom, who was clearly uncomfortable in it. She suddenly looked, to my dismay, sort of...*afraid*.

Rabbi Glickman asked her if she wanted me to become a Bar Mitzvah.

She nodded, but very cautiously.

"Why, Mrs. Schwartz?"

Mom looked at Dad and took a deep breath. Then, she said... nothing.

"What choice did you make—for your own life?" the Rabbi pressed.

"She has chosen the path of *Reason*."

"Michael," Mom said, "I can speak for myself."

My parents glared at each other again. I felt disaster was imminent, but before anyone could speak, the clanging came again from outside. This time it was so loud it couldn't be ignored. There was also, this time, the sound of a woman screaming something that sounded like my father's name.

"Oh, shit," my mother blurted, hurrying to the window. She'd spoken under her breath, but the curse was audible. I couldn't believe she said that in front of the Rabbi. Incredibly, he didn't seem any worse for it.

"*Michael Schwartz! Michael Schwartz!*" the voice cried. A woman was definitely screaming Dad's name, and something else, too, but her voice was muffled. My father and I walked to the window and leaned forward to see what was happening, but it was too dark outside to see. The streetlight in front of the Murphy's was burned out. My mother picked up the newfangled and very bulky cordless phone, but my father put up his hand.

"Maybe she'll go away," he said.

"*Michael Schwartz!*" the woman screeched again while dragging some sort of metal bar across the fence. Then it sounded like she called out, "YOU ARGAD!! YOU ARGAD, MICHAEL SCHWARTZ!"

"I'm calling the police," Mom said, but Dad shook his head.

"Maybe we should open the window to hear what she's saying," Rabbi Glickman suggested. I didn't realize he'd joined us. My parents looked at each other. Mom sighed and reached for the lock on top of the lower pane and then slid the window up.

"MICHAEL SCHWARTZ! YOU ARE GOD!"

I don't think any of us processed what we heard at first, because no one reacted. Another chance came quickly. "MICHAEL SCHWARTZ, YOU ARE GOD! YOUR MARY, YOUR LOVE, IS HERE!" Then, the clattering along the fence posts again.

No one said anything for several long beats until, finally, my father whispered, "I'll go talk to her."

"Michael," my mother warned, "she's liable to kill you. She's clearly insane. She obviously hasn't read your books."

"I UNDERSTAND YOUR SECRET CODE!" the woman bellowed, as if to dispel my mother's doubts. "COME DOWN AND GIVE ME OUR SAVIOR, MY LORD! MAKE ME A CHRIST CHILD, MICHAEL SCHWARTZ! I'M READY FOR YOU NOW!"

I didn't know why my father wouldn't let Mom call the police, though I suspected it had something to do with the Rabbi's presence.

It sounded as if the door to the Murphy's house opened across the street, and my father, hearing this, looked at my mother and then at the Rabbi. He put his head through the window, but before he could speak, another, much more resonant, high-volume voice ripped down over the yard. "PULL YOUR HEAD OUT OF

YOUR ASS, INKWHORE!"

It was Nadia, from upstairs.

Recoiling, my father banged his head on the bottom of the raised window. "Damn it!" he complained, hauling himself back into the room. He rubbed the top of his skull. I watched the Rabbi for a reaction to having been subjected to both of my parents and my sister swearing inside of two minutes, but none was visible. He was looking out in the direction of the shadowy figure at the gate, who'd gone eerily silent.

My mother, slightly pale, forced a polite laugh. "You'll have to excuse Nadia," she said. "She can be a little direct."

Rabbi Glickman flashed a reassuring smile. "I'm not sure I've had — the pleasure of meeting, Nadia," he said. "Or your other —"

"*God? Are you there?*" our visitor entreated. Unfortunately, Dad hadn't closed the window. "*I understand your ways! Only the true believers remain when you've proven their beliefs to be false!*"

It took a fraction of a second too long for Dad to realize what was coming next. He'd only just reached for the window when Nadia responded.

"WE'RE *JEWISH*, YOU IGNORANT SLUT! WE KILLED CHRIST TWO THOUSAND YEARS AGO, SO WHY IN HELL WOULD WE KNOCK UP SOME HO-BAG SKIMMER LIKE YOU WITH HIM NOW?"

The window slammed shut.

Mom jabbed wildly at the phone.

The Rabbi backed away toward the chair he'd left in order to bear witness to these profane events. My father, poker-faced, followed him and took a seat, so I did the same. I'd even forgotten about the clock.

No one spoke. Instead, we looked over at my mother, who was still at the window holding the phone, which she apparently never successfully dialed. After a long moment, she said, "She's gone," then walked demurely back to her seat.

Rabbi Glickman wiped some perspiration from his brow and said, "She assumed you were a Christian. That's—interesting—even with a name like—Schwartz."

"Someday names won't elicit any assumptions other than that they are attached to a fellow human being," my father replied.

With that, the two men were back into the flow of discussion as if nothing embarrassing had just happened. I was awed.

"Hitler didn't care how un-Jewish—people just like you were," said Rabbi Glickman. "He would consider you Jewish whether—you thought you were or not, like these hooligans in your mother's store. It's not so simple to jettison a historical—identity."

"My identity is what I make it," said my father. "Insofar as I have control over anything in this world, it is over my identity. It is *you* who have none. Under the clothing of your religion, you are naked."

I couldn't believe he said that. The edge was back in his voice. He was flushing again.

"Michael," my mother warned.

"Please," offered the Rabbi, "I fully understand—his passion. May I share something I recently read, Michael?" Dad nodded and settled back into his chair. "I just finished a wonderful book," the Rabbi told him, *"A Child of the Century,* by Ben Hecht. In many ways—he reminds me of you."

"Yes," was Dad's reply.

"Well, during the Holocaust, he was trying to raise money for those—sardonic advertisements he put in the papers—'Jewish souls for sale' and all that. Well, he went to a prominent Jewish movie producer with a—solicitation. This bigwig Jewish guy, like you, didn't do *anything* Jewish. The whole subject was—anathema to him. So he told Hecht to get lost. But Hecht knew this man to be a—gambler, so he made him a bet."

Dad offered no reply to this, but he did scratch his beard.

"Well," the Rabbi continued, "Hecht told this bigwig guy — to give him three names — the names of the three people who knew him best in the world, not — including his family. Hecht said — he'd ask these friends whether they considered the producer a Jew — and if any one of them said no, he'd leave him alone. Otherwise, the guy would give him — twice the amount of money he came for. Do you know this story?"

My father remained silent. He just sat there scratching. My mother was sipping lemonade again and watching him warily, like a parent might watch a child walking on a wall. Finally, and suddenly, Dad looked at the Rabbi and said, "I will take that challenge."

Rabbi Glickman and my mother said, "Pardon me?" and "What?" at the same time.

Dad got up, snatched the phone from the desk and handed it to the Rabbi. "Call Information," he said. "Ask for Hamil Graham. We grew up together." As far as I knew, my father didn't have any friends, or, all his friends were my mother's. But that must have been why he said to call Information.

"Mr. Schwartz, I didn't come here for this. It's not — necessary."

"I insist."

"Michael!" Mom was furious now. "You will stop this insanity right now. Maybe we should call it a night, Rabbi Glickman. I'm very — "

"You can leave, Deana," Dad said, "if you are not interested. Rabbi Glickman has intrigued me."

The look my mother gave Dad chilled me. She rose, straightened her skirt, then walked out of the room. I wanted more than anything to go with her. Ten minutes!

"Are you sure you want me to do this?"

"Hamil Graham."

"Whom shall I say is calling?"

Just then, Mom walked back into the room. "Let me handle it, Rabbi," she said, pacing up to him and taking the phone out of his hand. My father looked at her with mild surprise. She got the number, then dialed it.

"Hi, Mr. Graham? Yes, my name is Shira Cohen-Katz. I'm with the *Jewish Chronicle*. I'm so sorry to bother you at home. We're doing a brief write-up on Michael Schwartz. Do you think you could answer a question or two?"

We were all riveted by my mom's performance. She was using her advertising voice.

"Fabulous. Thank you so much. Actually, maybe you can settle something for us right off the bat. We're having a teeny-weenie debate here at the office. I'm thinking of referring to Mr. Schwartz in the article as an American Jew, but my colleague thinks Jewish American is much more appropriate — Actually, another colleague thinks we shouldn't even refer to him as Jewish at all since he obviously has a well-known stance on organized religion. What do you think? Interesting. Would you say most people see him similarly? Hmm."

I tried to watch my father, without being obvious about it, while my mother carried on this conversation. His face was utterly blank, but not in the manner of his ordinary non-committal expression. It was emptier. He scratched his beard.

"Let me ask you this," Mom continued. "If there were only space for one word, 'American' or 'Jew,' which would you choose? Okay, thanks. I've got a few more — Oops, that's another call. Mr. Graham? Hamil then. Do you think I could get back to you another time? You've been so helpful. Yes? Oh, you're a doll. Thank you so much. Bye now."

Mom hung up, then looked at my still-expressionless father and said, "He told me he admired the Jewish people, and that of course you were a Jew, no matter what your books are about. In fact, you are even more Jewish because of what your books are about."

There was the slightest clench in Dad's jaw.

Rabbi Glickman nodded, gravely.

"Kwazim Bardo," Dad said, "my editor."

Once again, Mother made the call. She asked for Mr. Bardo and then waited for him to come to the phone.

Dad scratched.

Mom did her routine perfectly and clicked off the phone. "Same answer," she whispered. It looked hard for her to say.

Apparently, that was enough. Dad didn't offer another name.

Rabbi Glickman looked at him tenderly and said, "There is a story—of a rabbi and a group of prisoners in a concentration camp who put God on—trial. They called witnesses and argued both sides of the case. The jury deliberated, and then rendered— a verdict. It was guilty, finding that God did not exist. Then the rabbi who organized the trial called it to an end because it was time—for prayers."

There was a moment of total silence when Rabbi Glickman finished this story. I was wondering what the heck it had to do with anything when, suddenly, my father exploded.

"HORSESHIT!" he roared, leaping to his feet. Then he snatched the phone from my horrified mother and began circling our chairs, brandishing it like a dagger. "Horseshit! Horseshit! Horseshit!" He must have shouted it twenty times. Then he threw the phone against the closet door, where it shattered a mirror and broke into bits. Then he stormed out of the room. Mom followed him. The Rabbi, ashen-faced, followed her. I brought up the rear.

We raced toward the steps leading downstairs, but as the Rabbi passed the entrance to the third floor flight, I heard high-pitched shrieking. My sisters appeared in a stumbling blur that collided with the Rabbi. I couldn't stop and crashed into them all. Bright flashes exploded in my eyes, and then I saw black. Several disoriented moments later, the front door slammed.

When my head cleared, I realized I was one of several bodies scattered across the second floor hall carpet. The others were Rabbi Glickman and both of my sisters. Before I could make sense of the situation, I heard hysterical female crying and the Rabbi's voice calling out, "Dearest God! Dearest God!"

I was only dazed and managed to achieve a sitting position, from which I could see, if not comprehend, what had occurred. Olivia was lying on her side in a nearly fetal position. Nadia was spooned behind her screeching in pain. It dawned on me next that Olivia was wearing a wedding veil and nothing but what appeared to be leather panties and a bra. There were distinctly dangerous looking spikes protruding from the waistband of the panties and from the center of the bra's cups.

"I'm dying!" Nadia howled. "Call a goddamn ambulance!"

Mom rushed out of the TV room, where she'd apparently run for another phone. "Help is coming!" she cried and rushed to the girls' side. "Don't move, Naddie. You're going to be okay!"

I realized then that Nadia had, to some degree, been impaled on Olivia's panty spikes. Olivia was silent and breathing slowly with her hands over her eyes under the veil.

My eyes moved across the floor to the Rabbi. He was crumpled along the banister holding his left foot—not unlike Milo would do in the not-too-distant future one floor above—and still muttering, "Dearest God—Dearest God," while staring at my sisters.

Still a bit woozy, I heard myself calling to him. "Rabbi Glickman?"

"Yes, child?" he managed.

"Do you know a Rabbi Polly Anna?"

"Dearest God," he moaned, as if I hadn't said a thing.

All I can say for certain is that no one was seriously hurt, physically. The paramedics arrived within minutes and, with rather impressive nonchalance, handled the crisis. This didn't mean the pair found it easy keeping their eyes in their skulls at the sight of Olivia, but they certainly didn't do or say anything inappropriate.

It turned out Olivia's spikes were made of a rather rigid rubber that pierced Nadia, but also bent, thus not skewering her to any dangerous degree. The wounds were painful, but superficial, and she was bandaged up promptly. My mother plucked the veil from Olivia's head and put a blanket over her as soon as she was able.

Rabbi Glickman, for his part, suffered a broken ankle. I don't remember him leaving, but he obviously did. I'm pretty sure he didn't say goodbye.

Mom and I carried Nadia up to her room. She was incredibly light—I could have carried her myself. Mom commanded Olivia to join us there after putting on some decent clothes because we needed an Emergency Family Meeting.

"First of all, young lady," Mom said when Olivia arrived, "we will discuss where you got those items and what the hell you were doing with them, later."

"Mom, I wasn't in the window. Seriously. I've never done that! I'm sick of Nadia's lies! I can't live in this house with her any more!"

I blinked at this outburst. It seemed to come out of nowhere.

"Olivia," Mom sighed, clearly unable to deal with this right now.

"She wasn't in the window," Nadia substantiated, looking much more coherent. "She was modeling that ridiculous ensemble for me when we heard Dad bust a gasket downstairs. She started running, and I was trying to hold her back. That's some tough leather—I'll say that much. I can't believe I didn't yank it off, or cut her in two, or both. The Rabbi would've loved that. I'm sure there'd've been a sermon in there somewhere."

"I wasn't modeling! I was just asking what you thought!" Olivia was rapidly losing her composure again.

"Why'd you ask me how many pounds heavier people look on TV?"

"I did not! *Mom!*"

Mom wasn't even listening. She looked sick. "What have I done?" she whispered.

"What's going *on,* Mom?" Olivia whined.

Mom looked at us. "This is my fault," she said. "I forced this on your father."

"But he's not afraid of debating anyone," I said.

"No," Mom agreed. "But he values his dignity more than anyone I know — it's something I love him for. He didn't feel he should have to explain himself for what Jon did — I know it was your grandmother," she added, no doubt seeing the look of outrage on my face. "And I made him agree to ask you girls to stay upstairs. He felt that was beneath him too, no matter how much you might, well — never mind. I just wanted things to — We couldn't refuse to see our rabbi!"

"Where did Dad go?" Olivia whimpered.

"I don't know. I've never seen your father like that. I don't know what he — "

The front door banged open so hard, we heard it all the way from downstairs. Everyone's head turned.

"Can you call it a night, guys?" Mom asked.

We all nodded.

She touched a finger under her eye, then walked slowly out of the room.

Nadia was the first to speak, and the first to shed the look of impotence we'd all taken on. "That was some zany shit down there," she remarked, sounding more impressed than disturbed. "And I'm talking about what went on *inside* the house. I would never have believed Dad could snap like that. And how about Mom with her ineffectual little golem ploy? They both lost their touch tonight. Very interesting."

"How do you know what happened?" I asked as the fear of Nadia crept over me.

"We were both listening," Olivia explained, rather despondently. "Dad must've left the intercom in there on talk-lock."

"Really?" I replied.

"Bummer for him," said Nadia, looking at me with unsettling scrutiny. "He should be more careful about that. Those buttons stick."

"What's going to happen?" Olivia asked.

"Divorce, obviously," Nadia replied. "Bitter recriminations. Custody battles. Therapy. Narcotics."

Olivia rolled her eyes, but they looked scared.

I finally remembered the game, so I ran out.

I caught most of the second half.

There was no discussion whatsoever of my family's display in front of Rabbi Glickman. As the weeks and months went by, I was expecting the Family Meeting to end all Family Meetings, but it never came, and so the Schwartzes resumed their routines. The only obvious change for me was my immediate removal from Hebrew School and a corresponding discontinuation of all Bar Mitzvah preparations. My mother sat me down in the kitchen and told me that if someday I wanted to become a Bar Mitzvah, I could, but that the current time wasn't best for the family. She looked sick to her stomach telling me this.

"No problem," I told her. "I have my whole life ahead of me."

Which seemed to make her feel much better.

What I didn't tell her was that the Rabbi made me realize the only reason I never stopped going of my own accord was that I knew she'd be disappointed. Nor did I mention how thrilled I was to find myself with more time to pursue points on the Purity Test with my friends, none of whom knew much of anything at all about their religions. Jake was Unitarian, which I understood to mean he could believe in whatever he wanted. Cory said his family was "Lapsed Catholic," and Milo was "Goulash," as he called it—which I suppose he did learn something about during his family "vacations" to meditation retreats, New Age seminars, and sweat lodges, just to name a few. But he might as well have learned nothing because he couldn't keep any of it straight.

We spent a lot of time at my house, but, as demonstrated by the "No-touch" affair, the place was as full of peril as promise. Jake's house was better for two big reasons. First, Mr. Baker died when Jake was one, and his mom had some kind of cancer that forced her to go for long stays at a special nutrition center in Arizona, so the house was unsupervised most of the time. Second, his washout older brother, Daniel, sometimes left alcohol around.

Jake could do his own laundry and even cook a little bit. We thought that might be the reason girls gravitated to him, but there was never enough evidence to prompt the rest of us to learn.

We sometimes went to Cory's house, but he discouraged it. Mr. Minor, an engineer at Westinghouse, had no faith in the public school system and was consequently always giving him "Bonus" math assignments. Apparently, the more it appeared that Cory had nothing better to do, the more assignments he got.

Milo's house was totally off limits. He claimed if we went there one of us would be sacrificed on some altar or shrine. He often cited that possibility as the reason he needed to lose his virginity as soon as possible. For some reason the girls he frequently petitioned never seemed interested in saving his life.

Dad seemed to revert to his normal self after the Glickman Debacle, though it was hard to be sure because, as per his normal routine, he spent most of every day writing in his garret, a little room above our garage behind the house that no one but him was ever allowed to enter.

We did notice one significant change over the next few months: Dad stopped making us discuss the latest headlines at dinner, something he'd done every night of our entire lives. At first, his policy changed to every other night, then once a week. Eventually, he gave up the enterprise altogether and just ate in brooding silence. No one mentioned it because we all hated those discussions — Mom included.

Nadia, who usually devoted her energy at dinner to causing a beverage to be expelled through one of her siblings' noses, turned her attentions to Dad. She'd say things like, "Some guy named Rocco called and said the money better be where it's supposed to be, Dad, or those story ideas they've been selling you will start involving the postal service and various fingers of a certain first born son." She was good at killing two birds. Or, referring to some flowers Dad had given Mom, "I saw you take those from that little roadside shrine for that dead girl down the street. Don't deny it, Dad – they were propped up against the cross."

But she got nothing.

By contrast, Mom experienced something of a personal high late that spring after devising a controversial citywide campaign to encourage the use of bicycle helmets. It was controversial because it used images of brutal accidents and injuries, though only in silhouette. Mom loved the debate it stirred. Her theory was that any attention paid to the subject was good news.

Nadia was skeptical, as she was about all PSA's. "You can't *make* people pull their heads out of their asses," she told Mom at dinner one night, "though if asses were helmets, your job would already be done."

Dad didn't even bat an eye at this. I couldn't believe it. Before my mom could react, Nadia added, "As usual, you've come up with a public *dis*-service campaign."

"What do you mean?" Mom asked.

"How does it serve the public to save the lives of people too stupid to wear helmets?"

Mom didn't have a good answer.

On the Fourth of July, Olivia divulged some surprising news. Jake was over. Both of us were already dressed in coats and ties for our Big Family Dinner, which I was dreading. We were in the den on the third floor, partly watching a movie on cable while we mulled over a dungeon we were considering collaborating on for the next D & D sleepover. I was looking for some graph paper in the closet when Jake complained that neither Cory nor Milo were coming.

"How is it my fault their parents are freaks?" I said from the closet. Milo was at a Zodiac conference of some sort. Cory was at home working on his dad's latest mathematical tortures.

"What's up with this stupid movie, anyway," Jake complained. "I thought this was *Skinimax!*"

As I emerged from the closet with a few sheets of yellow graph paper, Olivia marched in and unceremoniously flipped off the TV. Jake's pupils enlarged.

"What's going on with Dad?" she demanded.

"What happened?" I asked, alarmed.

"I was driving around with Marcus yesterday—"

"Who's Marcus?"

"This guy at Pitt, okay?" Olivia was starting to hang out with much older guys.

"You were driving around with him?"

"Shut up, will you?" she barked. "I was driving around with him in Dad's car. And I pushed the tape in. I thought it was mine."

"And?"

"It was one of those language tapes. It was Hebrew."

"That's weird."

"What does it mean?"

"I have no idea. Maybe he's doing research for a new book."

"Why don't you just ask him?" This was Jake, having found the ability to speak.

"He'd have to kill us," I told him. Dad never discussed his

writing while it was in process.

"I highly doubt he's planning to write a book in Hebrew, Jonathan," Olivia said.

"What does Nadia think?"

"I don't know. I'm not talking to that—"

"That's not nearly the weirdest thing," said Nadia, who was somehow suddenly standing next to us.

"What?" we all asked, trying not to look terrified by her dark powers.

"Mom and Dad haven't had sex in six months," she said, "not since the night of Olivia's little rabbinical bondage party."

"*Wha?*" Jake bleated, looking at me with anger and amazement. I shook my head at him.

"'Course it doesn't help that he's been meeting some new rabbi in the middle of the night," Nadia added.

"How in hell do you know about our parents' sex life?" Olivia demanded. I was wondering the same thing, of course. Only I didn't want to know the answer.

Nadia shrugged. "Mom takes care of herself these days. I think Dad's a little pent up."

None of us wanted to touch that, and we couldn't un-hear it.

"What's going on?" Olivia demanded.

"He's obviously having some sort of meltdown," Nadia declared. "And Mom's too busy to deal. She oughta whip up a PSA for all depressed husbands of hers to pull their—"

"What do you mean, 'meltdown'?" I asked.

"I realize that word is not in your vocabulary, Jonathan," Nadia said, "but that's no reason to act all high and—"

"KIDS!"

Mom was calling us over the intercom. She was at the front door, welcoming Leon and Myna. Out of habit, she made sure her father didn't have to ring the doorbell. It was something she had to do as a kid—always be ready when he was coming. It was no big deal at our house, though, since she was so often standing there keeping watch, anyway.

My sisters and I looked at one another with mutual certainty that an ordeal was about to begin. Nadia crossed herself, then headed downstairs. The rest of us followed.

After hugs were exchanged, we lavished some extra attention on Leon because, as we'd learned in a brief Family Meeting, he was not "right" lately. This, my mom explained, meant he was irate about having been fitted for hearing aids, and that he should thus be handled with complete deference, lest he do "strange things."

"How will we know?" I asked, in all sincerity. Olivia cracked up, but Mom got angry.

"Such a polite *boy!*" Leon proclaimed, spitting on me when I took everyone's coats. He was not wearing hearing aids, but his glasses were so oversized, I thought maybe they could accommodate two senses.

"Young *man*, Leon!" Myna corrected, rather loudly. "Tenth grade coming up! Are you ready, Jonson?" I nodded dumbly and shuffled down the hall with the coats. As we'd been instructed to do, everyone went right into the dining room. It was my mother's feeling that dispensing with the preliminary living room small-talk reserved for normal guests would be helpful because Leon was becoming increasingly impatient with almost all forms of light conversation.

Everyone settled around the table. I got stuck between Myna and Leon because they both wanted to be next to the "high honored guest." I'd forgotten that my report card came the day before (it having been lost in the mail for a few weeks). I'd earned a nearly perfect 3.95, which garnered me a spot on the High Honor Roll. (Olivia's grades always hovered around 3.0.) Thus, the dinner was also a celebration of my achievement. My seating predicament meant I'd be vulnerable on two fronts, which was worrisome. It also meant that Jake had to go it alone. He tried to land next to Olivia, but failed and wound up between Nadia and my mother.

"How's your boyfriend?" Myna shouted into my ear, referring to Jake. I supposed she'd been getting into the habit of raising her voice for Leon, so I tried to be generous about it. Both Nadia and Olivia sniggered.

"He's not my boyfriend, Grandma, and you can ask him. He's right—"

"Is he a *boy?*" Leon shouted into my other ear, spitting at me again. I knew I'd asked for it.

"Yes, Grandpa," I moaned.

"What?"

"Yes!"

"Is he your *friend?*"

"Yes, Grandpa."

"I'm fine, Mrs. Julianelle," Jake nobly called from his end of the table.

"He is a boy, and he is your *friend?*"

"Yes. Grandpa." I put a finger in my ear to dab the saliva collecting inside.

"Then don't harass your grandmother!"

Mom came in from the kitchen with the roast Dad had prepared and set it on the table. Then she stood behind her chair and said, "Jonson, your father and I are very proud of you today. You are an outstanding student. We hope, as you grow older, you won't lose your lust for learning—or your special gift for enjoying life."

I was embarrassed, especially because she used the word 'lust.' Mom seemed to be done speaking, so everyone naturally turned to Dad to see if he was going to add anything, but his thoughts appeared to be elsewhere. But then his dark brown eyes found me, and he smiled for the first time I'd seen in months.

"Jonathan," he whispered, "we are very proud of you." Then he fell silent again. His brevity was so unexpected that I actually wished for his annual speech on how ambivalent he was about Independence Day — he loathed nationalism, but loved America for allowing him to loathe it.

Mom interrupted then, or perhaps, I thought, tried to appear to interrupt because she knew Dad had nothing further to offer. "And *Nadia,*" she said with a flourish, "this is a special time for you as well."

"Leave it alone, Mother," Nadia warned.

"Nonsense," Mom said. "Nadia has received her diploma. She is now a high school graduate. Congratulations, honey."

Olivia turned to her older sister with undisguised joy and said, "Does that mean—?" But the withering look Nadia cast prevented her from finishing the question.

Leon bumped me rather forcefully. I looked at him in surprise, but he seemed not to have noticed. Too many strange things were happening, but then Mom told everyone to eat.

So I ate.

We all took very small portions when we ate with my grandparents because to push back one's chair with so much as a particle of food still on the plate was to incur the wrath of God, as dispensed by Leon. He and Myna (after she married him) would consume what they took completely, and only then take more, and I use the word 'completely' in its most literal sense, as in the plates looked like they'd just come out of the dishwasher. Leon was even known to pull a hunk of meat right off a roasted chicken and take it straight to his mouth, but my mother objected strenuously when he did that.

We all knew the way our grandparents ate had something to do with Leon's experiences during the war, something to do with his constant fear of having to flee at a moment's notice from the barn.

Sometimes Leon would put bits of food in his pockets. I know he didn't realize he did this because, later, he'd seem genuinely surprised to find food in one—after which he'd rant and rave about the laundromat, as if incompetence explained the presence of brisket or half a blintz in his blazer. Myna knew he did it, but she never said anything about it.

Taking small portions meant there was a great deal of passing dishes back and forth, and it was in this fashion that our Fourth of July feast progressed. Leon kept jostling me, but I was prepared to deal with it because everything else seemed relatively normal. Myna asked my mother about her work but didn't listen to any of the response. Nadia told Olivia she should join the Drama Club in the fall, and Olivia actually said it was a great idea. Everyone agreed. No one bothered to point out that she'd never acted in her life.

Nadia stood up and cleared her throat.

"Family," she said, "I've got additional news. Now that I've joined that revered fraternity of high school graduates, I will be going to college."

No one responded to this, though Olivia's eyes lit up.

"I've been accepted at Swarthmore, actually."

I snorted, since this was obviously a joke.

"What?" said Leon, because he couldn't hear. He bumped into me heavily for what seemed like the fiftieth time. I tried to inch my chair away, but Myna's chair was jammed right up against it on the other side.

"Naddie, what are you talking about?" Mom asked this in a tone that struck me as not unlike the one movie doctors used to humor the criminally insane.

"She's not feeling well," said Myna. "Sit down and eat something, darling."

Nadia's eyes narrowed, and it occurred to me that she really wasn't as skinny as she used to be. I wondered when that had happened. She managed to calm herself. I munched slowly on roast beef while Leon kept jouncing me.

"I took the SAT's earlier in the year," Nadia explained. "When Mr. O'Donnell saw my score, he said he'd talk to some admission people about considering me, even though I hadn't gotten my diploma yet. So they did, and I got an acceptance a few months ago contingent on me finishing my credits. So, I'm going to college."

I looked over at my mother, who looked more dismayed than delighted. "Why, that's wonderful," she said. Dad looked as if he were on another planet, mentally absent from all proceedings.

"What score did you get?" Olivia asked, trying to sound casual. She sipped her diet cola.

"1600," Nadia said, taking a seat.

Olivia spat her soda on the table.

"Holy *shit*," I inadvertently blurted, after which I was struck in the face with Leon's napkin.

"How dare you!" he demanded.

"I'm sorry, Grandpa! That's the highest possible score!"

Olivia slammed back her chair and ran from the table. Mom called after her, but she was gone.

"She's not feeling well," Myna explained.

"Olivia got 1050 on her PSAT." This information was courtesy of Jake.

"That's not bad, is it?" Mom asked, apparently unfazed that Jake knew this particular piece of information about her daughter. I hadn't known.

"If that girl put half of her attentions into school instead of all this meshugenah make-up," declared Myna, to no one in particular, "she'd be Albert Einstein."

"What?" shouted Leon, shouldering me into Myna.

"Einstein! Albert Einstein!" Myna bellowed this into my ear, as if intending to pass her voice through my skull.

"He was *Jewish*, you know," Leon proclaimed. He was looking at Jake, who shrugged, helplessly. "Now *that* was a smart boy."

"Here's one for you, Miss Sixty-three Hundred on the STD's," Myna said, apropos of nothing. "When a Jew looks into an ashtray, what is he doing?"

"Myna, please," Mom groaned. "Spare us tonight. We have a guest."

I looked at Jake because I'd told him a million times how Myna was, but he'd never witnessed it in person. He looked both excited and nervous.

"So, we're not so smart after all, eh?"

Nadia actually appeared to be pondering the question, evidently unconcerned that her big news had been so casually swept aside. I assumed everyone figured she was just trying to get a rise out of Olivia and that the truth would come out later.

We all knew the ashtray joke Myna told Leon the night my parents met, so I guessed Nadia was trying to connect them somehow. "I don't know, Grandma," she finally conceded. "I give up."

With a triumphant smile, Myna leaned forward and whispered, "Researching his family tree!"

"Myna, that's disgusting!" Mom cried.

Jake looked confused. He didn't get it.

"What?" Leon demanded, scanning the faces at the table. They were: nonplussed (Nadia), baffled (Jake), appalled (Mom) and apparently oblivious (Dad).

"*Tree!*" Myna screamed into my ear. "*His family tree!*"

I wanted to ask her if she was a Self-hating Jew, but I didn't have the nerve.

"Myna!" Mom shouted.

"ENOUGH!"

That was my father.

Everyone fell silent.

"GODDAMN IT! ENOUGH IS *ENOUGH!*" he roared. "This is a free country, and you can say what you like, but enough is enough." His voice trailed off to a whisper.

Leon's ears were evidently tuned with greater sensitivity to the sounds of disrespect. He leaned right over my plate, forcing me to grind shoulders with Myna, and growled, "Don't you *dare* talk to your mother that way, young man! Just who do you think you *are?*"

"Father!" Mom scolded. *"Please!"*

Leon turned on his daughter. "Don't you sass me, young lady," he scolded right back. "Do I need to take you *upstairs?*"

Mom went red in the face. I could see Jake mentally recording all of these events to tell the world later on.

Myna leaned over and put her hand on Leon's shoulder to calm him. Then she looked at my father and asked, "Did you know that there are only two kinds of countries in the world?"

"No," Dad replied, trying not to invite an explanation.

"There are the kinds that want to kick Jews out—and the kind that don't want to let Jews in."

My father stared at his mother, blankly. I was trying to determine whether Myna had told another "joke," but didn't have long to contemplate the matter, for just as my father was going to respond, Leon slumped over and fell directly into my lap.

Nadia turned white. Myna screamed. I remained frozen until Dad rushed over and pulled my grandfather off of me.

After determining that Leon was not choking, Dad carefully lowered him onto the hardwood floor. Leon's breathing was very shallow, his eyes were bulging, and his face looked blue. Mom rushed to the kitchen to call 911. Dad instructed me to take Myna away as he tried to make Leon comfortable, so I shepherded her into the living room and onto a couch. She was dazed and pliant. I sat down next to her, and she held my hands.

Myna began rocking forward and back, taking me with her in the motion. But, suddenly, she stopped. Without looking at me she said, "Jonson, the other day, I was watching you and your boy friend in the front yard playing football, running and smashing each other's brains—"

I was too disoriented to respond and kept craning my neck to see what was going on in the dining room. Myna didn't seem to need a reply, anyway.

"Did you know," she whispered, "the children of the ghettoes—these children, Jewish children, five, six years-old—they play games called, in English, 'Gas Chamber' and 'Gestapo Agent.' Did you know that, Jonson?"

I shook my head.

"And you shouldn't," Myna said. "Tell this to your teacher."

"But I don't go to Hebrew School any—"

"We do what God wills," Myna said. "There is no fighting it. There is no asking why." Then she said, "We live, we do what we must, and then we die."

The paramedics arrived, saving me from having to respond to this. They loaded Leon into an ambulance and rushed him off to Presbyterian Hospital. We followed as a family and sat red-eyed and silent on green couches and beige chairs in the waiting room. Despite the certainty I felt that Leon would be okay, the tension that gripped us as we sat there was nearly unbearable.

At some point, Olivia, who'd come back down to dinner looking remarkably composed only to find pandemonium, sounded as if she were crying. "Please don't let him die," she whimpered, loudly. "Please, God, *don't*—"

She cut herself off, and we all knew why.

The idea of a god who could be plied for personal favors, especially at a time of crisis, was another of Dad's big pet peeves. But he either hadn't heard or wasn't up to lecturing anyone about babies getting pitched alive into Nazi ovens.

Olivia put her head into her hands and lapsed into pained silence. My father did the same. I couldn't stand to be there, staring at them all, but I didn't want to leave, so I took a seat at the far end of the room next to a large planter and tried to clear my mind. Jake hadn't come along with us, having, I assumed, walked back to his own house when we rushed away.

Mercifully, I drifted off.

"Jonathan!" Someone was calling my name. *"Jonathan!"*

It was my father. I looked up, startled to find everyone standing up, staring at me. "Didn't you hear me?" he asked. "I've called your name five times."

"No, I didn't," I said. "I'm sorry."

"What in the world are you doing?" Mom asked. "Look at your hands!"

"What do you mean?" I looked down at my hands. They were clutching a clump of dirt.

"Why in the world would you take dirt out of the planter?" Dad asked.

Instead of responding, I tossed the whole hunk back into the oversized pot and tried to clean my hands over it. I was thoroughly embarrassed and confused. I had no idea what I'd been doing.

"Here," Mom said, opening her purse. "Some tissues." She dug around but found none. "I'm out," she told me. "Do you have a handkerchief in that sport coat?"

I reached into my pocket and hooted in disgust as my hand slipped into something cold and wet. Everyone walked over to me as I fished out four shreds of cold roast beef and several congealed hunks of gravy.

It took a second for everyone to realize how they'd gotten there, and for me to realize what was going on with all of Leon's shoulder-checking at dinner.

Mom was the first to giggle at the mess, then Olivia broke down, but it was Myna bursting into outright guffaws that sent us all into spasms. Even Dad was laughing. I guess it was the stress and fear we were all feeling because no one could stop. We tottered around the room, roaring.

At some point, Nadia tottered over to the planter to look inside, and I stopped laughing because I could see she was only pretending to be amused. I looked into it with her.

Inside was a small human-like figure molded out of dirt.

"Voodoo?" she asked.

Once again, it took me a moment to process my thoughts, but I realized what it was: a golem. I'd fashioned my own golem out of dirt from the hospital planter. Nadia seemed to be waiting for an explanation, but I wasn't planning on providing her with one.

It turned out I didn't have to because the doctor came into the waiting area. Everyone stopped laughing at once. He was gangly and awkward and had silver sideburns, and he told us that Leon had suffered a massive heart attack—and that he didn't survive it.

PART II

By the time I attended my first day as a tenth grader at Taylor Allderdice in the fall of 1983, the makeup of my household had changed dramatically. Nadia was gone, evidently already well ensconced in an apartment that had been arranged by another freshman she'd somehow connected with. It turned out that while secluded in her room all that time, along with memorizing the latest version of The Diagnostic and Statistical Manual of Mental Disorders, she was completing her high school coursework and mailing it in. Upon taking her leave, she told us she'd be done in three years or less with her B. S. I wanted to tell her she'd been born with that degree, but I didn't dare.

With Leon gone and Nadia out of the house, Myna moved in. It was Nadia's suggestion, a devastating parting shot Olivia and I hated her for. It wasn't that we disliked our grandmother, but the plan was for her to take over Nadia's room, which would have ruined our third-floor lives. Fortunately, the situation was saved when it was determined that she couldn't handle two flights of stairs. To accommodate her, my parents converted the TV room on the second floor into a bedroom. Myna sold the house she and Leon had been living in all those years and came to us with all her worldly possessions, the entirety of which apparently fit into two suitcases.

Rabbi Glickman conducted the funeral service, which was mercifully, though by necessity, short. In order to give eulogies for people he didn't know much about (Leon never stepped foot in shul), he depended upon information provided by the deceased's family and friends, but either the Rabbi didn't want to further jeopardize his health and welfare by approaching us for the necessary information, or my parents simply avoided providing it for him. Either way, it was fairly obvious he was talking in broad strokes about how if Leon was a hard man with the highest of expectations (everyone knew *that* much about him), then shouldn't we be that much more impressed? After all, here was a man who'd experienced unspeakable evil, yet who could not only look for, but *demand* the best in others? "You know," Rabbi Glickman mused, "I've been thinking. We often talk about 'Post-traumatic Stress Disorder' — but I wonder if I can reverse its meaning for — a moment. Consider many of us, the generations *after* such — Evil incarnate existed, *post*, this Evil, this traumatic — *Stress*. Perhaps we too are disordered being born — in its wake. Is there anything to be done — for us?"

It might have been the only pessimistic sounding thing I ever heard him say.

Myna didn't cry during the service. Instead, she rocked sadly to and fro in a melancholy stupor, nodding her head, though not, as far as I could tell, in response to anything Rabbi Glickman said. It looked more like she was heeding the words of some invisible interlocutor whispering consolations only she could hear.

The actual burial was brief — rushed, actually. It was only us Schwartzes and the Rabbi, which was hideously awkward because he seemed afraid to look at anyone, perhaps fearing eye-contact would send one of us off on some kind of psychotic episode. Not that I blamed him. I'm positive it was the fastest he'd ever spoken.

I noticed he had a bit of a limp.

The strangest part of the next few weeks was that nothing was particularly strange. At a Family Meeting just before Myna's arrival, my parents coached Olivia and me on what to expect from our grandmother as she navigated the grieving process. Dad told us to anticipate a short period of denial, followed by a possibly lengthy stage of anger before Myna accepted her loss. We were to treat her with "Kid gloves," which I had to look up.

"What about you, Mom?" Olivia asked. "You lost your dad."

"I know," my mother replied, "but don't worry — I took care of the anger stage while he was alive."

We agreed, such as we ever did, to have frequent, informal check-ins to update one another on Myna's progress.

It did appear as if Myna was in denial when she first moved in. While she certainly wasn't chipper, she didn't act the least bit morose either. And while she didn't talk to Leon as if he were there or set a place at the table for him at meals, she also didn't bring up the fact that he was dead. She simply began living her life at our house, which mostly meant taking over the cooking duties from Dad.

After a month, my mother began to worry Myna wasn't ever going to face the truth. "How could she act as if nothing has changed?" she wondered. "She's exactly the same."

"She stopped telling jokes!" Olivia suddenly realized. I hadn't noticed, but she was right. Myna hadn't told a single whopper since she'd moved in. Somehow, we hadn't noticed. I asked Dad what it meant.

"It means things aren't so funny when your husband is dead," was his reply, which seemed eminently reasonable. We agreed not to mention the change to Myna.

Myna was Myna then, with no jokes.

"You, darling, are the only one not acting silly. What are the others waiting for? I should act ding-dong in the head for them to treat me regular?"

My grandmother had corralled me walking past her room one Saturday morning. I was on my way over to Jake's to see about breaking into his brother's newly discovered *Hustler* stash.

"Uh—" I said.

"They are driving me up walls," Myna complained, "with the tiptoes and the What-can-I-get-you's all the time."

"I guess they think you should be sad," I explained, "about Grandpa dying."

"Jonson, I am very, very sad for this! I love Leon like life. But people live and die, and they must do what they must do between the two. It is not ours to question."

"Fate, Grandma? Are you talking about fate?"

"What choice do I have?"

I didn't know Myna believed in anything like fate, even though it was suddenly obvious it was fate she was talking about before we left for the hospital. I didn't even know she had much of a belief in God, and I was certain my parents didn't know either—fairly certain, anyway. Or, maybe believing in fate wasn't the same as believing in God. I didn't know. I wanted to ask her whether God or fate made her stop the jokes—or tell them to begin with, for that matter. Instead, I told her I had to get to Jake's to play some new Intellivision games.

"That's what I love about you, Jonson," Myna said. "You know from fun."

It was during the first week of September, just after school started, when Dad called the first full meeting of our newly constituted family.

"What is this?" Myna asked as my sister and I led her downstairs. "Is he going to pretend to be listening to our opinions and then telling us what to do, anyway?"

Olivia and I said yes.

The meeting was brief and non-confrontational, although very surprising. Dad informed us that he was going to Hebron to do research for a novel about the increasing militancy among orthodox Jews in Israel. He'd been in touch with an ultra-orthodox sect called Halacha for a number of months and managed to convince them that he wanted to join. He was using a false name, of course. They'd agreed to take him in for a trial period. The problem was that he wouldn't be back until Thanksgiving. *"And,"* he added, "I'm leaving tomorrow morning. They're willing to take me right now, and I can't risk losing the opportunity. *And,"* he added to his addition, "I won't be able to get in touch. These folks are, as they say, off the grid."

Olivia and I looked at Mom, who had a poker face. Since Leon's death, she'd appeared to be happily immersed in plans to expand her gross-out silhouette strategy to other PSA's, but Olivia told me she'd seen occasional moments of absence in which Mom's eyes would cloud over and she'd stare into the void for ten seconds or so. We agreed she was sad about losing her father, despite her own denial.

"Israel?" Myna said. "Such a distance to study crazy people! You don't need to go so far, darling. The Jews in Prague used to say—"

"Meeting adjourned," Dad announced.

I looked at my mother, expecting her to be cross, but she was still just sitting there, spacing out. It was the opposite of the Fourth of July dinner.

"The meeting is adjourned you say?" Myna asked.

"The meeting is adjourned."

Myna raised her upturned hands. "Because if the meeting is adjourned," she said, "the meeting is adjourned. No further business here if the meeting is adjourned."

"The Meeting. Is. *Adjourned.*"

Olivia and I raced upstairs. "What in the hell is going on?"

she demanded when we reached the third floor hall.

"I guess he's doing research for a book," I said. "What he said."

"Are you sure? When's the last time he did research outside of that stupid garret? I'll tell you when — *never.*"

"What else could it be? Those tapes — he was learning Hebrew for those people."

"Hmmm," Olivia grumbled. "All I know is that everyone around here is full of shit."

"What do you mean?" I asked, but Olivia didn't answer. She walked into her room and slammed the pink door.

Dad left the next morning without incident, though there might've been one. Myna wouldn't come out of her room to see him off. Only token efforts were made to lure her out because we all knew she was a nervous traveler, even when it wasn't she who was doing the travelling. I wanted to ask her why she was making such a fuss if it was my father's fate to travel to Israel, but I held my tongue.

Dad said goodbye through the door.

When the taxi arrived, Mom looked at Olivia and me. "Kids," she said, "say your goodbyes, then go upstairs and find something useful to do."

Olivia and I gave Dad a quick hug, then headed upstairs. I could see Olivia had tears in her eyes, but I didn't know what to make of them. I decided she was being melodramatic. Since school had begun she'd been talking non-stop about how glad she was she'd signed up for Drama, and how gifted the coach said she was.

A few minutes later, Mom came up and found us on the second floor, lurking by Myna's still-closed door. She didn't look as though she was or had been crying, but she seemed shaky. Olivia asked if what Dad was doing was dangerous. Mom said don't be silly.

Mom moved to knock on her mother-in-law's door, but it suddenly opened.

"Did he really go through with this *meshugas?*" Myna asked.

"Yes, Myna," my mother replied. "He really did."

Myna's sour expression intensified momentarily, but then it vanished. She shrugged and straightened up a bit. "So be it, then," she said.

My grandmother came out of her room, and our lives went on.

At lunch one day in late September, Milo abruptly announced that he was never going to step foot inside his house again because his parents had decided to make their home kosher, despite the fact they weren't Jewish. They claimed to have received a sign, which, Milo explained with maximum scorn, was in the form of one of the "cheap-shit flyers" they were always getting in the mail. After reading it, his folks cleaned out every speck of food from the premises, threw out all the pots, pans, and dishes, and sterilized everything nailed down.

"I now live in an insane asylum," Milo declared. "An insan*er* asylum."

"What's the point?" Jake asked.

"THERE IS NO POINT!" Milo agonized, attracting attention from everyone at the twenty-foot long table. "They got goddamn junk-mail that said kosher is the only 'cruelty-free' meat, and it had all these astrological signs and quotes from the Bible all over it. MY PARENTS HAVE JOINED A FREAKIN' MAIL-ORDER CULT! No offense, Jon."

I had no idea why he said that. We certainly didn't follow any dietary restrictions, religious or otherwise.

"Is the food any better?" Cory asked. Eating was becoming his main focus in life. He'd made the JV football squad and was apparently planning to eat his way up to Varsity. And there was also his abiding interest in anything of or related to Sarah Glickman.

A pair of girls sitting a few seats away seemed to be enjoying Milo's raving. I could see he was aware of this. "Listen," he whispered, loudly enough for them to hear, "I got me a pig."

"What?" I asked.

"It's in my garage. I'm going to let it in the house tonight."

The girls giggled and stopped pretending not to be eavesdropping.

"I'm going to slather it in half and half and then let it into my parents' bedroom."

They laughed some more. I tried to stop listening since I knew what was going on, but I did sense distress in Milo's tone. I wondered, as I often did, why he even mentioned his parents' antics if they embarrassed him so much. He was behaving like an ass as far as I was concerned. I looked away.

"Then I'm going to kill it," Milo declared. "With an ax. And then I'm going to smear the blood all over the porcelain Aztec Calendar on their headboard."

The girls were suddenly un-amused. They gathered their red plastic trays and left the table.

"Airheads!" Milo shouted.

"What's wrong with you, man? Cory asked, liberating a conglomeration of soggy French fries from Milo's tray. "That's some sick shit to be thinking about."

"Ah, bite me!" Milo snapped. "Why don't you go calculate the square root of the hairs on your ass." He grabbed his tray and headed off.

"What's eating him?" Cory asked.

"Probably *you* if he sat there for another five minutes," I replied.

"Funny, Schwartz. How come your parents don't keep kosher? Don't you have to if you're Jewish?"

"My dad would rather starve."

"I don't get it."

"Get what, Cory?"

"Some Jews keep kosher and some don't?"

"Right. You do get it."

"So you don't *have* to? It's, like, optional?"

"I don't know—it's complicated. You don't even really have to believe in God, I don't think."

"What?"

"It's really complicated, Cory. Why don't you go talk to your girlfriend about it?"

Cory ignored the jab and pressed on with an obviously self-interested question. "So, is it the same thing like how come some Jewish girls won't date boys that aren't Jewish, but some will. You don't care about the girls you date, right? I mean, if you had a date, you wouldn't—"

"Right. Some of us don't believe in that, *okay?*"

"What the hell? Can you make up your own rules? Seems to me you either get with the program or you don't."

"Thank you, Rabbi Lombardi."

"Anyway, *is* the food better?"

That same night, while Myna, Olivia, and I sat eating dinner and wondering why Mom was late, she came in bleary-eyed and red-faced. Her hair was tied back in a ponytail, and she'd obviously attempted to wash mascara stains from her cheeks.

"He'll come back to you, darling," Myna promised.

"What is that supposed to mean?" Mom demanded.

"Bike helmets," Olivia said.

Surprised, Mom turned to Olivia and nodded, dejectedly. She tried to suppress tears, but they came, so Olivia got up and hugged her. "The numbers aren't good, are they?" she asked.

"How in the world did you know that?"

"Nadia called the other day to ask if they'd come in yet. She said they'd be bad."

"She's right," Mom admitted. "The initial results were fantastic—through the roof! But now they've gone off a cliff. My detractors are swooping down like vultures. It's a feeding frenzy! The campaign's been yanked, and now my smoke-detectors and fetal alcohol PSA's are at risk. And it seems the Ad Council is backing away from me, too." Mom put a napkin to her face. It was her dream to do a campaign for the Ad Council. I didn't know they'd been considering her.

"People *like* having their heads up their asses!" Olivia suddenly shouted, "and until they're actually sewn shut, they'll never learn!"

I cringed, but Mom actually smiled. "You have Nadia down pat, honey," she said. "That Drama coach is really good, isn't he?"

Upon reflection, I had to admit she did nail our sister, the sardonic intonation and everything.

"Thank you, thank you," Olivia purred. "No applause. Just throw money." She curtsied and sat back down.

Mom blew her nose. "I'm starving," she said.

Mom seemed strangely buoyed by Olivia's performance. There were no further tearful entrances or breakdowns, though that didn't mean she was her old self. On the contrary, she was changing. First, she started cleaning things more than she used to. It wasn't that the house was ever sloppy. Olivia and I were actually rather neat, and Myna was constantly tidying up. Even so, Mom seemed to be cleaning whenever she was home: vacuuming, dusting, wiping, polishing, rearranging, and generally washing. It started off unobtrusively enough in the form of a little extra table scrubbing after dinner and some late night dusting in the family room, but soon enough, things escalated to the point where no one would dare set a glass down because, empty, half full, or overflowing, Mom would have it washed out and deposited in the dishwasher before your next sip. Sometimes she just stood at the sink and washed dishes clean without ever putting them into the washer, which was something she never used to do.

Another, more ominous, change occurred at the dinner table in mid-October. We were sitting down to lamb chops when something detonated inside Mom. She put down her glass of wine, looked at Myna, and calmly enunciated the word, *"Bastard."*

"No, darling," Myna protested. "He will be back soon."

But Mom was not talking about her husband. "Myna," she said, "my father was not a good person."

"Don't say such things, Deana," my grandmother warned.

Mom looked down at her plate and squelched whatever she was going to say next. Olivia and I looked at each other and then went back to work on our food.

I was laying on the second floor hall carpet, throwing playing cards at my overturned Steelers cap and listening to Casey Kasem one Sunday afternoon, when I heard Mom in Myna's room expressing more specific reproaches. Her voice was simmering. "He was the worst father a child could have! The worst! *The worst!* He hated me. He treated me like dirt! There was nothing between us but *rules!* Myna, he wouldn't let me take Dance because I had to wear a leotard in public! The only people he treated worse were the women stupid enough to try to become his friend. I wanted a mother, Myna. And for that matter, I wanted a father!"

"You've got a mother, darling. You must not say such things."

Soon enough, exchanges like this were occurring nearly every night, but I was the only one forced to witness the majority of them because Olivia's Drama obligations kept her tied up every evening, sometimes past eight or nine o'clock. For the first few weeks, she came home looking wiped out and went straight to bed. Mom, for her part, didn't seem overly concerned, though one night, when Olivia tried to hurry past her up the stairs, she pulled the vacuum cord out of the wall and threatened to call the coach. "I don't care how good he is, Olivia," she said. "This is too much. You look like you've been sobbing."

"Mom," Olivia sighed, "we're working on *Despair* this week. I happen to be the best one in the entire group." She produced a dazzling grin. "Next week we do Fury. It's the most fun I've ever had."

"Hmmm."

A few nights later, Myna corralled Olivia when she came in and forced her to eat. "What, are you taking over for your sister around here? Is that who you're still acting? Act like you're hungry," she ordered.

I was in the hall and walked into the kitchen. Olivia looked nauseated and somehow older. "Don't the signs in the cafeteria say Drama meets Monday, Wednesday, and Friday?" I asked.

Olivia's eyes darkened. "That's for school, stupid," she said. "I'm also doing dual-credit at—through Pitt. Just butt out, *all right?*"

"Whoa," Myna interjected, "act like you like each other."

I kept out of Olivia's way after that and, soon enough, she was herself again, full-time. Myna started having warm dinners ready for her when she came home, and Olivia gobbled them down with gusto, as if compensating for the meals she'd missed.

"So, how's Mom?" Olivia asked one night, digging into Myna's re-heated Cornish hen.

"She told Grandma that Leon used to demand to know everywhere she ever went and everything she ever did, and he'd slap her sometimes if he didn't like her answers, not really bad, but for real—and then he would cry for days at a time and not do any work. Mom had to skip school and do all the sewing for his shop herself when that happened. I didn't even know Mom could sew."

"Old news."

"What do you mean?"

"That's why Mom never interrogates us when we go out."

"Oh, yeah, right," I said. *"Duh."*

Four days before Thanksgiving, Mom called a Family Meeting. She summoned us via the intercom in a voice that sounded fraught.

"Nadia was right!" Olivia said when I met her on the steps. Her jaws were clenched. We ran into Myna as she came out of her room.

"About what?" our grandmother asked. Her hearing was excellent.

"She thinks Mom and Dad are separated," I explained in the best *Isn't-that-just-ridiculous* tone I could muster. Nadia had been calling to predict this regularly.

"Oy," Myna replied, straightening the red scarf on her head. "I'm afraid this is so."

"What? How can you say that?" Olivia demanded.

"How does my saying make it so or not so?" Myna retorted. "A husband doesn't do research so long away from his wife unless he's researching the wrong things."

"You didn't exactly try to keep him here," Olivia pointed out. "You didn't even say goodbye."

"I was trying to keep him here, young lady. This is why I didn't say goodbye."

"And now you don't care?"

"Of course I care! Who says I don't care?"

Before Mom could even open her mouth at the card table, Olivia began babbling. "What is going on, Mother? You owe us an explanation. Just how are we supposed to feel about never knowing what's going on around here? What is going on, Mother!"

Mom looked at Olivia with real sadness in her eyes. "I am so sorry," she whispered. "I don't think I'm handling this situation well at all. Please forgive me."

Olivia's outrage fizzled. "What situation, Mom? *Please*," she begged.

"Your father," Mom said. "He is such a wonderful man."

"This sounds like a funeral," said Myna. "Is this a funeral?"

Mom let this pass. "After our meeting with Rabbi Glickman," she explained, "your father started doing some serious soul searching."

"What's he really doing in Israel, Mom?" Olivia asked. "Is he having an affair?"

"He told me what he told you, that he was doing research. But I wonder now if it's not really for a new book."

"What do you mean?"

"I think he's researching a new life. I think he is considering actually joining this group he's living with. I received a letter from him today saying he'll be staying with them for another three months."

"What?" Myna croaked, standing up painfully. It wasn't a Family Meeting if someone didn't get to her feet. "Is he meshugenah?"

"Oh, my God," was what Olivia said.

I heard myself announce, to no one in particular, "He was meeting a rabbi at night—not Rabbi Glickman."

"I know," Mom muttered. "Rabbi Speigleman."

"You know?" Olivia cried.

"Who's not to know?" said Myna. "He stomped past my room every night like elephants."

"He wanted to keep the meetings a secret," Mom explained. "They were about these types of groups in Israel. He was worried if the press found out they'd start writing that he'd changed his mind about religion."

"But he did!" Olivia cried. Then she whined, "What are we

going to do?"

Mom put her hand through her hair. "I booked us a flight over Thanksgiving weekend," she said. "Maybe I'm overreacting, but I want him to see us before he makes this kind of decision."

"I can't go," Olivia said, almost too quietly to hear.

"What do you mean, you can't go?"

"I just can't go, that's all." Olivia wouldn't look at anyone.

"You're going."

We watched my sister stomp away, then Mom looked to me for an explanation she surely knew I couldn't provide.

The evening before our scheduled departure for Israel, Cory, Jake, and Milo were over. We'd spent hours in the den on the third floor playing KABOOM! on Atari — until I achieved a score high enough to win a prize. Instructions on the box indicated that to claim my (unspecified) reward, I would need to submit a picture of the TV screen showing the points total. We wasted nearly an entire role of Polaroid film trying to produce one, but no matter how we lit the room and from whatever angle we snapped the camera, the TV looked off. I was just about to give up when Cory got an idea.

"Hey," he said, "what if we video the screen and send in the tape? They'd have to accept that. You guys have a camera don't you?"

"Genius," I declared and immediately headed downstairs to find the video camera my mother had recently brought home from work. It took a while, but I found it on the top shelf in her office closet. I ran it back upstairs, only to discover there was no tape inside. "Shit," I grumbled. "I didn't see any tapes. I really want that prize."

"Ah—" Jake said, "there are some tapes in Olivia's room."

"How exactly do you happen to know that?"

Jake flushed. Milo cocked a brow. Cory raised his hands as

if to indicate he had no part in something I wouldn't appreciate.

"What?"

"Milo dared him to steal a pair of her underwear," Cory confessed. "I told him not to do it."

I looked at Jake and then at Milo, who, to demonstrate proof of the deed, produced a black thong from under the couch cushion. He threw it at me, but missed. "Licorice," he said. "It's edible. Baker took a bite." There did indeed seem to be a chunk missing.

I was much too concerned with my KABOOM! score to be distracted by this nonsense. "Where are the tapes?" I asked.

"In her underwear drawer," Jake muttered. Milo found this hilarious.

"Sick," Cory decreed.

"Go get me one, and hurry up because Olivia will be back from Drama soon."

Jake ran out, then sprinted back thirty seconds later with a silver video box. He slid the tape out and handed it to me. I popped it in the camera, hit record, and aimed at the TV.

"Why are you taping a video game?"

Olivia was in the room. I had no idea how my sisters did that. I nearly dropped the camera. Jake was so startled that he fell over the Atari console, disconnecting it from the TV.

"Crap!" I cried.

"You idiots better not damage Mom's—"

Olivia caught herself up short because she'd spotted her masticated thong on the floor. Then, in what I perceived as slow motion, she slid her eyes along the carpet to the empty silver box at my feet, after which her face drained of color. It took another second for her to realize I had the tape in the recorder.

"That's my tape!" she screeched, leaping at me.

I eluded her with a shoulder fake.

Olivia fell past me and crashed right on top of Jake, who hadn't gotten up. I made a beeline for my bedroom, and, once inside, slammed and locked the door.

"_Please,_ Jonathan," Olivia whined through the keyhole. "Give it back. It's only an audition tape, but it's totally lame and embarrassing. I don't care if you ruined it. _Please._"

"Only if I can watch it first."

"No! Just destroy it. I don't care."

Going straight for the jugular, I said, "Either I watch it and give it back, or it goes to school with Milo next week."

"Damn you! _Wait!_ I'll pay you for it."

"Nineteen trillion dollars."

"Damn you, Jonathan!" Olivia sounded halfway berserk, but then her voice went calm. "Okay," she said. "What do you want? Anything—I'll clean your room for a year."

"Ten."

"Please, Jonson. Be a pal. I love you, you know. You're my best friend, and I need you to do me this favor." She had that throaty voice she sometimes used, though never on me. I made regurgitation noises through the door.

"Fine. I don't give a flying fuck."

I came out holding the tape in both hands behind my back. Olivia made a lunge for it, but I checked her out of the way. "Milo!" I called.

"Okay! Okay!" Olivia wasn't crying, but her face was alarmingly twisted. She really looked as if she were suffering, but I told myself not to be taken in. Milo, Cory, and Jake were already in the hall, having watched the scene at the door. I told them to hit the road, and they agreed without protest. We'd been through many potential blackmail scenarios at various friends' houses. Everyone knew the drill.

"Wait, guys!" Olivia shouted as they headed downstairs. Cory was in front and stopped dead. Jake and Milo would've knocked him down the steps if he weren't so big. They all turned around with big eyes.

Olivia looked at me and then back at them. "I'll make you three stooges a deal," she said. "If any one of you gets that tape for me, I'll strip naked for all three of you right here and now — *totally buck-fucking naked.*"

The world went still and quiet as my three best friends contemplated the situation. Olivia's eyes toggled between them.

No one moved.

We were at an impasse.

"You don't believe me?" Olivia asked. "I'm *dead* serious." She un-tucked the silk blouse she was wearing and let it hang over her jeans, which she proceeded to open and let fall to the carpet.

The word *kamikaze* entered my mind, probably because he was screaming words that didn't sound like any language he or I knew.

It was Jake.

He was flying down the hall, coming at me with a grotesquely contorted face, clearly intending to pry the tape from the grip of my carcass if he had to — but he stepped on one of Olivia's pant legs and fell on his face right in front of me. I leapt over him and into the den. Then I slammed and locked the door.

"You dumb, *shmuck!*" I heard Olivia scream. "Get the hell off of my jeans!" I heard some fumbling and incoherent apologies. "Get out of here!" she bellowed. "All of you! OR I'LL RIP YOUR LOUSY BALLS OFF!"

Frantic scampering down the steps.

"Let's just get this over with," Olivia said through the door. I could tell by her voice that she'd given up, so I let her into the den. She slumped into the couch as I switched the TV over to VCR, popped the tape in, and hit rewind. When it clicked, I hit play and sat down.

My KABOOM! score came up — totally distorted. "Son of a — !"

I swallowed my outrage because suddenly I was looking at a

shower house full of stark naked girls. "Holy —!" was all I could say at first. "What is this, a bootlegged copy of *Porky's?*"

Olivia was staring at the screen, stone-faced.

I looked back, and to my shock, *there she was.*

She was the last of seven girls in a row of showers, soaping and laughing like the rest of them. I blinked several times and shook my head, but it was absolutely her. I looked at the other girls, hoping to see Olivia's friends, but I didn't recognize any of them, which worried me. One had a yellow waterproof radio and turned on some dance music. The camera kept panning, but it was clearly returning frequently to Olivia. I was dumbfounded at the sight of her, completely nude. She grabbed her shampoo and squirted it at the girl next to her. Then all the girls were squirting shampoo at one another. Then they all started running around, half fighting and half dancing to the music. Some had shaving cream and started spraying it in all directions.

Then they were sliding onto the floor and rolling around in the slippery mess. I couldn't help getting an erection and crossed my legs to conceal it.

"Seen enough, pervert?" Olivia said, ejecting the tape. The sound brought me back to my senses.

"Olivia," I spluttered, "what — why — how could —?"

"I'm not really doing Drama at Pitt," she explained, sinking back down into the couch next to me. "I got hooked up with these guys who do these tapes."

"But — *why?*"

"Oh, don't pull that holier-than-thou shit with me, Jonathan! You spend half your life trolling for skin on *The Booby Channel.*" But then she calmed down. "Look," she said, "I've been doing this for a few months now. Why don't you take a guess how much money I've made."

"I don't know, but a few hundred bucks is hardly worth —"

"Try almost fifteen thousand dollars."

My jaw unhinged. "But—but—you looked so shitty when you came home all those nights. You—"

"So it took some getting used to. It's nothing now. We have fun."

"But—"

"This company—it's not porn. It's all girls on the tapes, and the videos get sent to Europe, to places where it's legal. It's the easiest damn money in the world."

"But *why?* What do you need that much money for?"

"Wake up, Jonathan! Men will give me money to take my clothes off. It's a joke! It's the biggest joke of all time! I know how the real world works now, and since Mother's not about to give me money for anything but tuition, there's no point in wasting my time with my head up my ass around here anymore. I think this weekend might be the time to clear out—soon as I'm done with one last job. Those guys are scary about girls missing shoots."

So that's why she couldn't go to Israel.

"What do you mean?" I asked. "Clear out for where?"

"LA. One of the girls knows some people out there with connections to movie agents."

"You can't be serious." I was starting to suspect this was all an elaborate practical joke devised to make me feel stupid. People didn't *really* do these kind of things, certainly not people in my family.

"Does that tape look like I'm kidding around?"

"But, Olivia, you're naked in there—"

"I'm playing the cards I was dealt, Jonathan. And I've got a winning hand. I've got a royal fucking flush."

"But—"

"These guys don't even know my real name, and they don't want to either. I'm Liv Shimmer. Nice, huh?"

"But—"

"I'm going to be famous, Jonson. These two scout guys with

connections to producers who make big time porno movies are always coming to the shoots—to see me!"

"How do you know who they are?"

"'Cause they offer me thousands just to do a test shoot! Not like I'd ever do that in a million years, but still—"

"But they could just be deviants or something. How do you—?"

"Gimme a break, Jonathan. *You're* the deviant. Hiding the fact you want me is eating you up, admit it!"

"*What?*"

Olivia laughed. "Maybe we should just do it so you can get on with your life. We're both virgins, so it would be sweet, don't you think?" She laughed harder.

"Very funny, Olivia. How will you get out of going tomorrow?"

"I'm not sure exactly," she said, suddenly concerned. "I think I'll go along to the airport and then back out when it's too late to stop me."

I guess I looked skeptical or otherwise unsupportive because Olivia put her hand on my arm, squeezed slightly, and said, "Jonson, I really need you to keep all of this between *us.*"

I looked down at her hand and then up at her again. I rolled my eyes, which caused her eyes to narrow sharply. She grabbed me by the skin on top of my shoulders, dug her nails right through my shirt, and put her face directly into mine.

"If you breathe one word of any of this—to anyone—including your brain-dead friends," she warned, "*I will kill you.* I will make your life a living hell from now until the day you die. Do you understand me, Jonathan? I will give my fifteen thousand dollars to one of those producers or their knuckle-dragging friends to castrate you."

"What the hell do I care?" I replied, with all the machismo I could muster. "It's your stupid life."

"Good."

Olivia shoved the tape back into the silver sleeve, scooped her thong up off the floor, then left the room.

But I did tell my friends about the video.

Jake nearly imploded when I admitted giving it back. Milo was surprisingly philosophical about the decision, saying only that he had no doubt another such opportunity would arise for us if we just hung around my house long enough. Cory told me I did the right thing.

The night I watched Olivia's video, I dreamt a golem. It climbed out of the hospital planter, a full-sized dirt replica of Leon, glasses and all. It sat down and put its arm around me, then said, in Olivia's throaty voice, "How 'bout next time you hook me up with a set of *bodacious tatas?* If incestuous intergenerational necrophilia is on your little test, we can score *big!*"

I didn't know how to feel about Leon's death. Something felt unreal about the fact that I'd never see him again, but I didn't experience any real sense of loss. He was the cause of my mother's tirades about her suffocated childhood. He was a prickly character who made us nervous in public—and that was it. His absence, I was sorry to note, hit no harder than the weeks following the final episode of an amusing but also tiresome sitcom. I was vaguely ashamed of this.

I woke up from the dream in a cold sweat. It was two-thirty in the morning, and I had a powerful urge to march downstairs and inform on Olivia.

I marched downstairs, but instead of going to my mother's room, something impelled me to knock on Myna's door. She answered it surprisingly quickly in her gray robe. "Jonson!" she said, pulling me into her room, "what dybbuk disturbs your sleep tonight?"

"Um—"

"Your father will come home, darling, when he finishes with this silliness he is doing."

"But, what is he doing, Grandma?"

"Your father, I think he has no middles. Jewish, *not* Jewish—"

"What do you mean?"

"I mean with him it is all or nothing because in the middle it is hard to make sense."

I wasn't exactly sure what this meant. "Do you like being Jewish?" I heard myself ask.

Myna looked up at the ceiling and sighed. "Like? Not like? I am what I am, Jonson. Liking or not liking—what's the difference?"

"You never go to shul, and you tell—or you used to tell—Do you think we shouldn't go?"

Myna closed her eyes and shook her whole hand in the air. "Your mother needs to do this, I am thinking."

I felt a rising antipathy toward both my parents for upsetting our normal lives, but then I remembered why I'd come downstairs in the first place.

"Grandma?"

"Yes, darling?"

"If someone related to you was doing something you thought was really dumb and—or—is just about to go away and do something even dumber, what would you do?"

"About their dumbness," Myna replied, "first, I would talk to this relative."

"After that."

"I see," she said. "Of course, in the end, you must do what you must do. This is what I am saying."

"But—" Myna was talking nonsense. I wanted a straight answer, but I didn't know how to ask for one without divulging the details of the situation. Nonetheless, I resolved that it was, in fact, my destiny to go and wake my mother to tell her everything—

but I asked one more question. "What if someone was just jealous?"

"Jonathan," Myna whispered, "a person can only *hope* that what she does is from love. Now run along."

"Thanks, Grandma," I whispered back, though I had no idea what exactly I was thanking her for.

I went into the hall.

I stared at my mother's door for a few minutes.

My desire to inform on Olivia was, I was pretty sure, not motivated by love. A large part of me was envious of her audacity—and no matter how hypocritical it was, I didn't want her getting naked in movies. I wavered as I stood there on the carpet, waiting for the hand of fate to move me one way or the other.

Nothing happened, so I went into the office to look up the word *dybbuk* in the giant dictionary. I learned it was an evil, wandering spirit of Jewish folklore capable of entering a person and controlling his or her actions until properly exorcised. Here, finally, was the first reasonable explanation for my sister's behavior—both my sisters' behavior, and my father's, too.

But I still didn't know what to do. Finally, I decided to sleep on it. Once back in bed, I fell immediately into a deep and, mercifully, dreamless sleep.

"Emergency Family Meeting," Mom whispered when Myna stepped into the bathroom during breakfast the next morning. She wanted to confirm that we remembered our duties, devised in years past to prevent our grandparents from lousing up our trips. My usual task was to loiter near Myna and Leon at all times to prevent any wandering off. Olivia's was to supervise all small details, like whether the proper medications were packed and all bags actually made it to appropriate vehicles at the proper times. Nadia's job had been to manipulate conversations with Myna

such that our unsuspecting grandmother might reveal whatever ludicrous ideas she was hatching about unscheduled detours. Mom made us repeat these assignments and divided Nadia's role between us.

After everyone's baggage was loaded and Olivia gave the signal that Myna was properly equipped, we hit the road. Tension was thick. Mom was silent, lost in her own thoughts. Olivia, apparently worried I'd have a change of heart at any moment, kept throwing me threatening looks from the front seat. I stared out the window to avoid them. Myna was unusually quiet, too. She was watching us all.

We were booked on a 12:30 flight to New York and a 5 p.m. flight from there to Tel Aviv, from where we were to take a bus to Jerusalem. We made it to the TWA check-in counter at 11 a.m. Mom handed our tickets to an extremely young ticket agent while I was eyeing Olivia, wondering when she was going to do whatever she was going to do.

"Let's see," the agent said, but then she cried, "*Oh, no!* Excuse me, please," and promptly disappeared for nearly five minutes. "I'm *so* sorry," she said when she finally returned. "I put the wrong tags on that last set of luggage! I'm a little nervous," she admitted. "My first full day on the job—that would be just my luck, too."

"Not to worry—Misty," Mom said, smiling at the girl's nametag.

"So—right," Misty said, taking up our case again. "I'll just need to see everyone's identification to check you all the way through to Tel Aviv."

While Mom was laying out our passports, I noticed Olivia starting to breathe heavily. Her eyes were closed. She was conjuring something. Her face grew pale, and she started fluttering her eyes, but before she fainted, Myna inexplicably announced, "Of course I am a citizen, but me and my first husband—we make a big escape from Czechoslovakia!"

Olivia opened her eyes.

"Excuse me?" said Misty.

Mom's cheek twitched. "Don't mind her," she sighed. "My mother-in-law is a nervous traveler."

"Well, it wasn't like Adolf was chasing us himself," Myna clarified. "He would have heart attacks, that fat fucker of mothers like the young people say. Just in time, we get out."

"Really," said Misty, picking up a phone.

"Please," my mother begged. "She's harmless."

Misty didn't put the phone down, but she didn't dial it, either. It was sort of hovering between the two states.

Olivia was temporarily stupefied, like I was, but now she closed her eyes again and started turning green. I had no idea how she was doing it.

"There's certain things she can't say," Misty whined.

"If he were on the plane with me today, I would pray for a bomb, a nice terrorist with a big bomb in the back! *Boom!*"

"Myna!"

This was too much for Misty. She dialed. I, for one, couldn't blame her. "I'm *really* sorry," she whispered.

A middle-aged man with a disproportionately large belly arrived behind the counter. "Is there something I can help with?" he asked. He was looking at Olivia rather than Mom, but that was normal. Half the time women did it, too.

"It's my mother-in-law," Mom said. "She has episodes. It's really nothing." The man looked highly skeptical, so Mom added, "It's a form of early Alzheimer's. She could say anything."

Myna had her arms crossed and one side of her mouth scrunched up as if to demonstrate she was used to tolerating her daughter-in-law's disrespect.

"Ma'am?" the agent offered, looking at my grandmother.

"What's the big deal?" Myna asked. "So my husband and I

escaped to come to this country during World War Two. I said nothing about spying."

"*MYNA!*"

"Could you all step this way, please?"

Events took on a surreal aspect. The man, who looked to me as if he'd swallowed a bowling ball, led us into a small, whitewashed room and asked us to take seats. There was a long empty table at the far end of the room with two metal folding chairs behind it. A collection of identical chairs faced it from the opposite side. We all sat down and stared at the table. Mother was fuming. Olivia seemed bemused. Our grandmother had a look of vapid contentment.

When the man left, Mom lit into Myna. "What in God's name was *that?*" she demanded. "Have you lost your mind?"

Myna smiled, dumbly. I thought for a moment she'd gone senile or actually had developed Alzheimer's right there in the check-in line. "They always seem to want to know these things," she replied. "I just don't want to make any troubles."

My mother laughed. "Why did I let you come along?" she moaned. "I only have myself to blame. *What the hell did you say about spying?* Who said anything about spying?"

"No one said anything about spying?"

"No, Myna, no one said anything about spying."

"I thought someone said something about spying. It wasn't you, Olivia, darling?"

"No."

"Jonson?"

I shook my head.

Mom looked at Myna with outright malice, but spoke no further on the matter. We sat in silence then. The only audible noise was the sound of my mother periodically jamming up her coat sleeve to look at her watch. Olivia didn't seem to know how to react to these developments. She checked her watch a lot, too.

Thirty minutes later two different men entered. They didn't look like policemen in their suits and ties, but they flashed official looking badges. One was tall and thin, with a long braid of thick black hair plummeting like an anchor behind his head. His partner was short and stocky, but solid, like a low retaining wall. The men took seats in the empty chairs behind the table, laid our passports down, and began scrutinizing them silently.

After an inordinate amount of time, the short man looked up at Olivia and said, "Hi, my name is Officer Thomasino. This is Officer Sky. I'd like to ask you a few questions—" But then he seemed to realize he was interrogating the wrong person, so he looked at Myna. "Mrs.—Julianelle. In what country were you born?"

"Czechoslovakia, young man."

"In what year?" He was looking at Olivia again.

"Nineteen hundred and seventeen—*Oy vey!* So long now."

"Mrs. Julianelle," Thomasino said, "when did you come to the United States?" He seemed to be in no hurry. I could see my mother chewing her lip.

"I come to this wonderful country in 1939," Myna told him. "We make escape when Adolf's cronies came—a curse on those black-hearted barbarians! *Ptuuuf!*" She made a phony expectoration toward the floor.

When she was finished, Officer Sky said, "You say you 'escaped.' How do you mean?" He was looking at Olivia, too. She appeared utterly bored by the attention.

Myna shrugged. "I mean we applied for the visa, and then we pray. They arrive to us six weeks later, and we are leaving to America. So much luck, we didn't deserve."

"I see. Did you have a different name when you arrived?"

"Yes. It was Schwartz."

This seemed to confuse both men, who looked between all our passports. Thomasino said, "You had the same name as your current daughter-in-law?"

"She is also my step-daughter."

Eyebrows were raised. "Can you explain that, Ma'am?"

Mother let out an exasperated sigh. Both men looked over but ignored her. Thomasino shifted his chair underneath him and stole a quick look at Olivia, who seemed to be growing less anxious by the minute.

"What's to explain?" Myna asked.

"What was your maiden name, Ma'am?" Sky directed this question to my mother.

"Julianelle," she intoned. Eyebrows went to full mast. I thought maybe we were being unmasked as a family of moles. "Look," my mother said, "she married my father, okay? My husband's father married my mother—I mean, I married my husband's father. Shit! IT'S NOT ALL THAT COMPLICATED!"

I was sure we were going to jail, but the men let this pass. It took a good ten minutes to sort out our family tree, after which Officer Sky asked Myna when she'd become an American citizen.

"That ridiculous test!" Myna complained. "Why with that silly test? I don't need papers and pencils to show I love America. You boys should make a call—"

"What year did you become a citizen, Ma'am?"

"*Acch.* I finally made good—I don't know—in 1949, I think."

"What was it you said about spying?" asked Sky.

"I only want to say there was no spying."

"No spying?"

"No spying."

"Hmmm," both men said together, perhaps unconvinced they weren't dealing with a wily old international operative.

For a few minutes, the two men silently analyzed the situation, after which Thomasino said, "I guess that will be all then."

Mom leapt up and dashed out of the room. Olivia followed, already looking ill. I did my duty by staying behind Myna, who stopped in the doorway. She turned back to me and her old eyes screwed up a bit. Then she said, way too loudly, "Good I say nothing of those old papers from the war, no?"

Thomasino and Sky were standing right behind me.

To make a long story short, we missed our flight.

It took Myna another half hour to convince the officers they'd misunderstood her use of the word 'papers,' that she had only been referring to the old newspapers she brought from the homeland wrapped around her more fragile possessions.

Olivia could barely suppress her glee when the clock passed 12:30.

Mom looked amused, but insanely so.

When we were finally released, we returned to the ticket counter, whereupon we were informed by a more self-assured agent that, while it would be easy enough to get us on a later flight to New York, there was no guarantee when we'd be able to catch another flight to Israel.

My mother stared at the lady for several moments.

"Ma'am?"

Instead of responding, Mom spun around to us and said we were going home.

"Tomorrow?" I asked.

"We're not going at all."

"But what about Dad?"

"Your father will be home soon."

That was evidently all she had to say on the subject because she turned and walked on ahead of us out of the airport, dragging her rolling suitcase behind her.

Myna turned to Olivia then and said, "Nobody goes?"

My sister looked at her long and hard. Then she looked at me and back at Myna. "I guess not, Grandma," she replied. Then she ran up ahead to catch Mom.

When we hauled our luggage back into the house, we were met with a surprise. Nadia was sitting on the second floor steps like she sometimes used to do.

"Nadia!" Mom said. "You must have left Philadelphia at the crack of dawn! Is something wrong?"

Nothing was wrong. Nadia was taking a double course load and wanted a break over the long weekend.

"I wish I could look so fresh after a seven hour drive," Mom marveled. "You look wonderful!"

Since Mom mentioned it, I looked closely at Nadia and saw that she must have put on fifteen pounds since she left for college. She looked, frankly, beautiful. Her face, less pale than I'd ever seen it, seemed fuller, and its length, rather than producing its previously haunted effect, seemed exotic.

"The question is," Nadia said, "what are *you* doing here?"

"Your grandmother caused a slight delay," Mom said in a surprisingly cheerful tone. "But I changed my mind about going. I think you were wrong about surprising your father like that. It seems unfair."

"Sure, Mom," Nadia said. "I'm sure your sense of fair play will be a great comfort to you when you're growing old without a husband."

A flash of something frightening crossed my mother's face. Nadia maintained her neutral expression as Mom walked down the hall toward her. I held my breath, fearing something awful was about to take place, but Mom walked right into the kitchen.

The look Olivia and I exchanged when Mom revealed that the trip was going to be a surprise—and that it was apparently Nadia's idea—told me she hadn't known either, but we didn't have time to discuss it. We both raced upstairs past Nadia. I got to the phone first and called Jake to tell him we didn't go. He told me to come over right away.

"Dude!" Milo cried. I'd just come down the steps into the basement. "Listen to this," he said. "It's my bloody fluppin' masterpiece!"

I looked at Jake and Cory. Both reluctantly nodded.

Milo was holding our sword. He had it upside down and cleared his throat into the handle, so I knew one of his "Milo-ized" lyrical stylings was forthcoming. He cleared his throat again, then began to sing in a god-awful caterwaul. *"Sometimes when we fuck, the chafing gets too much, and I have to close my thighs aaaand cry. I want to fork you 'till I die, 'till we both break down and die, I wanna fork you, 'till the beer in me subsides!"*

Cory and Jake clapped. Milo bowed. We all hated that Dan Hill ballad, but he'd fixed it. I had to admit it was his best work.

"Damn straight it is."

Milo walked over to the boom box sitting awkwardly atop a pile of laundry on the dryer and flipped the radio on. "Anyway," he said to me. "Speaking of beer. We're having a bit of a *tit-a-tit* over here."

It turned out the three of them had been debating the wisdom of stealing an entire case of Iron City beer from the refrigerator. Cory wasn't keen on the idea.

"Those stinkin' math assignments are rotting his stinkin' brain!" Milo railed after bringing me up to speed. He turned to Jake and asked, "When's the last time Daniel was here?"

"A week or so."

"You think he remembers that case?"

"Probably not. He's pretty much only into pot and tattooing himself these days."

"He tattoos *himself?*" I asked. I'd seen some on him, and they were pretty bad.

"That's why he doesn't have any on his right arm," Jake explained. "Didn't you see all that weird stuff in the kitchen?"

"*Anyway,*" Milo said, refocusing us on the inexplicable behavior at hand. He looked at Cory and said, "This is a golden opportunity, man. *No* – this is an *Iron* opportunity, and all you can say is, 'Well, gee guys. I don't know'! No one ever drowned in beer, Minor!"

"All I'm saying," Cory replied, "is that I'm uncomfortable with *stealing,* not with *beer.*"

"All right, I call your bluff," Milo challenged. He was fishing some crumpled bills out of his pocket. "We can leave this in the fridge. And if you don't go for this, you might as well just admit you're a lightweight – a heavyweight lightweight."

I thought Cory was finally going to give Milo the thrashing that was coming to him, but instead he said, "You ever do a shotgun?" Without waiting for an answer, he added, "Go put the money in the fridge and bring down a can opener or some keys with the beer. Then we'll see who's a lightweight."

"Now that's what I'm talkin' about!" Milo handed the cash to Jake, who ran it upstairs.

Cory delivered a short seminar on the subject of how to "shotgun" a can of beer. It was apparently the football team's preferred method of imbibing. "You got a can opener?" he asked Jake, who threw him one. Cory turned the beer sideways and carefully punched a hole in the lower part of the can. Then he enlarged the crevice and worked around its edges, turning down sharp ridges. "Ready," he said.

I'd never seen this before, and I was certain that whatever he was planning wasn't going to work.

Cory held the beer up and put his mouth over the newly created opening. The top of the can was above his nose. He felt for the depressor with his free hand and opened it. There was a hiss. Cory's eyes bulged. Small streams of beer leaked from the corners of his mouth.

The next thing I knew, he was crumpling the empty can.

"Holy shit!" we all cried. Cory's face assumed a triumphant aspect. He raised his bulky arms and began walking victory laps around us, pumping his fists in small circles as he went. We were all too impressed to complain, even when he started belting out a mangled version of *We Are the Champions*.

Jake went next. He performed competently but spilled a fair amount of beer down the front of his shirt. *"In* the mouth!" Cory teased. "The beer goes *in* the mouth." Milo did an admirable, if much slower job on his, letting out an impressive belch when he was done.

I took my can and gingerly attempted to poke a hole in its side. "Jesus, Schwartz, this isn't brain surgery," Cory complained. "Stab the damn thing!" He was feeling important. I got the aluminum punctured and turned down the torn edges. Then I set it up over my mouth and held it.

And I held it.

"Come on!" Cory shouted. "Show some balls!"

I opened the top.

A flood of freezing cold fizz roared into my startled gullet. My eyes felt like they were going to explode. Then I thought I was going to retch, but before I could consider how serious a possibility either was, the can was empty.

"Look at his face!" Milo howled. "He looks like he's taking a massive dump!"

Hello by Lionel Richie came on. Jake threw his crushed can at the radio, so we all did the same. Then we each shotgunned two more beers.

Shortly thereafter we were slumped on the two tattered and torn couches by the back wall.

At some point, Cory passed gas rather loudly and looked momentarily sheepish about it. This wasn't acceptable to us—the sheepishness, that is—so we made him do another shotgun.

"Hey," I said when he was done, "is that how you warm the

bench?"

"Funny, Schwartz. Real stinkin' funny."

Cory couldn't help laughing at his choice of words—neither could anyone else. We snorted and giggled like fools.

Cory was a tight end—in name anyway. He'd gotten in for maybe half a dozen plays by then. The three of us were starting to suspect he just wasn't any good, but none of us ever mentioned it because he always responded to the merest whiff of criticism with one or another of his inspirational quotes, as he did on this occasion. "Winners never quit, boys," he counseled, "and quitters never win."

"Thank you, Vince Lombardi!" I said, holding up my end of the ritual exchange.

"Actually, that *was* Vince Lombardi."

"*Duh.*"

We talked for a while about school. Milo claimed one of the more attractive student teachers was checking out his ass, so we made him do a shotgun. Jake, who'd been talking earlier in the week about a freshman named Kelly Kroeger, admitted they'd kissed the day before and that he'd gone up her shirt in her back-yard—but also that he'd broken up with her after the fondling.

"Why the hell are you always dumping perfectly good girls?" Cory asked, sounding genuinely concerned.

Jake only shrugged and said that as soon as he knew a girl wasn't the right one for him, he ended it. "Why waste my time?" he asked.

"*Waste your time?*" Milo roared. "Are you telling me that feeling a girl's *tits* is a *waste of time* if you don't want to freakin' *marry* her? DO TEN SHOTGUNS, ASSHOLE!"

We only made Jake do two, one for each wasted…opportunity—which he acquiesced to only after Milo threatened to scream 'tit-waster' at him for the rest of the night.

Milo settled down when Jake finished and offered his opinion that the girls at Allderdice were all stuck up. Cory said a lot of the cheerleaders really would lay any player on the team, but he had to wait until they were done with the starters. We made him shotgun for that, even though we thought it was probably true.

The rules for this new game were fairly loose.

I didn't know how to feel about the girls at Allderdice. I'd received some attention because I was Olivia's brother. Some were nice, and some were really beautiful, but I didn't think they'd be interested in dating me. I made no comment on the matter as we'd all been drinking plenty in the regular fashion while we talked. My head was starting to spin.

We Got the Beat came on the radio. Milo sang, *we beat the meat* to it for a while, then said, "I wish I could pork all the Go Go's—at once."

"SHOTGUN!" we all screamed.

"I wish girls could play football," Cory announced, "'cause then you could feel 'em up when you tackled them."

"SHOTGUN!"

"Dudes!" shouted Jake. "Did anyone see *Wonder Woman* the other night?"

"Holy Shiite Muslim!" Milo shouted back. "That freakin' wetsuit!"

"What?" I asked.

Jake elaborated: "Oh, Man, it was frickin' *awesome*. She had to chase after these guys on jet skis, right? So when she spun around, she didn't get her regular—whatever you call it, what she wears. She was in this skin tight Wonder Woman wetsuit."

"Wow," I said, and meant it.

"Did you guys ever see the one with the motorcycle suit?" Jake asked.

"That was awesome, too!" Milo whooped.

"Like you can see shit on that crappy-ass TV," Jake said. Milo only had a little black and white he'd smuggled into his room because his parents thought Satan broadcast over the airwaves.

"True," Milo lamented. "But you can see Linda Carter's tits pretty good."

"You can see Linda Carter's tits *on the radio*," I put in—which nearly got beer out of Jake's nose.

Milo's eyes lit up. "How awesome would it be," he said, "if she spun around—and—and—came up with *nothing*—just freakin'—Wonder Tits in the wind!" He employed dual hand gestures to indicate what such a thing might look like.

"SHOTGUN!"

Despite his superior girth, Cory was the first to pass out. Milo went next, followed by Jake.

Some time later I found myself drifting in and out of consciousness in a pleasant, floating sort of way while I contemplated my progress on the Purity Test.

But then I heard crying.

I scanned the blurry room.

Jake was awake, sitting on the bottom basement step, sobbing.

I snapped my eyes shut. How long he'd been there, I had no idea. I peeked again.

Now he had his head hanging between his knees. It occurred to me that I'd never seen any of my friends weep in such an unselfconscious way, even when they were seriously hurt. I didn't know if he would want me to talk to him if it meant he would know I saw him like that, so I didn't do anything.

My head was swimming again, so I fell asleep.

Banging on the screen door in the kitchen above woke me another indeterminate amount of time later. Everyone else, including Jake, was unconscious. He was back on the couch, slumped over Cory's shoulder. Milo was snoring loudly. I felt too woozy to get up, but I heard the door open and shut, then footsteps, and then a thick-soled black shoe appeared on the steps. *Nadia.* I couldn't believe my bleary eyes. She came downstairs and surveyed my comatose friends.

"*Exactly* what I thought," she said. "Nice fucking science project."

I'd told my mother we were working on something for class — my standard ploy.

"What are you making a model of, *puke?*"

"What?" I asked, managing to sit up. My mouth was pasty and disgusting.

"Let me start by asking a general question that might cover everything I need to know."

"Yeah?"

"Just how far up your ass is your head right now?"

"Huh? Listen, Nadia —"

"All right. I figured that would be too abstract. Let me be more specific, and I'll try to use one-syllable words. First of all, why did Myna have to nearly get herself arrested or committed to prevent something you could have stopped yourself last night by telling Mom?"

"I — She —"

"Or were you just going to let Olivia go? Live and let live, is that it?" I didn't have to answer this because, just then, Cory passed gas again on the couch across from me. Nadia looked at him, scornfully. "Olivia promised she wouldn't go anywhere until at least the end of this year —" she said, "until she gets her diploma. She wouldn't tell me what she was planning, though. What is it? Is she going to run to Hollywood to be an actress?"

"Yeah," I mumbled, cowed.

"And she has funds, I assume. What's she doing, freshman peep shows?"

"Videos," I said. Nadia was making me feel completely ashamed, as if I were doing the things Olivia was doing.

"Wow," was her reaction. "Porn?"

"No, it's just girls." Then, for some reason I added, "She's still a virgin."

Nadia shook her head.

"Yeah. That's what I think," I said. For once, we were in agreement.

But then Nadia bore down on me. "Oh, stifle it, you sanctimonious twit. *Oblivia* is only stupid because she thinks being the Princess of Perversia is the same as being Queen of the Universe. She has no idea the population is repellent and the weather sucks."

"Ah—"

"Anyway," Nadia said, "she moves out over my dead body — or yours. Do you understand me? She obviously trusts you enough to tell you all of this, so don't screw that up. And if Myna has to do anything like that ever again, I will personally see to it that you die an agonizing and humiliating death."

"Fine," I muttered, realizing that both my sisters had now threatened my life. What in the world I'd done to deserve such treatment was utterly beyond me. I considered pointing out to Nadia that Olivia seemed to hate her, but I didn't bother. There was no point in trying to understand anything she said or did.

"And another thing," Nadia said. I'd forgotten she was there. "What's up with the wino?"

"What do you mean?"

Just then, Milo shifted violently in the corner of the couch. He mumbled something incoherent, but the word 'Mommy' was clearly audible.

Nadia walked over and leaned toward his ear. "Mommy's here, sweetie," she said, rubbing his back. "I'll touch you in your special place tomorrow night." A contented smile passed over Milo's face. "*I'm* the one who's going to puke," my sister said, straightening up.

"Okay."

"Hmmm," she replied, mounting the steps. "Go back to your

drunken stupor, then."

"Done," I said to the room after she'd gone.

We woke up with our first genuine hangovers. My eyes ached, my teeth tasted like death, and for some ungodly reason my scalp burned and itched where it seemed I'd cut myself a bit overnight on one of the springs sticking out of my couch. But compared to everyone else, I got off easy. Cory couldn't move until noon, Jake puked all morning long, and Milo had explosive diarrhea.

They took comfort, though, in the fact that their greater suffering was worth more points on the Purity Test.

Winter vacation came and went. Olivia seemed to have increased her "Drama" commitments and began making only intermittent appearances at home. The Allderdice Drama Club had its first production during the week before vacation, and I had to admit that Olivia was singularly impressive. They performed *Grease!* Olivia played Sandy, and though she wasn't the best singer in the show, she clearly had something not one of the other cast members had: charisma. No one could keep their eyes off her.

Another reason Olivia was around with increasing irregularity was that Mom was at home much more than usual. She was there when I returned from school several days a week, and the only explanation she offered was that she'd gotten her work done early. And I noticed she had a glass of wine in her hand most of the time. After a week, Olivia got her to admit that both the smoke detector and fetal alcohol PSA's had been scrapped before they ever got off the ground. Mom was being pressured to put her energy into regular ad campaigns, which she called "pitching the awful offal." Instead, she was cutting back her hours.

Mom snapped at Olivia over small things, like leaving a light on or rolling her eyes at Myna, things she didn't sweat before. With me, there were constant objections to my going out in a baseball cap or with the hood of one of my many sweatshirts on.

And she cleaned even more, if that was possible. Eventually, I started going straight to Jake's after school, and it became, almost exclusively, our private domain.

For several weeks preceding winter vacation, we'd been batting around the idea of throwing a party at Jake's. We finally decided to schedule it for the Friday before we returned to school, hoping to start off 1984 with a "bang," as Milo optimistically put it. I tended to stay away from the party circuit, though I knew carloads of kids between the ages of 14 and 19 cruised between such events every weekend. We didn't expect a horde because we'd only managed to reach a dozen or so friends and acquaintances each, but we just weren't sure. These things were unpredictable. We were prepared, though, thanks to the increasingly self-tattooed Daniel Baker, who bought us six cases of Milwaukee's Best for the occasion. We had to buy him two.

As I was getting ready to walk over to Jake's on the day of the party, my mother called a Family Meeting over the intercom. I was sure something was about to come up that would keep me from the festivities. Olivia was home and already downstairs. But we didn't even make it to the card table because Mom was too excited. "Your father booked a flight home!" she cried. "He talked to Myna! He's done with those people! He's coming home in March!" She was holding up a pad of paper on which, I gathered, Dad's flight arrangements were jotted.

I was elated. Olivia seemed thrilled as well. "Is it really true?" she asked.

"True as a knock in the head," Myna said from the leather ottoman in the back of the room. I hadn't noticed her. She sounded happy, though she looked pained.

"Myna?" Mom asked. "Are you okay?"

"Okay, fine. I think maybe more bran flakes for me, no?"

Mom declined to pursue that line of conversation. "Have

fun at Jake's on your science project," she told me. "You really shouldn't put off your work so long. You're supposed to be on vacation."

"Ah—English," I corrected, realizing there was no reason on Earth to have told my mother we had schoolwork to do this time. "We did the science one already," I added. "We just have to write some stupid skit. It won't take very long."

"I hope there won't be any drugs or alcohol in your skit," Olivia said. "Those don't go over well with teachers."

"How about the ones with gratuitous nudity?" I shot back. Olivia took in a breath, surrendering.

"You two," Mom sighed.

Once outside, I began feeling like things were soon going to return to normal. A weight seemed to lift from me as I walked down Wilkins Street in a lightly blowing snow.

Two hours later, Jake's house was, to our surprise and delight, overflowing. I was playing Quarters with a baseball player named Jeffrey Shepherd.

"Hey man, what's up with your sister, anyway?" he asked after I bounced my quarter into the shot glass for the twelfth straight time.

"I don't know, man," I replied.

"I guess you wouldn't, though, you being her brother and shit. Total waste, man." He took a slug from a Rolling Rock he must have brought himself, then said, "If there's one girl in school who shouldn't be a virgin, that's the one. She's *mint*—you know what I'm sayin'? In first lunch, sometimes she sits alone and sticks those popsicles all the way down her throat. That's just cruel, you know? My whole team worships the *Big O*." He took another slug, then added, "What a cock-teasing, blue-balling, frigid, ice-queen *bitch*." Shepherd got up, evidently too distraught to continue the game. "Still," he said, staggering away, "sign me up any day."

I leaned back in the chair and looked around the room. Cory

was in the kitchen with Milo and two girls. Milo was gesticulating wildly as he expounded, I assumed, on some nonsense. The girls, one blonde, one brunette, apparently weren't offended by lies or innuendo-laden come-ons, but I figured it was only a matter of time before one of them slapped him. Cory was standing next to Milo, grinning and nodding like an imbecile.

Gradually, I took notice of two things: First, Cory was drinking what looked like a milkshake. Second, the brunette was Sarah Glickman. I had no idea she went to parties. She was drinking a diet soda. I watched for a while, hoping to witness the breakthrough moment when Cory finally uttered a syllable to her, but all he kept doing was grinning and nodding. Eventually, I gave up on him.

Jake was sitting behind me on the steps to the second floor, under the masking tape cordon we'd put up. He had a girl on his lap, and she wasn't the one he'd groped or the even more recent one he'd dumped. I didn't know this one.

I wondered again what attracted so many girls to Jake. He was, I supposed, handsome, but not unusually so. He was smart, but also not in any distinguishing way. It was curious. One ex-girlfriend of his told me he had a "sexy dark side," but I had no idea what that meant.

I looked up at the ceiling and closed my eyes.

Everyone was singing along to *Blister in the Sun*. It was the whispery part. I joined in at the shouty part.

Everything in the world was perfect.

But the Violent Femmes stopped singing, and the mixed tape clicked off. Jake clearly didn't want to detach himself from his girl to deal with it, so I hauled myself out of my chair and stumbled past him up the stairs.

In Jake's room, I sat down in front of his crate of tapes. I was uncomfortable invading his bedroom, but too woozy to worry about it. I pulled Squeeze out, stuck it in the stereo, and hit play.

Then, sensing someone else in the room, I looked to the door. A girl I didn't know was standing there watching me. She was my height, with hazel eyes and a petite, ski-jump nose. Her hair was blonde and short, curling outward just above her chin. She was wearing faded jeans and a black vest over a long sleeved button-down shirt fastened all the way up. She looked older than me in her eyes. I blinked instead of greeting her.

"I know you," she said, shutting Jake's door behind her. She had to push it hard to get it over the extension cords that ran out to the speakers we perched at the top of the steps.

"You do?" I said, getting awkwardly back to my feet.

"My name is Darby."

"I'm Jon."

"I know. *Jonson.*"

I was nervous, so I reached down and plucked out a pen wedged in the tape crate and began flipping it around through my fingers. I wanted to play it cool. "Do you go to *Dice?*" I asked.

"No. I know your sister—from Drama."

"From Drama? But you just said you don't—"

"I don't."

Darby stared at me, waiting for me to get it. I finally did—she was the girl in the shower with the yellow waterproof radio. I lost control of the pen, which flipped upward into the air. I made a clumsy wave at it, which only served to spin it wildly upward again. Then, despite the astronomical odds against such a thing, it landed squarely behind my left ear, point forward. Darby's mouth dropped open.

"Holy crap!" she said. "Do that again."

I demurred. Instead, I said, "Is it true Olivia gets offers to do pornos?"

"Yeah," Darby confirmed. "These two guys are there every time with wads of cash, but they're totally smarmy. She's way better than that. They can't get enough of her, apparently." Darby looked at me significantly and added, "But I can. What I'm interested in is you."

"Me? Why?"

"Olivia talks about you."

"About how she'd like to tear my heart out and make me eat it while it's still pumping before I die?"

Darby laughed. "She thinks you're strange," she said. That sounded more like it. "She thinks you *know* things."

"She thinks I *know* things? What things?"

"She says nothing gets you upset or angry. She says you are the only human being on the planet she can't get to do whatever she wants, and that includes your mental-case older sister and both your weirdo parents. Anyone who wouldn't pay to lick the bottom of Olivia's shoes is worth a look to me. I was watching you downstairs playing Quarters," she added. "You have a calm about you. I liked it. I found it—*arousing.*"

I choked on my own spit, but circumspectly.

Darby turned around and locked the door. The last thing she said before flipping the light off was, "Get rid of that pen and put the stereo on automatic reverse, would you?"

The moment I accomplished these tasks, she was on me. We fell back on Jake's bed and started yanking each other's clothes off. The world felt like it was circling around me, like I was inside a whirlpool. I knew it was the alcohol, but it was also relief. When my father returned, life at my house would go back to the way it used to be.

We were kissing as Darby's hands opened my jeans. I could barely breathe with all of this happening so unexpectedly, so quickly. I was ticking off yeses on the Purity Test faster than I could count.

"Take me," Darby whispered.

And then someone knocked on the door.

"Oh, man! Ah, shit!" It was Jake, sounding as if he were

talking to himself. I rolled off the bed and went to the door.

"What!"

"Dude! I'm really sorry about this. I heard that girl in there, and I saw the lights were off and, aw, my bad."

"What the hell do you want?" I hissed. My eyes had adjusted to the dark, and I looked back at Darby. She was sitting up on the bed smiling at me. Her bra was back on. It was pink and lacy. My temples were throbbing, but I forced myself to appear calm.

"It's your sister, Jon."

"My sister? What about my sister? Olivia?"

"No, Nadia. She called. She says it's a family emergency, and you better pronto your ass home. I had to tell you, didn't I?"

"Yeah, shit," I said, already scrambling back into my clothes. As soon as I could, I bolted into the hall, stumbled downstairs, and flew out of the house.

I burst through the front door with grape Bubble-Yum juice sluicing down over my chin (four cubes was considered the minimum for masking alcohol breath), only to find Mom asleep on the couch with an empty wine glass on her chest. Olivia was sitting next to her. She looked up at me and laughed.

"Are congratulations in order, then?" she asked.

"What? What's the emergency?"

"What do you mean? Didn't Darby find you?"

"What? Nadia called and said there was an emergency at home!"

Olivia laughed again. *"Ooh,"* she mused, "you must have pissed her off good. That girl was a sure thing. She's the biggest slut in the history of the world."

I sprinted back outside, but stopped before I reached the front gate. I doubted Darby would hang around that party. I stood there, seething, until I looked up at the Murphy's house and saw binoculars in one of the darkened upstairs windows. There was a renter in there, but he never showed his face. Something in me snapped. I turned around, dropped my pants, and mooned the bastard. Then I turned around and shouted, "Feast your eyes on that, fucker of mothers!"

The binoculars withdrew, so I went back into the house and told Olivia her new Peeping Tom was waiting for his show. She acted like she had no idea what I was talking about.

I never saw Darby again—in real life, anyway.

On March 11th, 1984, at around three in the morning, I was wrenched from deep sleep by another golem. Just its head and torso came out of the planter this time, but it was Darby in her lacy pink bra. She begged for help, claiming to be possessed by a dybbuk. She stretched out a hand and grabbed my crotch, only to yank me halfway into the dirt by it. I fought my way free and woke up on my bedroom floor.

Disturbed, I stumbled all the way down to the kitchen for a drink and a couple of Ho Hos. The back porch light was on, which drew me to the door. Before flipping it off, I peeked through the blinds. My mother was outside in her robe and slippers, standing motionless on the walkway facing Dad's forbidden garret. I hadn't turned the light in the kitchen on, and she couldn't hear me, so I just stood there and watched. The sound of crickets chirping loudly forced its way in from outside. Mom didn't move for several minutes, but then she approached the garret door and began depressing buttons on the lock.

She opened the door, but didn't go inside.

The phone in the kitchen rang. Mom whipped around and ran toward the house. Something compelled me to hide, so I hurried into the laundry nook before she got back inside. I listened to her answer the phone.

"Nadia?" she whispered.

There was an eerie silence that extended for far too long.

Then I heard the phone smack a countertop.

Then, shattering glass.

I lunged out of the nook, groping for the lights. After managing to flip the switch, I found my mother slumped on the floor against a row of cabinets with her hair covering her face. She'd pulled a glass cake tray off the counter-top when she fell, and she lay in the debris. I had no voice, but I ran to her.

Myna's voice rang out over the intercom. "What's this? What's this?" she cried. "I will call the police!"

Then I heard crashing footsteps — Olivia flying down from the third floor. Seconds later, she was in the kitchen. "Oh, my God!" she gasped. "What happened? Is she drunk?"

I still couldn't speak, but was able to help Olivia maneuver Mom up and into a chair. She did smell of alcohol, and I hoped that mere drunkenness was the cause of this episode. But I knew it was not. Olivia wiped Mom's face with a wet dishtowel. Her eyes were open, but glassy, and, like me, she couldn't speak.

Myna made her wobbly way into the room, terrified. "What's this?" she shouted, teetering. We had to get her into a chair so she didn't wind up on the floor as well. Mom was trying to talk, but nothing coming out of her mouth made any sense.

Eventually, unfortunately, words came out that we could understand.

"Michael!" Mom shrieked. "He's — he's — *dead!*"

Myna let loose an inhuman wail.

Olivia burst into tears.

Mom collapsed on the table. "Why?" she cried into her arms. *"Why did I lie?"*

"What happened?" Olivia begged, though she could barely be heard over Myna's keening.

Through wracking sobs, Mom managed to tell us that an Israeli journalist trying to find our number had tracked down Nadia's in Philadelphia instead. He told her Dad had been killed patrolling the borders of Hebron, which was evidently surrounded by hostile Arabs.

Myna kept howling.

"I killed him!" Mom wailed. Her hands were flailing wildly — now they were pulling at her robe, now they were in her hair. She gripped the edges of the table and shook it violently. "I killed him!"

"What are you talking about?" Olivia screamed.

"Those phone calls!" Mom screamed back. *"Neither* of them said he was Jewish! I lied because I thought it would make him accept Jonathan's Bar Mitzvah. I thought it would make him soften his attitude about our religious life. AND I DON'T BELIEVE ANYTHING! I was too much of a coward to tell him what I'd done. HE WAS COMING HOME!"

Mom turned gray and lunged for the sink.

Myna suddenly went quiet. "No, darling," she said in a strangled whisper. "Michael — he wasn't coming home."

My mother, who was retching, turned from the sink to face my grandmother, apparently surprised enough to calm down for the moment.

"What?" she said.

Myna was rocking again. Then she whimpered in a voice almost too soft to hear, "Michael. He wasn't coming home. Not yet, but he was going to come."

"What are you talking about, Myna?"

"He didn't call."

"He didn't call? What do you mean he didn't call? Of course he called. You gave me the flight information!"

Myna kept rocking. "He never called," she repeated. "I wrote this down because I thought you were acting crazy, darling, with so much of the drinking. I had a plan to bring him home."

"You had a *plan?* For the love of God, Myna, what did you do?"

"They would not accept you!" Myna shouted, standing up.

"I know this kind of people!" Anger was forcing its way through her shock and grief. "I found an address, and I wrote a letter of the truth so they would send Michael away, and he would come home. They've known my letter for weeks, but still they kept him there. They sent him into danger to die! It is me who killed my son!"

With that, Myna's eyes rolled up in her head. Olivia and I caught her before she collapsed and eased her back into her chair.

I got my grandmother a glass of water. She drank it very slowly while Mom sat down and watched her with something like violence in her eyes. Finally, Myna put the shaking glass down. She looked like she was going to faint.

"So you told them his real name," Mom said, but she didn't sound angry. She didn't sound sane either, though. Her voice was scarcely recognizable. "There's no reason to think that would make them —"

"I told them about your mother!" Myna cried.

"What? Myna, you're not talking sense!"

"I promised your father."

"My *father?* I'm losing patience, Myna! Michael — my husband — is dead!"

"You know how your father survived the German occupation, yes?"

"Of course! He was hidden by a Protestant family on their farm."

"Do you know anything more of this?"

Mom looked flabbergasted to be talking about this, but she said, "No. Father never told us the name of the family. He claimed to have blocked it out. Do you know it?"

"No," Myna said, waving a hand to indicate she had other revelations to share. Olivia hadn't moved or spoken. She was in some kind of trance. For some reason, I got up and went to the back door. I pulled up the blinds and stared out at the sprinklers now watering the grass.

"I know he lost his parents and my mother in an accident just after Liberation," Mom said. "They hit a mine on the road."

"Yes. This is true, this mine."

"So what are you going to tell me?"

"This is also true that his parents are killed."

"What are you getting at, Myna? Has my mother been alive and living in Monroeville all these years? Am I about to get her in exchange for Michael?"

"Yes and no," Myna replied. She was turning her head side to side, as if stretching her neck muscles. I could see her reflection in the door's window.

"What does that *mean*, Myna? I can't deal with this right now!"

"Your father told you that your mother's name was Suzanne, yes?"

"Yes, Suzanne Blum. He said her entire extended family was murdered in Auschwitz."

"There was no such person."

Mom's right eye popped wide. "What are you talking about?"

Myna inhaled deeply. "Your father had no wife. He was never married before to me." I checked Olivia's reflection. She was still somewhere else. "He and his parents stayed on the farm together," Myna explained. "There was never this—Suzanne."

Mom's face was blank.

"Your father and his parents," Myna continued, "your grandparents—they are hiding for nearly three years on this farm. Your father was twenty-two years old when he went there. The prime of a young man's life—to spend this in a filthy barn!"

"And?" Mom said. Her voice wavered.

"About a year before the Liberation, the wife of this farmer— she becomes pregnant."

"Oh, my God."

"This is not why I am telling you this, to shock you."

"Go on, Myna."

"Your father—he told me this the night we all meet, the four of us."

"He *what?*"

"Do you remember, at the end of the evening, he brought me into the house while you and Michael made kisses in the car?"

"He told you the night you met him?" Color was pouring over Mom's cheeks now. "He told you something he didn't tell his own child, *in his entire life,* the day he *met* you?"

"This is why I am telling you this. Let me tell you."

"Tell me."

"You see—not at first. At first, we talked about you."

"Me?"

"You and Michael—how we thought you were perfect for each other—*besheret,* my parents used to say, soul partners. So, we decided to give you some time. So, we started to talk. I think my joking about the Jews—I don't know how to say. It made him feel better."

"And?"

"Your father's parents. They were very strict—nothing like these American parents today—nothing like he was for you. Trust me, darling." Mom flinched a bit at this and let out an exasperated huff. "There would be no tolerating a baby from outside of marriage," Myna explained. "A bastard, forgive me—with—from a married woman and a—And of course, telling the truth, that the farmer's wife seduced him while she teaches his English lessons? Impossible! The farmer's goodness to Jews would have finished, no? He would send Leon and his parents to the Nazis, God forbid. Your father lived in torture for those nine months, and the few after you were born."

Myna took a deep breath and went on. "Early in the pregnancy, this woman, she tells your father she is thinking of destroying the baby. Leon, he thinks of taking his own life. But as time passes, the farmer, he suspects nothing. Even so, Leon — of course he can never know his child, even if the war is to be over. His family would shun him forever for what he did. He and his child would be dead to them and all the relatives. He didn't know what to do. And so the baby was born, a healthy, beautiful girl."

Mom drew in a sharp breath and said, "And then Liberation."

"Yes. Just before, every night, he prayed and prayed for a miracle to his problem because he didn't think he could go on living."

"The accident," my mother croaked.

"Yes, then this accident. *Ach,* I can't explain a man with so few words, but you see, your father, he lived with such a big guilt over his shoulders. He told me while you made kisses how he prayed and prayed for something to make life with his daughter possible. One night, in a moment of weakness, he wished for the Nazis to take his parents away. He didn't mean this of course, but he prayed it anyway, like a foolish child. He lived his whole life sorry for this prayer. He punished himself for it. And, Deana, darling, I am so very sorry he punished you, too."

Mom looked helpless. "I — I don't understand why you're telling me this," she whined. But then she said, "*No,* I do."

Myna nodded.

"My mother was a Christian," Mom said. "I'm not Jewish to Orthodox Jews — or even the State of Israel."

"And neither are my children."

"My plan," Myna said, "is they will not have him for marrying to a non-Jew. Or they would not let his family come and he must go home to them."

"Unless we converted."

"Never!" Myna cried, her face crumpling up with rage. "Never! Never!"

Mom seemed to understand this.

"You didn't kill him," she said.

There was more talk and more crying, but it all began to blend. I was still at the door, staring through the glass, focusing on nothing. The sprinklers turned off, which snapped me, momentarily, back to attention. I noticed the door to the garret was still open.

When I stepped outside, I heard my mother say, "He's strong. Give him some space."

The garret was smaller than it looked from the outside. My heart pounded. It was about as big as our living room and carpeted in taupe. Countertops ran along the length of the two side walls. There was a main work area in the back left corner where a computer and printer rested. A leather rolling-chair sat on a plastic mat in front of them. The wall facing the door, from floor to ceiling, was lined with built-in shelves crammed with books: encyclopedias, desk references, handbooks, guidebooks, manuals, almanacs, history texts, and grammar guides. There were books with a year written on their spines dating back three quarters of a century. There were individual books on each of the fifty states and what appeared to be nearly every country in the world. There were weather books, books on presidents, art, music, philosophy, sports, and hobbies. There were field guides to trees, flowers, wildlife, and stars. Then I saw the dictionaries: abridged, unabridged, college, children's, rhyming, etymological, and visual. There were dictionaries of symbols, anagrams, the theater, the ancient world, literary terms, the occult, art and artists, Shakespearean quotations, archaeology, industry, advertising, saints, psychological terms, automotive terms, and half a dozen foreign languages.

There was nothing in the spacious center of the room except two small gray couches facing each other from either side of a blockish wooden coffee table. I walked over to see what books were stacked on it. There were five: a Hebrew Bible, The Talmud, The Mishna, The Zohar, and a Hebrew-English dictionary.

How was it possible, I wondered, for someone to believe something with every fiber of his being, then so suddenly and so completely change his mind?

He rejected the only version of himself I knew.

Therefore, he died without me knowing who he was.

I wondered if such a thing could ever happen to me. Could I suddenly throw over everything I believed in? No chance, I decided. But before I could figure out why, a chilling ululation drew my attention to the window.

It was my mother.

On a rampage.

She'd thrown open the back door and kicked the screen off its hinges, screaming bloody murder. Her hair whipped about her head in frazzled strands. She snatched a bottle of lighter fluid sitting atop the grill, shook it wildly, then flung it at the yard. From the hollow sound it made when it hit the cement path, I could tell it was empty. Then she ran right down the path toward the garret. I looked for a place to hide, but she didn't charge in. Instead, she ripped open the door to the garage.

When she went down the steps, I leapt outside and sprinted toward the house, but turned back when Mom reemerged with a canister of gasoline. Olivia and Myna arrived on the back porch just then. They cried out together, but their voices were drowned out by my mother's rage as she stormed into the garret.

"Do something!" Olivia screamed. She shoved me brutally from behind, sending me pitching face-first into the yard. I got up spitting dirt and swiping wet chunks of grass off my face.

Fire leapt to life inside the garret.

My mother walked out of it looking entirely calm, but entirely demonic with flames climbing the walls behind her. For all the world, I thought I was witnessing a fiend from *Dungeons and Dragons* emerging from the infernos of hell.

Mom helped me up and walked with me to my grandmother, who appeared petrified. The garret was fully ablaze by the time we climbed onto the porch. I could hear Olivia in the kitchen making yet another emergency call from the Schwartz house.

The fire was controlled with relative ease, though everything inside the garret was destroyed: the computer, the furniture, every book and paper. A reporter must've overheard the address of the fire on police radio and somehow knew whose it was, because journalists were swarming around us even before the flames were doused.

The exact details of the fire's immediate aftermath are impossible to recall because, in effect, there were no details that night.

PART III

In the flurry of attention, our address somehow became public. Consequently, telegrams, express mail letters, bouquets, and gifts poured in from all over the world. Mom wouldn't even touch any of them, and since Olivia wasn't doing anything but walking around the house like a zombie when she was home, I had to lug it all into the dining room every day.

Nadia showed up exactly seven hours after delivering the Bad News, but didn't stay long. She didn't say much of anything to anyone, not that there was much opportunity to, as a silence rule seemed to be in effect. She showed no interest in all the mail either. After surveying the situation, she pretty much holed up in her room like she always used to. Two days later she abruptly announced that she had to get back to school before she got too far behind on her work. And then she left.

I didn't read any of the letters, nor open any of the packages, but I did note where they came from before eventually throwing them away.

There were no letters from Dad explaining himself.

But I appreciated the mail for distracting me every day. It meant not having to dwell on my father's death.

Or on the fact that I was angrier about his changing than his dying.

I didn't know the man I was supposed to be grieving for.

And I hated him for that.

Rabbi Speigleman, the orthodox rabbi my father had been meeting, called many times over those first few weeks, but Mom wouldn't talk to him. She wouldn't take calls from anyone. Myna didn't discourage any of this behavior, as she'd barricaded herself in her room before the first fire truck arrived.

I was at the door scooping up the latest load of mail when I heard a crash upstairs. It was followed by something sailing over the railing from the second floor down onto the steps: a large book. It thumped down the stairs and landed on the entry hall floor. Several more books followed in the same manner, after which something heavier came down, something silver that cracked a tile: a menorah. I'd never seen one in our house before, as we didn't celebrate Chanukah (though Mom bought us gifts). More projectiles rained down, mostly books, but other silver items, too.

With all the bump and clatter, it took me a moment to realize someone was ringing the bell. My instinct was to head directly upstairs, but I opened the door instead.

It was Rabbi Glickman.

"Hello — Jonathan." He was holding a large bouquet of white flowers. Another crash from behind me startled us. "May I speak with your mother?" he asked, looking over my shoulder.

"Ah, sure," I said, turning round as three more oversized books flew down the steps.

As it turned out, I didn't have to retrieve my mother because she appeared on the landing just then, wholly disheveled in her robe and struggling with a large box. Her hair fell in wild strands over her throbbing face and bloodshot eyes, making her look cer-tifiably insane. I knew she was drunk.

"Mom," I said, "the Rabbi's here to see you. I'll just go up-stairs and find something useful to —"

"*Perfect!*" she barked. Then she hurled the box down the

steps. Books and various small objects burst free and crashed to the floor. Rabbi Glickman rushed to rescue it all.

He still had that limp.

I changed my mind about going upstairs. Instead, I backed slowly to the still open door.

"Mrs. Schwartz!" Rabbi Glickman cried, picking up a book and kissing it. "This is a holy text! These are sacred objects!"

Now I could see among the detritus a set of candlesticks and a silver Kiddush cup. Mom stood on the steps peering through the scraggles of her crazed hair while the Rabbi struggled to put everything back into the box.

"Take it! Take it all back!" Mom screamed.

I was ready to run for it, but I hesitated, wondering what she meant.

"Can I help—you, Mrs. Schwartz? I can see you—are in— grief."

"TAKE THIS GARBAGE BACK AND GET OUT OF HERE YOU SLOW-TALKING SON OF A BITCH!"

Rabbi Glickman slouched a bit. "Mrs. Schwartz, I know—you are in pain," he said, marshaling his best bedside manner. "The anger is—natural. And I—I can't help but feel that—I—in some small way—I thought we might discuss funeral arrangements—"

"There won't *be* a funeral!" Mom roared. She was leaning dangerously into the banister. "My husband's will explicitly forbids it, which I'm grateful for because it's about the only thing left to recognize him by! Thank God you didn't get your hands on my baby! BUT IT DOESN'T MATTER ANYWAY BECAUSE WE AREN'T *JEWISH!* DO YOU UNDERSTAND ME?"

I didn't wait for the Rabbi to register his comprehension. I'd heard enough, so I eased my way out of the house and walked straight to Jake's.

It turned out Mom had been having some secret meetings of her own to prepare for my father's return.

There was no funeral, nor any other sort of ceremony, and the decision was lauded in the papers as an appropriate epilogue to the life of a literary man who, "In his quixotic mission to enlighten the masses, shunned ritual in favor of reason." Dad's body was flown home and Mom had it cremated according to his wishes, or the wishes he used to have, anyway. He'd also instructed Mom to have the funeral home dispose of the ashes, so that's exactly what she did.

Dad was killed — shot — on one of the unauthorized patrols the Halacha conducted along Hebron's volatile border. He'd not only gone along — he was carrying a gun. The press was amazed at his willingness to risk his own life to understand the "other."

Mom didn't remain long the way Rabbi Glickman found her, meaning she tidied up and stopped throwing things. The cleaning and the drinking, however, did not abate at all.

Myna ended her self-imposed exile the same day Rabbi Glickman visited, but seemingly only to escalate the morbid and destructive debate with my mother about which of them was more to blame for my father's death. I thought about asking her what happened to fate being "not ours to question," but of course I didn't.

Family Meetings ceased that year, and the house took on a perpetually funereal air. During those first months following the ill tidings, I made every effort to avoid everyone by staying away as much as possible.

Not that anyone tried to keep me around.

I don't remember much about the summer after my sophomore year, or the first few months of my junior year. Jake's house was almost constantly stocked with beer by that time, so the three of us, along with Cory on the increasingly rare occasions he was able, practiced our shotgunning as often as we could. By winter break of our junior year, we'd reached our peak. Jake and I tied at 4.4 seconds.

Some combination of us saw two or three movies a weekend all year long — *Bachelor Party, Hardbodies, Revenge of the Nerds,* and *Reckless,* to name a few. One of Jake's ex-girlfriends worked at the Manor Theater, so not only could we get into R-rated films, we usually got in for free.

I never discussed my father with any of my friends — not once.

Olivia didn't take off for LA, but rather wound up accepting a drama scholarship to Carnegie Mellon in May, and though she didn't seem thrilled with the idea of living so close to home, she agreed to move into the garret when Mom promised to have it converted into an efficiency apartment with its own phone line, and to let her live rent free, of course. We had a minor celebration in honor of the scholarship, but it felt forced. We hardly ever saw Olivia to begin with, and once her apartment was ready, almost never. She may as well have moved three thousand miles away.

Nadia called on Halloween. Unfortunately, I picked up the phone.

"Trick or treat? Is she getting better or worse?"

"Why don't you come home and find out for yourself?" I snapped, then immediately regretted it.

"I don't need to come home to be home," was Nadia's cryptic reply. "I'm always home."

"Ah — okay."

"What's Myna doing?"

"Nothing really, besides convicting herself of murder every five minutes."

"Olivia?"

"Still renting out her clothes, I guess. I have no idea."

"What are you doing?"

"Packing my bags for college a year early."

"You should go to Pitt, like Dad, and become a writer."

"Why?"

"You know, footsteps and all that."

"I want to go to Michigan," I said, which was true. It was high on all our lists. Michigan Stadium seated over 100,000 rabid Wolverine fans. I'd heard that when half the crowd yelled, it actually pushed the other half back into their seats.

"How much are you drinking, by the way?"

"Why!" I snapped, unable to help myself again. "So you can call and ruin my parties!" I'd not forgotten about Darby.

"Is that what I did?" Nadia asked, innocent as can be.

"Just forget it."

"Interesting," Nadia replied. "One might think," she added dryly, "if one didn't know better, that you were going through something."

Because Olivia didn't go far, and because we didn't spend *all* our time at Jake's, we were occasionally still subject to questionable goings-on at the Schwartz abode. In March of 1985, during spring break, Jake and I were drinking in the third floor den on a Saturday night. Over the first half of the year, Milo had pilfered a dozen bottles of wine from his parents' supply. They'd developed a keen interest in the beverage because they somehow came to believe various vintages possessed certain mystical properties. He was on a wine-tasting trip with them that break, the first trip he'd ever not fought tooth and nail to get out of. We'd also built a fairly impressive stash of the miniature liquor bottles sold on airplanes. This was Cory's contribution—his dad traveled a lot and came home with them. Predictably, Cory wasn't there that night either, this time because he'd made himself sick drinking too many protein shakes. He'd ratcheted up his efforts to bulk up ever since learning he was going to be on Varsity as a senior despite the fact he never played more than a few downs on JV.

Jake had begun to fancy himself a bartender and was forcing

heinous concoctions of mixed alcohol upon anyone he could. The two of us were watching one of our all-time favorite movies, *Personal Best,* while getting buzzed on a blend of vodka, tequila, bourbon, and apple juice. When one of the lesbian sex scenes ended, Jake said, "Oh, dude, you ever do an upside down gin and tonic?"

"Nah," I replied. "I can never get the gin to go in the glass when I turn it over, but maybe I have some kind of drinking problem."

"You've got some kind of problem, that's for sure."

Jake insisted I sit in the black recliner and tip it all the way back. I followed his instructions with great reluctance since they required me to slide up to the end of the chair-back and hang my head over the nearly horizontal top. Jake positioned himself over me with a mini gin bottle in one hand and some of my mom's tonic in the other. I opened my mouth and closed my eyes, bracing for the rush of pungent liquid, but a drop of something hit me between the eyes.

"What the heck?" I complained, sitting up.

Jake hadn't poured anything. What hit me was a tear. He collapsed onto the couch, crying.

I didn't know what to do, and having seen Jake in a similar state in his basement didn't help.

"My mom," he moaned. "I think she's gonna die."

"How do you know?" Jake hadn't said anything about his mother in ages.

"Because we got plane tickets to Arizona." Tears were running freely down his cheeks. He made no attempt to disguise them. "She must be dying."

"Oh, man."

"I can't go," Jake whined. "I can't see her all withered away and shit. I can't do it. You were lucky your dad just went away and died." He was too upset to realize how that sounded, but I didn't mind. "I'm scared," he croaked, getting up to pace around the room. "I don't think I'll be able to handle it like you do. I'm so fucking *scared.*"

"Yeah, but I—"

"It's not like my life will be any different," he rambled. "I do everything for myself anyway. She's got money to get us all the way through college—or get me all the way through college while my stupid brother drugs and tattoos himself to death to punish my parents for both dying. I hardly talk to my mom—but I'm so damn scared anyway."

I was amazed to learn there was a reason for Daniel Baker's self-destructive behavior, other than plain stupidity. "I didn't know that about your brother," I said.

"He's got it all wrong, though."

"What do you mean?"

"He sits around all day thinking about death and the meaningless of it all. And all that gets him is pissed off at the world and the urge to screw up his life even more."

"How come you don't do that?"

"Because I'm like most smart people—I don't think."

"What do you mean?"

"I'm serious. I don't think about anything, ever. I just do whatever it turns out I'm going to do. People who think too much end up like Daniel, or Nadia." I wondered whether he thought I did much thinking. "But the problem is," Jake added, "now that she's going to die, I can't help thinking about it."

"Are you sure you're right about this?" I asked. "Maybe you're making a big deal out of nothing?"

Jake walked to the window and looked out over the backyard. He kept talking as if he didn't hear me, and I didn't repeat myself. "A void," he said, "a fuckin' *void.*"

"Avoid what?"

"A *void.* I'll be living in a void without my mom. No matter what I've ever done, even if she didn't know about it—which was almost always—it was different. It was different 'cause she *could* know, 'cause she was alive. I'm fucking scared."

Olivia's voice came over the intercom just then, from the garret. "Hey," she said, "I need some help."

Jake's eyes dilated.

"With what?" I asked, offering no enthusiasm whatsoever.

"My dress. I need to be zipped."

"Please," Jake begged, dropping directly to his knees. "Sweet Mary, mother of God. In the name of all that's holy. *Please."*

"Send your little butt-buddy if you don't think you can keep your hands to yourself."

Jake blundered out of the room and, judging by the sound of it, almost fell down the steps. I heard him swear a blue streak, but keep going. Moments later, I saw him burst into the backyard. He tried to compose himself before walking down the path to the garret. Olivia opened the door in a little black dress. She looked up at me for a split second before she and Jake disappeared inside.

I was sure some new low was about to be reached.

"What took so long?" I was irate by the time Jake finally reappeared in the den. He'd stayed inside the garret for nearly ten minutes. There were no stains on his pants, and he didn't look especially rapturous. In fact, he seemed more than a little disappointed. "What'd you think?" I jeered. "She was gonna open your zipper after you closed hers?"

"I don't know," Jake said. "You never know."

"So what took so—Wait a minute! What did she ask you to do?"

"Nothing," Jake said, rather defensively. "She asked me to move some furniture in there."

That made sense. I realized I hadn't seen the garret since it was renovated. "What did you talk about?"

"I don't know, *BS.* She just asked me about school. About our college plans. Listen, man, I gotta go home and pack for tomorrow."

"Oh, yeah, right."

"Well—I'll call you when I get back."

"Okay."

Jake's mother was not dying. In fact, her health was actually improving, so she wanted to start seeing more of her sons. Upon his return, Jake was positively chipper and didn't seem interested in talking any more about the subject. I assumed he was happy to stop thinking again, and we got on with the business of being upperclassmen.

Fortunately, the final few months of our junior year granted us a reprieve from tragedies of all sorts. My mother and grandmother maintained their battle of self-recrimination, Olivia found alternative zipper support, and I heard nothing at all from or about Nadia. Even Milo's parents helped out by staying fixated on wine. Our only disappointment was that we rarely ever saw Cory outside of school—at least until the Semi-Formal dance began looming in late April.

We were all sitting on various pieces of secondhand exercise equipment in the Minors' unfinished basement. Cory had refused to meet us at Jake's to hear Milo's latest scheme, so Milo made us all go to him—Mr. Minor's assignments be damned—insisting he needed all of us to help. He'd begun revealing his plan, albeit in a circuitous manner.

"So, anyone have dates yet?" he asked. "Baker? Anything lined up? I'm thinking it could be any girl on Earth except for whoever you're molesting right now."

"Funny, Milo," Jake grumbled. "I'm going with Kendra." Kendra Talinbach was a senior he'd starting seeing the week before. She'd already let him go down her pants, and we were unspeakably jealous. Jake seemed confident this one would last.

"What about you, Big Man?" Milo asked, turning to Cory. "If you take a fat chick, you can bench press her all night."

"That's totally obnoxious, Milo," Cory complained. He was sitting on his bench press, tossing our sword from hand to hand like it was made of balsa. He'd made us all wait outside until his parents left for a movie because he was afraid his dad would assign us *all* some math. This worked especially well for me because whenever I saw his mom, Corrine, she always asked me a million questions about my mom. They'd grown up together as close friends but rarely found time to socialize.

I was lounging on a treadmill, looking around idly until I noticed some sort of signs were taped to all the equipment. One hanging from the treadmill's handrail said, *"The only discipline that lasts is self-discipline – Bum Philips."* There was another quote taped to the bench press. *"If at first you don't succeed,"* it quipped, *"you're doing about average."* There was no citation for that one. Yet another was taped to the bare wall at the bottom of the steps. *"The athlete who says something cannot be done should never interrupt the one who is doing it – John Wooden."* I wondered what kind of athlete Cory thought he was. It was no secret by then that he was worse than terrible.

"He's taking Sarah Glickman," Jake was teasing when I tuned back into the conversation. Cory dropped the sword. His ears purpled up, but all he said was, "I wish."

"And what about you?" Milo queried, turning to me.

"I'm still reviewing resumes and checking references."

"Don't brag, Schwartz—it doesn't suit you."

I had no idea what he meant by that. To make my jest clearer, I added, "Yeah, the interview process is a bitch 'cause I need at least thirty minutes off between each one. I'm thinking group sessions are the way to go."

"Rub it in, Schwartz. It won't last forever."

"What are you talking about, Milo?"

"All right, I'll play along—Janice Walker, Marissa Crowley, Betsy Rooker."

I turned to Jake and Cory, who both looked at me as if I were playing dumb. "What about them?" I asked.

"Nice try," Milo said, "but I still offer something. You know you're guaranteed a date with any one of them, but will you promise right here and now to help me with my plan if I tell you which one isn't a virgin and frequently makes sure she doesn't somehow revert into one again?"

"Ah—sure," I muttered, suddenly lost in the face of my apparent good fortune. Betsy was in two of my classes and had been my Biology lab partner in ninth grade. Marissa and Janice were sophomores who'd been in the Ski Club with us for three years. All three were attractive and nice, but I'd never considered any of them potential girlfriends.

"So you're in? No matter what?"

"Fine, I'm in."

"Guaranteed?"

"Okay, already. Guaranteed. I'm *in.*"

"Well, you might assume it's Betsy since she practically slobbers on you in Kolbridge's class and wears those raging C. F. M. boots all the time. But you might think it's Marissa since she always has bed-head, even when we go night skiing. All freakin' three of them have tried to bribe me to get you to ask them, like I'm your freakin' pimp or something. Your little playing dumb scheme is a work of genius, man. Anyway, it's actually Janice! You gotta take her—you're a shoe-in, Schwartz—a *dick*-in. Are you hearing this? Do whatever you want, but a deal is a deal. *Now,*" he declared to the rest of his audience, "while Monte Hall here chooses, I need everyone else's help, too."

"Monte Hall doesn't choose," Cory said, mostly to the floor. He was lying face down now, tracing a finger up and down the sword, which was now under the bench. He seemed nervous to me, probably that his parents would come home early.

"Thank you, Vance Lombardi," Milo sighed.

"*Vince.*"

"Who gives a rat's ass! I'm about to let you losers in on the single greatest booty bounty scheme in the history of the world!"

"For crying out loud, Milo," Cory moaned, sitting up again. "What the hell do you want?"

"A date with Kimo Dáte."

We all laughed at that. "Yeah, right," Jake snickered. It was patently ridiculous for Milo to suggest such a thing. Kimo was the closest thing to Olivia Allderdice had to offer since my sister graduated. She was an unapproachable beauty who consorted exclusively with the school's best athletes, which obviously didn't include Cory—and certainly not Milo either, who could barely "catch his own balls," as he liked to say, "despite all the practice."

"I'm serious," Milo insisted. He got up and started walking around the exercise machines. "This will make me king of the school. I've been thinking about my legacy, my responsibility to posterity—and I ain't talkin' about mooning anyone. I want to be a legend *before* I'm a senior, and it's all so stinkin' easy, I can't stand it." He sounded like Nadia, which disturbed me. "This isn't even about Kimo," he continued. "This is about long-range planning. This is about getting myself an all-you-can-eat pass to the Freshman Buffet next year—not that a little *Kimo-therapy* wouldn't come in handy."

Milo's face froze, and we all looked at Jake, but he rolled his eyes. "This ought to be good," he said, releasing us from the moment. Cory was on his back now, staring up at the ceiling. I followed his line of vision and found another quotation, this one in large letters on a poster board taped to an exposed beam. *"There is no substitute for hard work and effort beyond the call of duty. That is what strengthens the soul and ennobles one's character—Walter Camp."* What I wanted to know was how could someone gain all these glorious attributes if he never actually played. It struck me that Cory might be crazier than Milo.

"Here's what I need—listen," Milo was saying. "We're going to have a party at Jake's with, like, a hundred people. Every one of them is going to be a plant. Everyone except Kimo."

"What?" the three of us said.

Milo continued, undaunted. "Jake," he ordered, "you provide the house and you have, like, nine hundred ex-girlfriends who can help out. Tell them to bring their girlfriends because it's girl-kind's first and only chance to get back at Olivia Schwartz for making their boyfriends call out her name while they screwed them for humpty-nine years. *Humpty*-nine! Get it?"

"What does Olivia have to do with it?" I asked.

"Hold on now, Monte," Milo scolded. "Cory, you bring the football team. The baseball team, too, if you can. Tell them an exclusive, smokin'-hot X-rated video of Olivia Schwartz will be showing if they play the parts they're given. Kimo will be there in a heartbeat if they come. Jon, you need to get that video back, or a new one if she's into hardcore now. Everything everyone says that night is about me: I'm God's gift, rich, brilliant, athletically gifted, freakishly well-hung—the whole she-bang! *She...bang!* Jesus, I'm good!"

No one replied to this. I think we were all taken aback by how asinine it was, but also by the fact that it sounded at least remotely possible to pull off.

"You swore you were in, guaranteed, Schwartz," Milo reminded me. "So?" he said, "Jake? The house and girls?" Jake nodded, which looked awkward because he was shaking his head. "Right on!" Milo cried. "You the man! Schwartz? The tape? Can you rustle one up?" I hesitated to get tangled up with Olivia again, but Milo had given me information that could potentially change my social life, and I did make a promise. "You owe me, man," Milo prodded. "That was legitimate intel I got for you. For all you know, this will make you Screw-ball number one out of all of us, which would be a stunning upset of the Human Dumpster over there."

"I'll see what I can do."

"Sweet." Milo looked at Cory then. "Big Man?" he said. "Can you produce the players? They'll never believe me if I tell them about the video."

"No."

"What?"

"I'm not doing it. Tell them yourself."

"It's the easiest frickin' job!" Milo wailed. "They won't come if any of us invite them! They'll probably beat the shit out of me if I get anywhere near them!"

"I'm not doing it," Cory repeated, clambering to his feet, "and I need to work out now. So, if you all don't mind—"

"AHHHH!" Milo screamed. "Help me out here," he implored, turning to Jake and me. We shrugged, so he turned back to Cory. "Why the hell do you work out so hard for a team that never lets you play!" he bellowed. He knew his plan was going down in flames. I was greatly relieved.

Cory fixed Milo with a rather intense stare. Then he said, "Working out clears my head, which is something you could use maybe more than anyone on the face of the Earth. A healthy body is a healthy mind, Milo."

"Work *this* out!" Milo snapped, violently flipping Cory off with both hands. It was the fancy Euro kind of flip-off, with fingers bent on either side of the bird. Then he stormed upstairs.

Jake and I were halfway up the steps when Cory said, "You can't let him pull this kind of shit anymore." We turned to look at him. "You know what his problem is, don't you?"

"Dane-bramage," I said.

"No fear of failure."

"What do you mean?"

"If you have no fear of failure," Cory explained, "then you have no sense of shame. And if you have no sense of shame there are no limits on how low you can go because there is no such thing as low. And if there is no such thing as low, there is no such thing as high, and then you have nothing to shoot for in life."

Jake and I looked at each other, back at Cory, and then at each other again. I think we were both surprised to realize that the only proper response to Cory's semi-articulate speech was to think about it.

"You may be right, Big Man," Jake replied.

"I'd try to stop him," I said. "But I fear I will fail in the end."

"Ha, ha, Schwartz—always with the joke."

That stung a bit.

"Stop *Vance Lom-farting* around down there," Milo said, appearing at the top of the steps. "Let's blow this popsicle stand. Speaking of that, sorry about the mess in your bathroom, Cory, but there was a Victoria's Secret catalog under the sink."

I did wind up going to the Semi-Formal with Janice, but I was so intimidated by her furious intelligence that I was tongue-tied all night. I learned later she thought I didn't say much because I'd considered her too dumb for me. We never went out again.

Early in my senior year, my mother came across a competition sponsored by the *You Scream Ice Cream! Company* for twelfth graders to devise an ad for them. The grand prize was a four year scholarship to college, provided the winner agreed to major in Business Marketing. I entered solely because Olivia had recently declared that ice cream was the one thing in life she could never give up. I got the idea almost instantly: *You Scream Ice Cream — Finally, a Habit You Can Lick.*

When I shared the idea with Mom, she teared up and said I was going to win. Then, for some reason, she asked, "Do you know what first attracted me to your father?"

"No," I replied, uncertain whether I wanted to hear the answer.

"We fell in love right away—you know that story," she said. "In October of 1962. We were pretty sure the world was going to end, which probably sped the bonding process up a bit."

"The Cuban Missile Crisis, right?"

"Yes, but I was talking about Myna meeting Leon," Mom joked. Her eyes seemed clear. "Your father and I became friends because we had several history classes in common, and he let me drag him to a few war protests even though he was opposed to them at first. I think he was impressed with the flyers I designed."

"So he was for the war at first?"

"Absolutely. He wanted to go fight the way our country didn't to defend the Jews of Europe during the Holocaust. He was gung-ho."

"But he never got drafted."

Mom gave me a perplexed look. "Of course he did, honey," she said. "But by that time we'd all learned enough to know we weren't fighting for anything noble in Vietnam. You can't imagine the agonized nights. It turned out he had flat feet, but that made his agonizing worse. Did you know when he was in high school, he taught himself how to run a business to keep Myna's store from going under?"

"No," I said. This was the first I'd ever heard of it. "What was wrong?"

"Everything," Mom said. "After Nathan died, Myna ran the store on whim. They managed to get by, but barely. And when your father got old enough to realize who the scary men were that came to bother his mother every month—her creditors—and that the business was constantly on the verge of bankruptcy—Well, he took over. How could I not fall in love with a man like that?"

"Why didn't Dad ever tell me this stuff?"

"I don't know, Jonson. Did you ever ask?"

In late January of 1986, I was named the national winner, and *You Scream Ice Cream!* offered me a scholarship to the school of my choice, as long as I was accepted there on my own merits. It happened during dinner. Myna and I were eating silently when my mother picked up the phone. Neither of us paid much attention as she listened on the receiver, but when she put it down she starting crying.

"Oh, dear God!" Myna bleated, perhaps ready for the final blow. The debate with my mother had finally petered out. She didn't speak much at all now.

"You won, Jonson," Mom blubbered. I could see she was shedding tears of joy, but it took me a few seconds to realize what she was talking about.

"You Scream?"

"Yes!"

"This silly contest for college?" Myna asked, brightening up.

"You won!" Mom sobbed.

"Wow."

"My blessed child," she sniffed.

All four of us were accepted through Early Admissions at Michigan. Milo was the only surprise. His acceptance was a bit of a coup because his grade average was only 3.3 (I had a 3.85 at the time), but he scored 1350 on the SAT's, which was only slightly lower than what I got. Several friends of ours, all girls, didn't get in though they had similar statistics, including extra-curriculars that didn't involve sucking beer out of gashed aluminum cans. Milo kept telling them he had some qualifications he submitted in photograph form and that he'd be happy to share the evidence with them in private. One of them gave him a black eye.

Milo and I immediately returned our acceptance forms. Jake did too, though he'd also been accepted at Cornell, where it turned out both his parents went. We all said he'd be crazy not to go, but he didn't seem torn about the matter at all. Of course, we didn't try very hard to change his mind.

Cory's decision was the toughest. Besides Michigan, he was accepted by Penn State, which offered him a partial scholarship based on his outstanding AP and SAT scores in math. And despite his father's evil campaign to make him a math genius (which clearly paid off), Cory was attached to his parents and wanted to stay relatively close. So, after a bit of anguish, he settled on Penn State. I was glad he harbored no pretenses of playing football there. He'd played some as a senior, but only when games were lost beyond hope. I don't think he ever caught a pass.

We abused him mercilessly when we found out Sarah Glickman was going to Penn State, too.

Naturally, the rest of senior year sailed by in a blur. College occupied our thoughts almost exclusively. With early enrollment confirmed, Milo, Jake, and I began devoting even less attention than normal to academics. Without concern, I watched my class standing drop from number eleven out of four hundred and twenty to number twenty-one. We spent most of our time together talking about the upcoming year, even to the exclusion of doing our weekly shotguns. This is not to say we refrained from drinking. The three of us checked off a coveted Purity Test item by mastering the "Century Club" that year, a drinking game requiring one to take a shot of beer every minute for one hundred minutes. It took months before any of us could reach the end of the game without throwing up. Cory refused outright to try, though he didn't mind serving as timekeeper when he was there.

Though it was hard for us to part with Cory, our goodbyes were casual. He left almost immediately after graduation, having enrolled in several summer math courses. We made ridiculous promises to alternate monthly road trips between Ann Arbor and

State College when he left. Before he got in the passenger seat of his dad's van, we all shook his hand and wished him best of luck.

On August 20th, two weeks before classes began, Jake, Milo, and I drove off together in a U-haul we rented in Daniel Baker's name. Before we left, Olivia made me swear I'd put her in an ad campaign, Myna made me promise to phone home at least once a week, and my mother wept uncontrollably. Nadia called to tell me not to be too hard on myself if things didn't work out for me that far from home.

Jake had only Daniel to bid farewell. He didn't tell us how that went.

Milo convinced his parents to drop him off halfway down the street, so I didn't see how their farewells went either. He looked upset, which surprised me.

"The party's tonight, you lush!" Jake shouted, startling me at the wheel. He'd turned around to find Milo in the back seat sneaking a sip from a champagne bottle. He'd been quiet in the hour or so since we'd left, but all of us had.

"Ever heard of the Head Start program?" Milo asked. Then he let out a hideously long belch.

"Wait a minute," I said, catching his red eyes in the rearview mirror. "Just how much of a head start are we talking about here?"

"Had a bit of a going away party for myself this morning."

"What a moron!" Jake cried. I think he was going to say more, but Milo passed out.

The rest of the drive was uneventful. The only thing I remember Jake and I discussing was whether we should strip Milo naked and leave him smeared with cow shit in some Ohio pasture. Otherwise, I spent my time thinking about how great it was finally to be free from the madhouse I'd left behind.

Ann Arbor was a sea of twittering freshmen, or "first year students," as I was tersely instructed to call them at a gas station by a young woman in a "Go Blue" bicycle cap. She was filling up a little Volkswagen that appeared to be jammed with at least nine of her friends. It seemed as if every station wagon and mini-van on the planet had converged on the area, crammed with crates full of lamps and hot pots. Soon after arriving, we were grateful that my mother had already arranged to rent us an apartment. It had three small bedrooms, one bathroom, a kitchenette, and one large living room/dining area. None of us cared even the least bit what it looked like.

We arrived in the early evening and had everything unloaded by eight o'clock. Jake volunteered to take the van to the local outlet, and when he left, Milo and I hunkered down on the living room carpet with our course guides. We were eligible to register the next morning and none of us had the foggiest notion of what courses to take, though I had required Business Marketing classes.

Milo was flipping through his guide, though his eyes were unfocused and his head seemed less than entirely stable on his neck. I realized he must've kept drinking when he woke up in the car. "Hmm, no Ass-rolology," he slurred. "Gracious, do you think it's not a valid field of snudy? Should I smell my folks?"

I'd never heard Milo too drunk to speak, and it occurred to me that none of us, to my knowledge, had ever gotten drunk alone. I leaned over to look closer at his eyes. Milo saw this and, in an awkward, sudden motion, head-butted me. He hit me directly over my right eye, hard enough to make me see stars.

"What the hell did you do that for?" I demanded when I could see again. Milo was massaging a red splotch above his nose.

We were all occasionally known to declare a "deadleg" or "redneck" war with an actual punch to the thigh or slap to the back of the neck, but head-butting was not one of our competitions.

"What the hell did you do that for?" I repeated. "That *hurt.*"

But Milo wouldn't respond. He was hanging his head over the catalog, covering his eyes with his hand. A tear dropped heavily onto the open page underneath him.

"Milo? Are you okay?" I was afraid to see another friend weep openly in front of me, though I thought it wouldn't be so bad if he had a concussion or something.

Without looking up, Milo barked, "You are *so* damn snupid!"

"What?" I stood up and walked across the room. "Who do you think you are, Hulk Frickin' Hogan? Why'd you head-butt me?"

"I didn't."

"You didn't think you were Hulk Hogan, or you didn't head-butt me? Tell that to this freakin' lump on my eyebrow."

"I didn't try to head-butt you, you snupid iniot."

Annoyed, I retreated to the kitchen area to see if there was any ice. "Whatever," I muttered, opening the freezer door. "Tell it to the judge."

The ice tray was full. I'd just taken it out when Milo half whimpered, half snarled, "I was trying to kish you, you *ash-hole.*"

In response to which I dropped the tray. Ice cubes exploded free, raining on the linoleum like slippery little bombs.

"What?" I was still standing in front of the open freezer, hoping Milo's inebriated speech impediment was worse than it sounded. I put the empty blue tray back in and carefully closed the door.

"So snupid. You're such a dog-namned—*snupidhead.*"

"Why?" I asked, not wanting to know, not wanting to continue this conversation one second longer.

"Because of the way you are."

"What are you talking about?"

"You can *handle* things," he whined.

"What things?"

"Everything! Your dad gets offed in some Israeli cult, your sisters are insane, your mom's turning into an alchy, and your grandmother's whacked in the head." Milo's outrage was apparently overpowering his drunkenness. "Girls like you, but you act like you could take them or leave them," he continued, picking up steam, "you get good grades without ever lifting a pencil, and you won a fucking scholarship from *You Scream I Creamed My Jeans Ice Cream!*"

While Milo ranted, I'd been peering down at the ice cubes shifting around in their own tiny puddles, but then the obvious hit me. "Wait a minute!" I cried, at last thinking again about that singular night we all seemed to have put out of our minds. "What about that time with Shoshana Silver in Olivia's room? You lost it all over your freakin' pajamas! And at every party you tried for girls! What about the freshman buffet and Kimo Dáte and leaving a goddamn legacy?"

Milo didn't say anything for a minute. Then he croaked, in a very small voice, "Yeah, well—maybe I'm bi-snexual. Ever think of *that,* Mr. Effing Snow-it-all?"

Before anything more disturbing could occur, Jake burst into the apartment with a twelve pack of Molson Golden. He flung the door open too hard, though. The doorknob broke a hole through the wall. "Ah, *shitbird,*" he said. "At least we don't have to worry about the security deposit now." He shrugged apologetically in my direction.

Milo was lying on the living room floor and hadn't responded to the crash. Jake walked around me and held up his prize, purchased by an of-age entrepreneur in front of our local party store buying liquor for a long line of minors for double the price. "Beer's here!" Jake announced, but Milo didn't look up. Jake walked over and prodded him with his foot, but to no avail. Milo was passed out again. When Jake looked back at me to register my reaction, he noticed I was standing amid a floor full of scattered ice cubes. "Oh, honey," he said, "don't tell me you're getting cold feet!" He nearly fell over Milo laughing at himself and couldn't understand why I didn't find the joke funny at all.

The fact that Milo remained unconscious well into the next morning convinced me he wouldn't even remember our little incident, and this seemed confirmed when he didn't bring it up in the following days. I wrote it off to stress-induced temporary insanity. The issue seemed to disappear altogether as all three of us got swept up by campus life. There were parties every night. Once we were registered successfully in our courses, we had total freedom, and we enjoyed it. With so much time before classes started, we drank until we had to stagger home, met people with whom we promised to be best friends, and generally felt like we were on top of the world.

It was as if the whole city was Jake's house, or the third floor of my place—but better.

"Was anyone in our high school gay?"

I screamed this at Jake over the blaring synthesizers of New Order at a frat party. As was typical, the place was jam-packed. People were dancing everywhere, or twitching and bumping into each other, anyway.

I'd been watching Milo chatting up a girl across the room, the same way he had at every party we'd ever been to.

"What do you mean?" Jake shouted back at me. "Of course people were gay! Are you testing me or something?"

"Yeah! Who?"

"Well," Jake shouted, "Ben Jones was, for one!"

"What?" Ben Jones sat two seats in front of me in Calculus.

"Ben Jones! And Andy Hawkins!"

"What?" I could hear Jake, but I couldn't believe what he was saying. Ben was Class Treasurer. Andy was the center forward on

the soccer team.

"And Shelly Morgan and Sydney Friedman — they were a couple!"

"No way!" My astonishment, I realized, experiencing a sensation that was beginning to feel all too familiar, was not so much at the fact that I had homosexual classmates, but that they could have been so without my knowing it.

"What," Jake shouted, "you only see the true humanity in people, is that it? Cut the crap pretending you don't remember! People harassed them all the time. It was sick! Shelly and Syndey started wearing those bracelets with all the pink triangles after the Holocaust unit, remember? How many times did Ben get the crap kicked out of him?"

"I thought that was because he was annoying!"

I remembered the pink triangles, but I never thought anything of them. Lots of girls wore matching accessories — friendship bracelets, beaded or woven hair strings and the like.

Just then a rush of revelers surged between Jake and me. He was swept away, but I settled against a wall next to the kitchen nook. The three people inside the kitchen were intoxicated fraternity pledges, which I gathered from the sandwich boards they were wearing, stenciled with, "Intoxicated Fraternity Pledge #1," etc. They were preparing a new batch of "punch." The two couples who'd been dancing on the bar were taking a breather, so I could see the pledges working. They had a hose running in through an open window and draped into a large plastic garbage can, which it was slowly filling. One pledge was pouring grain alcohol into the vat from oversized plastic jugs while another dumped tin after tin of red Kool-Aide into it. A third was stirring the whole concoction with a golf club. There was a line of maybe fifty people waiting for the refurbishment to be completed. I leaned back against the side of the bar, out of the line, and tried to grapple with Life.

A song or two went by as I stood there, and then someone grabbed my elbow and pulled me into the crowd. Before I knew it, I was slow dancing, pressed up against a baby-faced young woman with long brown hair. She sang Depeche Mode lyrics into my ear, giving me to understand that she wanted to be cared for passionately.

"I've been watching you," she whispered with her lips actually in my ear. You looked all peaceful, like you were halfway to nirvana or something. It was so—Zen. Way cool. *Way* stimulating."

"I'm pretty drunk," I replied, awash in déjà vu.

"There's a room upstairs where everyone's doing lines."

"Actors?"

She flashed a smile full of white teeth and whispered, "I'm going up. Give me twenty and meet me outside. We'll hit Taco *Hell* and go to my apartment." Then she stuck her tongue in my ear, which caused me to snap into semi-sobriety.

She walked away, so I headed for the front door feeling like my time had finally come to take Rabbi Glickman up on his suggestion to leave childish things behind. *Tonight,* I thought, *it's adult things all the way.*

I had to struggle between sweaty bodies just to get outside, and the porch was no less crowded. The only alley for movement I could find was up against the railing, so I slid my behind along it until I hit a corner, then continued sliding. At some point, the railing disappeared, and I fell down the steps leading to the front lawn, where I lay disoriented, but unhurt. The grass was soft and slick with spilled beer. Before I could struggle to my knees, strong hands yanked me up.

"All right, *Mo-fo!* You next?" The hands belonged to a large, glaze-eyed fraternity brother in an over-sized Michigan hockey jersey bearing his Greek letters. He had a blue M cap on, pulled down and curved over intense eyes. He pushed me unceremoniously to the side of the porch toward two frayed and sagging recliners stretched nearly horizontal on the grass. I saw two guys prostrate on the chairs with their feet facing the street. Something flashed just above their faces, which drew my attention upward to a balcony overhanging the lawn chairs. A small cluster of frat brothers was perched on it, hauling up some sort of plastic tubing.

"Get those posers outta here!" one of them yelled. Three or four guys in Rose Bowl T-shirts rolled the two bodies off the chairs. The bodies, apparently not dead, struggled to their knees and feet and then staggered into the crowd on the porch. Someone was pushing me toward the recliner on the left. "Chicks totally dig this, dude," he whispered, forcing me down into the chair.

"Go for it!" a female voice yelled from the porch.

"Anyone else in?" someone called out. I hadn't resisted at all. Everything was moving in slow motion.

Moments later, a muscle-bound kid lay down next to me. He had a crew cut and wore a T-shirt with the sleeves torn off. The front had a picture of Calvin urinating on Michigan State's mascot, Sparty.

"Funneling is AWESOME!" he screamed right into my face.

Two thick tubes appeared over our faces as people raised the backs of our chairs a bit. They caught the tubes and inserted the ends into our mouths. The one holding mine was pinching it shut with some kind of clamp, just above my nose. I could see up to the edge of the balcony where many hands were holding up a gigantic cherry-red funnel, the mouth of which had to be as big as a garbage can lid.

I hoped Jake or Milo was watching because funneling was on the Purity Test.

There were random screams of support from the porch, and then, all at once, a chorus of voices began singing from above. "Twelve bottles of beer on the wall, twelve bottles of beer. Funnel 'em down, pass 'em around—no bottles—"

All noises ceased as an overwhelming torrent of cold liquid hit my mouth. I felt like a balloon filling up with water, but there was no pain. I saw and heard nothing for a length of time that felt endless. I was out of my body completely, somewhere else. For a split second, I was hovering above the frat house, looking down on my prone body.

Which looked dead.

Then I was in a courtroom. My father, who was a golem, was in the witness box. He was on trial. Globs of mud were falling off of him, and he was frantically trying to stick them back on. I stood up, pointed at him, and screamed "Fraud!"

Sounds re-registered at a deafening level. Hands hauled me from my chair like I was a rag doll. It was my euphoric funnel-buddy. "Yeah, yeah, *yeah!*" he exulted, slapping me on the back with a sledgehammer of an arm. I looked up and saw our tubes being reeled in. They were connected half way up. Only one tube led into the funnel, which meant I'd consumed six beers in a matter of—I didn't know.

A voice from above announced a time, but I didn't hear it. "Second best, you two!" it added.

"Fuckin'-A, *yeah!*" my new friend cried, nearly collapsing my lungs with a bone-crunching embrace. "We can do better!"

My head began to spin when he let me go, and I swayed toward the sidewalk. When I regained my balance, I noticed my Depeche Mode girl struggling to break free from the crowd on the porch. Her face looked white. Then it turned green. Then she threw up on someone's neck.

I hustled down the road, heading for home, but halfway there the sidewalk reeled up and hit me in the face. It was a ridiculous thing to happen, so I just held on. At some point I threw up. At some other point, a group of wandering partiers walked over and around me.

"Fight the power, dude," one of them advised me.

I don't know how long it took, but eventually I noticed the ground was back where it was supposed to be, so I was able to grope my way home.

After fumbling into the apartment, I collapsed on my bed and stayed there until the first day of class, which was two days later. Jake and Milo tried to pry me out several times, but I claimed to have the flu and just laid there in a state of suspended animation.

During that time I repeatedly dreamt about a golem and a dybbuk sitting on the carpet in my Pittsburgh bedroom rolling dice to create a character they were calling Jon-son. They laughed hysterically after each roll.

When I wasn't suffering through this dream, I had time to think about my classes. I'd enrolled in four. Two were for my major: Introduction to Business Marketing and Economics I. I couldn't decide what else to take, so I'd signed up for one class each with Milo and Jake.

Milo wanted to become the first person in history to literally major in "T & A," so he'd signed up for an art class that used nude models, Human Anatomy, a history class called, "Sex and Society," and a sociology course called, "Media Exploitation of the Female form." I'd heard plenty about the latter from my mother growing up, and I couldn't paint to save my life. History in general didn't interest me, so I chose Anatomy.

I took the T & A curriculum plan as further confirmation that the big bi-sexual revelation was just Milo being Milo.

Jake was pretty sure he was going to major in English, so he signed up for three related classes. We picked one together because it fit well into both our schedules, something called Introduction to Literary Theory — whatever that was.

Little did I know that in the schedule I'd so casually created for myself, I'd combined exactly the right ingredients for a very short stint in Ann Arbor.

Introduction to Literary Theory met Monday and Friday mornings from 8:30 to 10:00. Jake and I showed up early to the first meeting, blithe and enthusiastic. However, our enthusiasm was tempered almost immediately upon our arrival. The enrollment was evidently limited because when we walked into the seminar room we saw there were no more than thirty seats. I guess I was expecting a crowded auditorium I could blend into.

Jake and I took seats in the back of the room, behind a dozen or so students, and I immediately realized we were the only people in the room not garbed predominately in black. Just after we were settled, a woman with a shaved head two seats in front of me said to a woman with a buzz-cut sitting next to her, "I hear we don't have to read a single dead white guy in here. How sweet is _that?_"

Jake and I looked at each other, nervously. He leaned over and said, _"A Single Dead White Guy_ – who wrote that?"

"I have no idea," I replied. "I hope it isn't a pre-requisite."

A woman with a long blonde ponytail heard the first exchange. She leaned toward her classmates and said, "The canon is wide open here, _bay-bee._ I'm doing Virginia Wolfe and nothing else for four years. I checked it out with my counselor."

"Sweet," both the other women replied.

It occurred to me that not everyone there was a freshman, but I stopped listening because the professor walked into the room. He was holding a stack of syllabi and began passing them out even before approaching the lectern at the front of the room. He was the first professor I'd ever seen, so I inspected him closely. He looked to be in his mid-forties and had a square face, thinning hair, pale cheeks, and the first signs of paunchiness. He was wearing khakis and a sweater over a collared shirt.

When all the handouts were passed around, he went to the board and wrote, _"Meaning is exactly where meaning is not."_ Jake and I looked at each other and back at the board. The professor had jotted his name, "Donovan Clock," underneath the sentence, which I took to mean he was quoting himself.

I glanced down at the syllabus, which appeared to be in a language poorly masquerading as English. There were headings under each week's class with titles like, *The Fundamental Mythology of the Self, The Ideology of Ideology,* and *The Social Construction of Reality*. The topic for the first class was *The Non-existence of Language and Meaning*. I looked up when Professor Clock began speaking, ready to drop the class as soon as I could get out of there. Jake could be an English major on his own.

"We must begin with Saussure's insights about language," Professor Clock began in a rather attention-getting baritone. "Now, given his Structuralist bent, his project was to identify the stable systems he believed underpinned all phenomena, from mythology to psychology to political relationships—everything. And he was a linguist, so, naturally, he put most of his efforts into the examination of language."

I wished to God I had our giant dictionary there. I would have flipped it open no matter how conspicuously.

The professor walked to his podium and made eye contact with a student in the front row wearing a black jeans jacket. "How do you know what the letters 'c-a-t' signify?" he queried.

The student sat motionless, caught in full-on deer-in-the-headlights mode. I felt bad for him, but I was glad it wasn't me.

"Come on," said Clock. "It's not a trick question."

"It means cat," the boy croaked. "The furry animal with whiskers. It says meow."

"Well done—but, why 'c-a-t'?"

"Don't know. Arbitrary, I guess."

Professor Clock seemed pleased. He walked back to the chalkboard, whereupon he wrote the three letters in question. The way he wrote them, placing a slightly larger than normal distance between the characters, made the word look strange to me.

"There is no real connection between these letters and the animal with whiskers that says, 'meow,' yes?" Clock was addressing everyone, so we all nodded, albeit hesitantly. Then he wrote the words 'cap' and 'bat' underneath 'cat.' "'C-a-t' has identifiable meaning not because that combination of letters in and of itself corresponds to anything," he said, "but because it is distinguished from these combinations of letters." Clock was alternately tapping the board on 'cap' and 'bat' with a chalk stub. It started to hypnotize me. "Look again at the word 'cat,'" he instructed. Now the letters ceased to convey even a semblance of meaning. They looked like a picture or some sort of hieroglyph. "Where is the meaning here?" Clock asked. He was tapping 'cat.' No one responded. I didn't know what he was looking for, but I felt he was saying something vitally important to me. "Is there any meaning in these letters?" he asked.

"No," ventured some brave soul.

"Where is it then?" Clock asked with a smile. "Will a child who hasn't learned the alphabet make a connection between these three shapes and a meow-making feline?"

The woman with the shaved head said, "I guess the meaning is available only because of the other letters — in other arrangements. Is that it?"

Clock turned to face the board and smacked the smooth green surface with an open palm. Then he spun around and shouted, "Yes! Don't you see the meaning is in the differences? And where is that? Can you put your finger on it? Can you measure it with a scientific instrument? Can you?"

I'd never seen a teacher express such emotion before and found myself on the edge of my seat, despite the fact I wasn't comprehending much of what he was saying.

"Meaning, my friends," Clock concluded, calming down, "is exactly where meaning is not."

All eyes went to the sentence on the board and understanding swept the room, or at least an understanding of why the strange sentence was there. It felt like we'd just been elected into some sort of club.

Clock strode to the far side of the class, to my left, and approached a cowering boy in a black sweatshirt. "If you didn't know the meaning of 'c-a-t,'" he asked, "what would you do?"

"Ahh, ahh—" The poor kid looked as if he were facing his firing squad.

"Look in the dictionary, of course!"

"And when you did," said Clock, looking directly at me, "what would you find?"

Jake was gaping at me as if my head had just rotated around my neck in a full circle, and I looked at him in alarm, then back at Clock. I hadn't realized it was I who'd spoken. "The definition?" I squeaked, fearing a trap. But Clock wasn't out for blood.

"But the definition would be made up of other words, no?" he replied, thankfully turning his attention elsewhere. "And where do you go in search of definitions for any or all of those words in your definition? You would turn to other definitions, and still others, and so on and so on, *ad infinitum*. Words only point to other words. You would never reach a ground or find an original source anywhere—ever." Clock turned again to the board. "There is no essence in any word or in any letter," he declared. "Saussure didn't push it that far, but others did." Clock circled the word 'cap.' "I say again," he said, "there is no essence of any word or any letter. There is no essential *'cap'-ness.* Then he underlined just the letter 'p' and said, "There is no essential *'P'-ness.*"

This last exemplar temporarily stunned everyone. Jake looked down at his notebook, stifling a smirk. The professor seemed stunned himself.

"Tell that to my ex-boyfriend," said the woman with the ponytail, which uncorked the laughter everyone in the room was trying to bottle up.

Clock actually blushed, but then giggled in a surprisingly lighthearted way. "Thank goodness we get to deconstruct Freud in this class," he sighed. Everyone (but Jake and me) laughed again.

"Imagine we're on one of those rope webs the kids climb on at the fun parks," Clock continued, getting back to business. He started weaving through our desks as he spoke. "Only, it's so big you can't see the ends in any direction. We're in the middle somewhere, right on a corner knot, and we want to know what's supporting it because we're lucky enough not to have completely TV'ed our natural human curiosity. So, we study our little knot, quickly perceiving two ropes leading away from it in different directions at ninety-degree angles. We follow one and quickly find ourselves at another corner knot. Are you with me?"

The class nodded its collective head.

"*Ah ha!* we say. We think we see how this works, so we move around until we realize there are four knots, nicely, geometrically supporting one another—laws of physics and all that. Nicely, nicely then. But soon we're curious about the whole square, no? What's holding it up? So we push on outward and find more and more squares with more and more neat knots linking them together. Do you see what I'm getting at? Most people stop pushing out when things get shaky. They sense danger and don't want to get hung up on any loose ends. They can smell the abyss! But if you intend to be a part of this class, we will not lounge on a few squares as if they made a hammock in our Farmington Hills backyards. We will push further and further out on the ropes! Are you with me?"

Clock was pacing back and forth across the room now, gesticulating wildly as he spoke. "What you will find is that the whole vast net is floating in mid-air!" he cried. "Will you push out there with me?"

No one responded.

"You must understand that everything we know, we know through language — *words*. And we see in a matter of seconds that language, and thus the Universe as we *know* it, has no essence, no *ground*. This is its fundamental defect, this hidden, infinitesimal hole at the bottom of this monumental edifice we sit upon, and it is our gift because to *dis*-cover this tiny interstice offers us a rare chance to peer through it! We're going to see that we live on many different floating webs of language. There's one called gender. There are nets called sexual orientation, ideology, nationalism, Capitalism, Communism — and, my new friends, there is even one called the Personal Self!"

My pulse was racing.

"Will you push out there with me?" he asked again, "or is it the hammock for you?" Still no one said anything. "The push or the hammock!" he demanded.

"The push!"

I shouted this into the nervous silence filling the room. Then, before Jake's eyes could fall out of his head and bounce onto my desk, six or seven others echoed my call. "The push!" they cried.

"Good enough," Clock muttered, returning immediately to the cool demeanor with which he had begun his disquisition. "You should be off balance." I don't recall much of what he talked about for the rest of class, but at some point he said, "See you next class. Have the Eagleton book finished."

I found the Monday/Wednesday/Friday Anatomy lectures quite interesting, despite the fact that the only T & A involved was a morbidly obese Teacher's Assistant named Horatio. But the class was ruined for me when Milo started subjecting me to silent treatments. He insisted on sitting next to me but wouldn't utter a single word before, during, or directly after class. I assumed his behavior was related to what I'd begun to think of as the

"Bincident," but I wasn't about to let him goad me into broaching the subject. I figured if he had something to say, he could say it. After two weeks of his nonsense, I stopped going to class.

I was planning to change my schedule, but as it turned out, I found a better solution.

I also lasted only two weeks in Business Marketing, or "Bizmark" as it was affectionately known by those who had affection for it. The charts and graphs about supply and demand were absorbing, as were the various properties, tendencies, and idiosyncrasies of the market, but my interest died during the fourth meeting when the professor explained the class project.

The assignment was to write a business proposal for a product or service that we would subsequently provide for the campus over the second half of the yearlong course. I didn't realize it was a yearlong course until he mentioned this. It was to be a competition between the students in class: the most profit earned set the grading curve. The catch was that the product or service we designed had to be entirely original. We weren't allowed to sell homemade Hacky Sacks or U of M paraphernalia of any sort.

"Let me give you an idea of what I'm talking about," intoned the rail-thin, bespectacled professor. His name was Steven Deadmarsh. He had close-set eyes that punctuated his otherwise flat face. "The most successful project ever to emerge from this class was Love Notes, which was launched in 1982 and currently nets about twenty thousand dollars per academic year." A twitter rippled through the auditorium of approximately three hundred students at this news. "Love Notes is, of course, the note-taking service with which many of you are surely familiar," Deadmarsh explained, "especially those of you enrolled in this course and currently not here."

Everyone laughed.

Someone in the front row put up his hand and asked a

question I couldn't hear from my seat in the back.

"Yes, a real business!" Deadmarsh shouted into the microphone. "I realize this might be a novel concept for you kids, but this is education that has something to do with the *real world*. What you learn in here will make your lives easier. I'M TALKING ABOUT MAKING MONEY!"

A wave of enthusiastic murmuring swept the auditorium, but all I could think about was my father running Myna's business all by himself. I suddenly felt nauseated.

"Now, of course, most years a bona fide business isn't born," the professor warned, "though many projects earn a fair profit. The winning project from last year was this—" Deadmarsh held aloft and shook a plastic strip that looked like a rubbery yardstick, which elicited a smattering of chuckles. "I believe this low-cost item brought its designers nearly four thousand dollars last year." Deadmarsh proclaimed this like a proud papa showing off his son's first trophy.

"What is it?" someone shouted.

I thought I could see Deadmarsh flash a sly grin all the way from the back. "It fits in the space under a door," he explained, "to prevent—odors—incense and the like—from—offending others who might live in immediate proximity. It's called a Stick-it."

"What?" someone whispered behind me.

"It's a pot smoke blocker, *doofus*," another voice explained. "You stick it under your door in the dorm."

"And finally," Deadmarsh continued, sounding like a politician at a victory party, "there's the winner from two years back, best described as the Better Business Bureau for Lovers. It was a 900-line for former flames to lodge complaints against their exes so that prospective partners could review such information for a small per-minute fee. Unfortunately, there were legal issues that—"

I didn't hear any more because I'd broken into a cold sweat.

I had the uncontrollable urge to leave immediately, so I did just that. The last thing I wanted to do was run a business when I was supposed to be in school.

A girl in a "Harvard: the Michigan of the East" T-shirt was ascending the steps to the building as I was coming down them. She informed me that Love Notes operated out of a local copy store. I went straight there, and upon my arrival, discovered that one could subscribe to the service for a mere twenty dollars per course, thereby securing clearance to pick up each week's neatly typed notes (taken down by cracker-jack students hired by the company) every Sunday evening. I quickly revised my schedule-changing plans and signed on for notes from Anatomy, Econ, and Business Marketing.

As she'd done for Nadia and Olivia, Mom had opened a bank account for me, though of course mine only required money for living expenses. She wanted us to learn the responsibility of handling financial affairs. I considered the sixty dollars well invested.

And promptly stopped attending all three classes.

Notes were available for Clock's course, too, but there was no way I was going to skip it. It gripped me like nothing ever had before in school—it was almost as absorbing as D & D used to be.

Going to the class was like seeing a magician every week. I understood virtually nothing in any real depth, but in any case, I was beginning to comprehend the sheer vastness of the things I didn't understand. The vertiginous sensation caused by the dawning of this awareness was pleasing to me. Every "debunking" of commonly held beliefs was a revelation. If identity was a dubious social construct, what was the point of all that jibber-jabber with Rabbi Glickman? If pornography was neither the subjugation of, nor the seizing of power by women, why shouldn't Olivia make some easy money? If repressive ideologies of all sorts were imbedded in even the most benign media messages, why did Mom care what kind of ad campaigns she worked on?

If the family unit was the most basic model of pure exploitation, why did Jake care so much about being orphaned?

If religion was impossible without uncertainty — then my goddamn father was wrong on both sides of the fence!

Taking notes was futile, so I got into the habit of doodling elaborate pages full of mazes while I listened. Jake was also engrossed in the class, as much as I was, it seemed. We didn't get much time to talk about it, though, because he'd found a girl and was spending every minute he could with her.

Milo wasn't around much either, and when he was, he maintained the outright hostile distance he established the day I quit going to Anatomy. One rare evening when we all happened to be sharing a pizza, I asked him where he'd been hiding lately. His eyes narrowed as he told us about the bunch of cool fraternity guys he'd met in Art class. He said they were always asking him to hang out with them to see if he might like to pledge. I told him that was great, but he only cut his eyes further and shoved half a slice of crispy bacon and mushroom into his mouth.

After Clock's class one day, I was sitting dazed in the back row when Wanda, the girl with the buzz-cut, sat down next to me. I'd chatted with her several times before, so I wasn't caught too much off guard.

"Hey," she said.

"Hey," I said back.

"Are you interested in Foucault?"

I had no idea what that meant. "Why?"

"I don't know. I watch you back here. You don't say too much, but you're, like, scribbling everything down, and I know you're absorbing. And the guts you had on the first day when you spoke up like that — pretty great. *Unheard* of for a freshman."

"Thanks."

"As you probably know, Foucault believed one can go

beyond, outside the parameters of conventional thought by subjecting oneself to limit-experiences. There's an entire class on him here."

"Of course," I said, and Wanda looked pleased. She had a round face, made rounder by her lack of hair. Her eyes were almond-shaped and attractive. "Um—so, do you think I should sign up for that other course?" I asked.

"If you need it," she replied. Then her eyes took on a conspiratorial glimmer. "I was just going to tell you that I'm part of a group of Foucauldians that meets on Monday nights, really late— like, one in the morning."

"Foucauldians?"

"Exactly. Monday is a weird night on this campus 'cause there's nothing going on. Most of the upper-level theory classes are on Mondays, so people are geared up."

"What do you do?" I asked, wondering if she was pulling my leg.

"Experiment with limit-experiences—work like mad to shatter the false-consciousness we're all enslaved to in this demented culture. My sister, Genevieve, is one of the founders of the group. She's doing her Master's in Lit. Crit."

"Wow, I don't know." It all sounded impressive, but way out of my league.

"Tonight's address—no pressure," Wanda said, handing me an index card with green writing on it. Then she got up and headed out of class. Jake was standing at the door waiting for me, and when she reached him, she turned around and said, "You can bring friends if you like."

"By the way," Jake said while we were walking home, "that girl I've been hanging out with—"

"Let me take a wild guess, Jake—you dumped her."

"Yeah—"

"Big surprise. Thanks for breaking it to me easy."

Jake looked down at the ground as we walked on, then added, almost off-handedly, "Right after things got sort of intercoursey."

I stopped. "Wait—*what?* Are you saying you had sex?"

"Kind of. Yes."

"Holy shit! Wait, and then you *dumped* her?"

"I know, I know," Jake groaned, still looking down at his feet.

"You think maybe you might have a slight fear of commitment?"

"No, that's not it."

"I don't know what to say. Congratulations?"

Jake looked at me. "Thanks," he sighed, saving me from further floundering. "I don't want to talk about it. Do me a favor, will you? Don't tell Milo. I don't want to deal with him going ape-shit."

I couldn't get to sleep that night. At midnight, I got up and started leafing through the books for Clock's class, searching for information on Foucault.

The phone rang, so I snatched it up.

At first, I thought the call was a crank because I couldn't understand the voice on the line. It was garbled and breathy. But then I discerned something like, "Jonsthanan."

"Mom?" I gulped, and then I heard a long, wretched sob, then a click and the dial tone.

I immediately called Olivia in the garret, but a man answered in a panting state. "Hang it up!" I heard my sister hiss in the background—again, a click and the dial tone.

As a last resort, I called Nadia, afraid to wake her up. I got her answering machine, but I panicked after saying it was me and hung up.

A few minutes later the phone rang again.

"What's the damage?" Nadia asked.

"Mom just called me! She sounded insane. I couldn't understand a word she said. Then she cried and hung up."

"Did you call Olivia, or did you think I might run over to the house from Philadelphia to check on her?"

"A man answered the phone."

"That was probably Guy Peperchuck."

"Who?"

"The head of the Drama Department at CMU."

"Oh, Jesus."

"Wake up, Jonathan!"

"What?"

"How are your classes going, by the way? Any good ones?"

"I — ah — I like my Lit. Theory class."

"Literary Theory is just a sophisticated bunch of word games," Nadia declared. "Do me a favor and ask your professor why so many so-called deconstructionists write so many words about how meaningless words are. I dare you to tell him it's only their incompetence that proves their point. I bet he kicks your meaningless ass right out of class. Even if the basic point is right, don't be such a sucker. Are you drinking?"

"Look, Nadia—"

"Just don't do that stupid funneling thing that's all the rage right now. It's strictly for troglodytes. Why someone would want to lay down and slurp from the lowest gene pool on Earth is beyond me. Unless, of course, you want to get yourself sent home."

I hung up on her.

Harrowed, I went back to bed with no further investigation into Foucault. I still couldn't get to sleep, though, thinking about Olivia shacking up with some smarmy lech. Why did she need to do that? She was obviously a magnetic personality. She was going to succeed as an actress.

And why couldn't my mother just move on!

Like I had!

I felt like hurting someone, but all I did was just lay there, stewing.

I was still awake an hour later when the phone rang again. My hand clutched at the receiver as I assumed it was Nadia calling to taunt me some more with her psychic powers.

Only, it wasn't her. It was Daniel Baker. His voice, which was normally drugged into a sandpapery whisper, was crisp, clean, and utterly devoid of human resonance. It sounded like an automated voice intoning the words, "Schwartz, I need to talk to Jake. Right now. Put him on the phone."

I pushed Jake's door open, hoping he wasn't home. He was, a lump under his covers. I stood there without saying anything for a minute, but finally, I whispered his name. He didn't respond. I didn't want to invade his room, but I knew I had to, so I walked over to the bed and poked him a few times. A head emerged, and one groggy eye opened to me.

"Jake."

"Hmrm?"

"Your brother's on the phone."

He bolted upright, completely awake. It was startling, but I knew exactly what he knew. He picked up his phone and said, "Yeah?" but didn't utter another word before he put it down. Then he looked at me and said, "She's dead. She wouldn't let anyone tell us until it happened."

Jake sat on the edge of his bed and hung his head once again. I wanted to say something that would keep him from crying, but no words came, only the feeling that I was confirming the inadequacy of words.

Instead of crying, Jake looked up at me with a strangely calm expression and said, "You know what?"

"What?"

"*Relief.*"

"What?"

"That's what I feel—more than anything. Is that wrong?"

"I don't think anything you feel at a time like this counts for much."

"Good," he said. "You're a genius, Schwartz. Nothing you think counts after something shitty happens. It's later that counts, right? Like months, or a year—but it probably doesn't count too much then, either, huh? And if you're like me and you don't think, you're home free."

"Home free," I echoed, weakly.

An uncomfortable silence arose, but we were saved by the repetitive signal coming from the phone in my room. "I'll go hang that up," I announced and walked out.

Jake wasn't in his room when I returned. I assumed he was in the bathroom, so I sat down on his bed to wait. He came in with Milo, who looked stricken. His black waves of hair were pointing in random sleepy directions. He gave me an unpleasant, but ultimately indecipherable look that made me get off the bed. "Oh, man," he said, "this reeks."

"We've got to go do something," Jake declared. His eyes were dark and darting. "I can't just sit around here—not when my mom's dead."

"You want to go over to South Quad and hang out in the snack bar?" Milo asked. "Eat some cheese sticks and shit?"

Jake started pacing. "No," he grumbled. "I have to go *out*. Damn! Why does it have to be Monday night?"

I remembered Wanda's invitation, so I mentioned it.

"Do you still have the address?"

I ran to my room and found it in my jeans.

"What the hell is it?" Milo asked. "Jake said she's in some secret book club or something."

"I don't know."

Jake looked at the card. "I'm going home tomorrow to get

ready for the funeral," he said. "They're flying my mom back to Pittsburgh. So I am going out *right* now. You guys can go back to bed if you want."

Milo sighed, but I knew he wouldn't bail on us.

"We're in," I said.

We walked out onto Packard Street at 1:30. Milo knew the general location of the address. He said some of his new friends lived in the area, so it only took about fifteen minutes to find it. Our destination seemed to be a large, somewhat dilapidated country-style house out past the fraternities. There were no drunken revelers on the sizable wrap-around porch, or, apparently, in the main room on the first floor, as no one was visible through the thinly veiled front window. Whatever was going on inside, it was clearly not a frat party.

I stood in front of the house to take it in, but Jake strode right up onto the porch and in through the front door.

Milo and I looked at each other.

"We're still friends, aren't we?" he asked. He looked shamefaced and shy, which wasn't a demeanor I'd ever seen from him.

I nodded, but then scampered up the steps and into the house.

There was a card table set up at the bottom of a flight of steps just inside the front door, the exact type we used to have our Family Meetings around. An anorexic woman with long, carrot-colored hair was sitting behind it with a clipboard. Hanging from the front edge of the table was a butcher-paper banner on which was written in black magic marker, "Pot/pourri." The woman smiled and said, "Foucauldians? Lacanians? Deconstructionists or Derri-dadaists? Generic Theory-heads? Everybody's welcome."

Jake and Milo stared blankly. I said, somewhat randomly, "Yes. I know Wanda and—" I couldn't recall her sister's name. "These guys are friends."

"Great," the hostess said. "Have you already eradicated your false egos, or are you just starting the process?"

"Oh, well," I fumbled, "we're making progress, I would say."

"Great, great," she said, reaching into a blue and white box at her feet, from which she produced flyers for each of us. "Take a minute to get acquainted with tonight's lineup. It's the best stuff from last year." She tilted her head, causing her hair to swing out momentarily. Then she pointed both index fingers over the edge of the table at the banner. "That's why we're calling it Pot/pourri Night. Get it?" I smiled and nodded with, I hoped, something approximating amusement. Jake and Milo were perusing their flyers, so I did the same.

Our hostess suggested we sit in the lounge, which was the empty room we saw through the front window, to decide comfortably what we wanted to do. Milo and I went in and sat down, but Jake didn't follow. We craned our necks to see what he was doing. He said something to the hostess, then walked up the steps behind her.

Milo and I looked at each other again, then back down at our flyers.

Foucauldian Session #7 — Pot/pourri
Room 1: Pacification: suppression of the putative "self"
Room 2: Transcendence: de-reifying, deprivileging, and destabilizing hegemonic boundaries
Room 3: Deliquescification: from aggregation toward obliteration
Room 4: Suicide Room

"What is this *shite?*" Milo groused, looking at me with extreme perturbation. "Is this even English? Sounds like a bunch of suck-ass lectures. There is no way in hell I'm sitting in some freakish home school classroom listening to mumbo-jumbo with a bunch of fugly bush pigs at this hour of the night. And what the fuck is the 'Suicide Room'? Someone's idea of a sick joke?"

I knew Milo's reaction had to have something to do with his parents, but I wanted to get away from him. He was making me nervous. I told him I was going upstairs.

"Just make sure you watch Jake," he ordered. "He's completely mental right now, and frankly," he added, "so are you." I didn't know what he meant by that, and I didn't care. He got up and headed for the door.

I'd just re-approached the redhead at her card table when a minor commotion erupted behind me. A blonde woman in shockingly high-cut jeans shorts was pushing past Milo into the house. She was carrying an apparently heavy gym bag over her shoulder and was out of breath. Milo turned around and stared at her from behind as she elbowed me aside to talk to the hostess. She was wearing an open zip-front sweatshirt. Underneath she wore only a mesh shirt and no bra. I looked up to see Milo's reaction, but he was gone.

"Are you Cherry?" the redhead asked, rather tersely.

"Yeah," the new arrival said, cracking a wad of gum. "Sorry, I'm late." She was looking down at the banner, regarding it with a rather pronounced screwing-up of her thickly painted eyes.

"We need you in Room Two. It's been slow so far. There's no back-log, thank God."

"Super," Cherry replied with maximum indifference. Something made her turn around and look at me. I intended to say hello, but I handed her my flyer instead. She looked at me with disdain but glanced down at it. "Ohhh, no!" she spat. "Not *this* crap again!"

"What?" the redhead snapped.

"Trans-whatever, hedge-whoever? Got a migraine last time that lasted —"

"Listen, *bitch*," the redhead snarled, "if you want to get paid at all tonight, get your ass up there. Otherwise get the hell out of here and don't come back."

Cherry backed down. "All right, all right," she grumbled. "Jesus, Honey — no need to get your panties in a bunch. *Shit.*"

With that, she walked up the stairs, leaving me standing in silence, gaping at her behind, underwearless and visible through a multitude of tears in the shorts.

"Sir? Sir?" The hostess was talking to me again. She smiled a perfectly relaxed smile. "Are you ready?" I nodded dumbly and headed up the steps. "I definitely suggest starting in Room One," she advised. "And feel free to just watch in any room. Oh, and have fun!"

The steps led into a long and narrow hall of brown doors. Just to my right at the top step was the door to Room 1, adorned with a laminated sign repeating what my now lost flyer had so obscurely promised: *Pacification: suppression of the putative "self."* Ignoring the feelings of inadequacy aroused by the sign, I walked into the room only to be enveloped in a cloud, a cloud with a very distinctive odor. Seven or eight shadows were just visible sitting against the walls. A constellation of hovering sparks revealed that they were all toking. No one said a word to me, so I walked toward the back of the room. Just after I passed the first person, he or she got up and moved toward the door. I looked back to see the figure hunch down to put something under it — one of Deadmarsh's Stick-its. I must have kicked it aside when I came in.

The room was larger than it first appeared. Moving through it was like wading into a fog bank. At some point, I bumped into a table laden with rolling papers and what I assumed to be marijuana. I stared at it, getting dazed simply from breathing the air in the room.

"*Psst.*"

A voice hissed at me from somewhere nearby. It was Jake, so I walked over to him and sat down. He was smoking a prodigiously fat joint. "Do you believe I've never done this before?" he said. "I guess I'm going to have to break up with it when I finish."

"Shhhh!" This came from several places around the room.

I gathered there was a no talking rule in effect, so I leaned back against the wall and just inhaled. Soon enough, I began to feel loose and happy, as if the world were joyful and light. Suddenly, I turned to Jake, who was still puffing away, and said, "Pot-pourri? Get it? *Pot*-pourri?"

Jake looked at me, and we both giggled.

"Shhhhh!" came again, this time more forcefully. We stifled our laughter and tried not to look at each other.

"Come on," I whispered, "there are other rooms."

Jake shook his head and leaned close to me. "I think my mother's ghost is in here," he whispered back. "They gave her acres of weed. I'm gonna inhale her."

"Good luck with that," I replied, disturbed, but also amused. I got up and headed for the door, where I passed a golem in black stretch-pants coming inside. That was also amusing. I accidentally kicked the Stick-it into the hall and had to toss it back into the room. Hilarious!

The hall was empty, so I stood there with a hand on each wall until my head cleared. Then I managed a few unsteady steps until I found myself in front of Room 2: *Transcendence: de-reifying, deprivileging, and destabilizing hegemonic boundaries.* I knew from Clock's class (because it was the only time I recall he took the time to define a word) that 'reified' referred to an abstract concept that appears concrete only because one is never taught to question it— the concept of "race," for example, which he explained was only a few hundred years old. It can be seen as "controlling" because it governs the way millions of people interpret their experiences in the world. This was interesting enough, but he also added that the concept of the personal self as a forward-projecting, cohesive and coherent entity was no different, and that we could just as easily view humans as completely different people from moment to moment. Just because it's not practical to do so, he asserted, doesn't mean doing so is groundless.

It occurred to me standing there that Clock had given me a more plausible explanation for the behavior of—everybody I knew. There didn't need to be a dybbuk inhabiting my parents and siblings, because there really were no members of my family. There were only these people who did things that couldn't be predicted from one moment to the next because they were different people from one moment to the next—as was I. One minute my father is a famous author and a staunch defender of Reason, the next he's ready for the anonymity of black hats, sidelocks, and Holy Wars. One minute my mother is a happily married, high-powered business woman with respect for her Jewish heritage and a talent for protecting the public welfare, and the next she's an alcoholic, obsessive-compulsive Protestant widow who's work is a failure. So be it! Rather than loathe the chaotic nature of this random process, I decided to embrace it.

I felt as if I'd honed in on a real truth.

I went to open the door, but the moment I put my hand on the knob, I heard shouting inside the room.

"Don't you start that shit with me!"

It was Cherry.

"Please," a male voice whimpered, "turn the crank. Keep— turning—the crank. No—body."

"What did you say?"

"I—No body. Destroy—body—politic—"

"That's *IT!*" I heard the sound of someone jumping from a height. "If you say one more thing like that—I'm serious—I will fucking KILL YOU! And I'm not kidding around here. This is not part of the routine. I will kill you dead. *DO YOU UNDERSTAND ME?*"

The man whimpered something remotely affirmative. Cherry, apparently mollified, evidently climbed back up to wherever she was perched. There must have been someone else in the room because she barked, "You got any fancy college talk for me, honey?" I could just barely hear female moaning in response. It wasn't pained, though. It sounded more like purring. "Think I'm stupid?" Cherry sneered. "Goddamn bunch of spoiled bitches and bastards. Fucking Gross Pointe royalty — probably wanted to shove that silver spoon right up your asses, didn't you?"

I heard the sound of metal on metal, the turning of some sort of gear. Both the male and female voices inside screamed in what can only be described as blissful agony.

"Monty," I said to No Body, "I think I'm gonna have to take a pass on door number two."

That cracked me up for a solid minute.

When the laughing jag passed, I considered going home, but I remembered Milo's warning to watch out for Jake. The cloud in Room 1 was nearly impenetrable when I went back inside. I walked along the walls, tripping over people and whispering Jake's name. Someone grabbed my ankle.

I squatted down and peered through the fog to find Jake's glazed-over face. He was grinning so largely that his features were nearly unrecognizable. His head was slumped over sideways. "Mom?" he mumbled.

"It's me, Jake."

"But *I'm* Jake, aren't I?"

"No, Jake. It's me, Jonathan."

"Oh. You scared me for a sec."

I told him about Room 2, adding for effect that there were butt-naked babes romping all over the hall.

"You've got a knack, my friend," was Jake's reply, "a serious *knack*. But it's all good in here."

"You can't stay in here all—" I started to say, but someone shushed me again.

Jake leaned over and whispered, "Listen, Jon. I know you're worried about me. Tell you what. You go check out the other rooms and come back to tell me about them. Then I'll leave with you." I was going to object, but Jake looked me in the eye and said, "Shhhh!" as loudly as he could.

"Fine," I relented, "but I'll be right back."

I made my way to Room 3: *Deliquescification: from aggregation toward obliteration.* Some kind of cheesy music was playing inside. I rested my forehead on the door, wondering just exactly what I was doing there.

The door pushed open from the pressure of my lean, and I found myself staring at a huge, astonishingly hirsute man and a petite woman, both apparently naked. They were sitting on a blue gymnastics mat and staring up at a television monitor mounted on the wall. They were both taking notes on yellow legal pads resting on their laps. On the screen was an orgy, immeasurably more explicit than anything received by my family's cable subscription. My mouth dropped open as I unconsciously walked into the room. When the couple noticed me, they leapt to their feet.

They *were* naked.

"Finally!" the woman sighed.

"Here," said the hairy giant, striding over to me. To my dismay, he grabbed my shirt and starting pulling it up over my head.

"What are you doing?" I shouted through my shirt, which was already over my face. My arms were forced straight above my head. The only thing I could do was backpedal. I hit the doorjamb, then pulled my attacker into the hall, where it seemed we collided with at least one other person who grunted in annoyance but continued on his way. The next thing I knew, I was jerked back into the room as my shirt was yanked free.

The couple regarded me angrily. The woman said, "Well, we can't very well get started without you!" Her up-turned breasts seemed to point at me, accusingly.

"Ah, ah—" I stammered. "Did Wanda—or—or—*Genieveve*

tell you I was coming?"

"Yeah," said the hairy giant. "Wanda told us she invited someone who knew what the hell he was doing. So, if it's you," he added, chucking my shirt into the hall. "Let's get this show on the road."

"Wait!" I exclaimed. "Why do you need me?"

The woman sighed again and pointed impatiently toward the wall above the television set, at a sign I hadn't noticed. "This room for Aggregation only," it read. Then she waited for the look of comprehension I attempted to display. "That's why we're bored off our asses in here," she said. "Rules are rules, and two people do not an orgy make."

"Of course," I said, stalling, wracking my brains for a means of escape. I didn't want to flee like a child if it would get back to Wanda. "Before we get started," I said, trying to sound like my father as I bent down to unlace my Pumas, "would you mind sharing your thoughts on the process? I'm only asking because we really should be on the same page. Don't you think?"

"Yeah, sure," the hairy giant reluctantly agreed. "Why don't you start, Penelope?"

Penelope looked vaguely uncomfortable. "Well, from what I understand," she said, "the notion is to, sort of, dissolve one's individual self into the, sort of, collective — to obliterate the con-structs that, sort of, define our illusory individual selves. From aggregation toward obliteration — that means in the group we are destroying the individual."

"In an orgy," I said.

"Well, yeah," she replied, smiling. I had one shoe and sock off when she walked to me and unceremoniously grabbed my crotch exactly the way the Darby golem had in my evidently prophetic dream. I hopped backward and fell on my behind in the doorway.

"What the hell?" she demanded. The two irate nudes were standing over me then, scowling. I didn't know where to look, and I was out of ideas.

"This is bullshit, pure and simple," the hairy giant decreed.

A fortuitous choice of words.

"You two are way hasty," I declared from my seat on the floor, "and that gives me serious reservations. There are still only three of us, and everyone knows that a meh—a mena—" The Purity Test word wouldn't articulate itself clearly. "Everyone knows that a manage—a *menage-à-trois* does not an orgy make, either. Wanda told me you knew your ass from your elbow in here."

"Damn!" they both cried.

"Listen," I said, striking a conciliatory tone, "why don't you guys take some more notes while I go get my friend. He's even smarter than I am." This seemed to mollify the eager couple, and they returned to their seats on the mat. My heart was beating so fast, and I was so unsteady, that getting to my feet was impossible. So I slid backward on my behind until I was entirely in the hallway, then shut their door with my bare foot. Then I laid down on my back and sighed.

Screaming.

I jerked to a sitting position to see a door near the end of the hall burst open. The redheaded hostess ran out so frantically that she hit the opposite wall like a cartoon character. "Shit, shit, shit, shit, shit!" she screamed. Then she noticed me. "Get in there!" she wailed, rushing at me. She grabbed me by the face and yanked me to my feet. "He's going to kill himself!"

It was Jake.

He was standing on a radiator in the back of the last room with his belt looped around his neck, trying to get the rest of it over an exposed pipe. There was no furniture in the room and no other people. The redhead was still screaming when I helped him down. Jake didn't resist at all. In fact, he handed me the belt.

"Get the hell out of here!" the redhead ordered.

"Hold up," Jake protested. "It's the frickin' *Suicide Room*, is it not?"

"It's a *metaphor*, you idiot! It's a goddamn metaphor for a quiet place to come and live free from all the crap society shoves down your throat. You're supposed to kill your *false* self! FOR CHRIST'S SAKE! YOU'RE NOT SUPPOSED TO ACTUALLY KILL YOUR-SELF!"

I found myself indignant. "Isn't suicide the very definition of '*limit*-experience'?" I demanded. "How can you call it a *limit*-experience if you haven't gone to the *limit!*"

The redhead's authoritative posture evaporated. "Look," she said, "I'm not going to tell you what to do with your theory, okay? Maybe I don't even understand it all as well as I should." She came a little closer and whispered, "Truth is, I just agreed to facilitate tonight because I'm good at it—all this cloak and dagger stuff—I'm into it. If you're really going to kill yourself, will you just do it next week, when I'm off? I can hide paraphernalia, but I'm not prepared for *bodies*. I'm really sorry."

Jake was lucid then. "You mean no one has tried before?"

"No," she admitted.

"Very disappointing," Jake said. "But we'll cut you some slack."

"Let's go, Jake," I said.

"All righty then. Just as soon as you explain why you're only wearing one Puma and waving your Wonder Tits in the wind."

I found my shirt in the hall but thought it best to forego the Puma, which was still in the orgy room. Jake and I made our unsteady way out onto the porch of the Foucauldian's lair, but we had to sit down.

We didn't speak for a few minutes, until, finally, I heard myself ask, "Were you really trying to kill yourself?" I didn't want to know the answer, though.

"Yeah, I think so," Jake replied. "But not because I wanted to die or anything."

That's the last thing I remember clearly. We walked — I guess I hopped — home in a daze.

I woke up at noon the next day, still in the same clothes, wearing the one shoe. I staggered that way out of my room to find Milo glowering into a cup of coffee. With one leg crossed tersely over the other, he impatiently flexed his ankle.

"Did Jake go already?" I asked, rubbing the bleariness from my eyes. I was dizzy and ravenous.

"Took a cab to the airport at 9:30."

"Oh, damn!"

"Whatever."

"What's wrong with you?" I asked. Another question I did not want the answer to.

"Why don't *you* tell *me?*" Milo sneered. His hair was a tangled mess of black curls, indiscriminately crushed and bulging all over his head.

"Look, Milo, we had a really weird night. I'm sure Jake didn't expect me to —"

"You have to have *everything*, don't you? You have to have the most interesting life — not even table scraps for us losers. The unfazed Master of the Universe. He-*Asshole* himself."

"What are you talking about?" Ominous moisture was gathering in Milo's eyes.

"I tell you I'm *bi*," he said, "and you act like it's nothing, like I told you I'm secretly Canadian or something." Now he was starting to breathe heavily.

"But —"

"So *what* do we find just a short while later, *hmm?* Suddenly, Mr. *Schwartz* is a bi-sexual. Well, isn't that interesting. What an original and groundbreaking decision."

"*What?* What did Jake tell you, Milo?" I sat down at the table, exhausted. My stomach was churning, and I was so hungry that I thought, paradoxically, I was going to vomit.

"He said you were having, like, acrobatic sex with a hot chick and some hairy Neanderthal last night. What a wild, amazing *coincidence.*" Tears suddenly cascaded over Milo's swelling face. There were no preliminary dribbles, just an instantaneous downpour.

"Milo, nothing happened," I heard myself say. "I got sucked into something. I—I was in there for, like, two minutes." At least I was hoping such was the case, but I realized I had no real sense of time the night before. It occurred to me that the hairy giant and I must have collided with Jake on his way to the Suicide Room when we careened into the hall.

"Damn!" Milo sobbed. "Why did I leave? What is wrong with me? I do everything back-asswards!" He banged his forehead on the tabletop. "I'm so full of shit," he moaned.

"What do you mean?"

"I had a feeling that kind of shit was going on in there."

He said this to the floor beneath the table. I could barely hear him.

"You did? So then why did you leave?"

"BECAUSE I'M CHICKEN-SHIT, FUCKWAD!" Milo looked up at me. Tears were flowing in torrents. I couldn't look at him. "I never think anything like that is really, *actually* going to happen," he admitted. "I'm such a poser."

'Milo—"

"There's something I never told you about that time in Olivia's room."

"What?"

"When I realized it was for real—once I got inside—I totally bolted."

"Wait—are you saying it didn't happen? That can't—" I was suddenly sure he was going to tell me he wet his pajamas in the bathroom.

"Oh, it happened all right," Milo assured me. "Your *other*

freakazoid sister accosted me in the hall. She said I better go back in there and cream myself ASAP or she'd tell everyone I was a phony. She said she was tape-recording the whole thing over the intercom. I guess I yelled 'mommy' or some shit like that before I hightailed it out of the room. She tried to get to Cory before he went in there, but he was too scared of her and she couldn't stop him. Guess it didn't matter with him, anyway."

"Oh, my God." I didn't want to think about Nadia, but she was always there, always haunting me—and something told me I wasn't gleaning the true essence of the conversation.

"Shoshana wasn't wearing lingerie either," Milo confessed, "just some frilly nightshirt. Pretty hot, though. It was over fast, so I waited in the hall for a while afterward."

"What are you telling me, Milo? Are you *not* bisexual?"

He blew his nose, then said, "Not so much."

"What?"

"Bite me!" Milo snapped. Then he said, "Look, I was drunk off my ass sitting there in the car for five hours—not to mention all night the night before—panicking about how the hell I was going to establish myself with thirty-five thousand people who couldn't give two shits about me—knowing full well that asking my professors if I could do a report on *Lake fucking Titicaca* wasn't going to cut it. And then I'm over there on the floor, looking at you act like the devil himself farting in your face couldn't make you break a sweat—just like you are right fucking now. So, I decided to kill two birds: find a new, more sophisticated angle for me *and* give Mr. Cool the shock of a lifetime—BUT NOT ONLY DO YOU NOT BAT A FREAKIN' EYE WHEN YOUR BEST FRIEND PUTS THE MOVES ON YOU, YOU PRETEND IT NEVER HAPPENED—AND *THEN* YOU HAVE THE UNMITIGATED BALLS TO STEAL THE IDEA!" Milo had worked himself into a frenzy, but just as quickly calmed down. "At least that's what I thought," he said. "So, you're not stealing my angle, then?"

"I don't believe this, Milo. What angle?"

"MY ANGLE ON LIFE, *BANUS!* We don't have any bisexual friends yet, I don't think. I thought I'd take the role."

"But you like *girls*, Milo. You're majoring in T & A, remember?"

"So fucking what! You gotta do what you gotta do!"

"Jesus, Milo, you don't need a *role.*"

"He was totally off, you know."

"What? Who was totally off?"

"Cory. I heard his little speech to you guys about keeping me under control. He said I have no fear of failure, and that's why I act like an idiot all the time. Trust me, Jon, there is no one on Earth with a bigger fear of failure then me. What does that do for his little theory, that overgrown, number-crunching butt-munch."

"I don't know, Milo. I didn't really think about that theory very much."

"That's because you don't listen to bullshit. That's why you have it all together."

"Milo—"

"Listen—there's only one thing you don't seem to know, and it's because you don't *need* to know it. You're a lucky bastard, so kick ass for you. But most people feel the need to be *interesting.* And it's not easy! Why do you think Jake dumps so many girls? Every time he gives another one the boot, more want to go out with him. It makes him *interesting*—they're all, like, *Why does he think he's so much better than these girls? There must be something.* Cory tried football and working out like a freak. Who knows, maybe he's doing the nasty with every Pythagorean ho in State College right now. And *you*—you've got the *I'm-not-interested-in-all-the-stupid-things-people-do-to-be-interesting* thing going on—and it makes you interesting, you stupid fucking asshole."

"Milo, you're perfectly interesting."

"I know!" he cried. "You don't understand the pressure! I was in third grade the first time I asked my teacher if I could do a report on Lake Titicaca, but I was *serious*. We were studying the region, for Christ's sake. I liked the sound of it! I wasn't trying to be a smart-ass, but a couple of the more mature kids cracked up. The teacher assumed I said it to make them laugh and got pissed at me. I didn't back down, which meant the whole class thought I was cool. So then I had to live up to that, and the next thing I know I'm calling Kentucky Fried *Bitchin'* every other day to ask how large their breasts are. And then, *voila!* That's me, *Milo,* saying stupid shit and doing even stupider shit. That's what people expect. Look," he said, calming down again, "just don't let me chicken out next time, okay?"

"Okay," I promised, though I was feeling fairly certain there would never be another time.

"Fine."

Milo headed off to his room, so I ate seven bowls of corn flakes, took a shower, and then went for a walk in another pair of shoes.

I heard the hullabaloo well before entering the "Diag," a grassy hub behind the two university libraries. A protest was going on. People were waving signs and shouting. I tried to weave my way through the crowd, but only got tangled in it. Someone grabbed my shoulder.

"*Dude!*" he said. It was a kid wearing a sweatshirt featuring Bart Simpson wearing a U of M shirt.

"*Ah,* yeah?"

"Tommy Davis," he said. "Clock's class?"

"Oh, right," I said, anxious to get away. I didn't want to think about Clock, or anything else for that matter.

"Dude," he said again. "Exam's coming up."

"I know," I replied, though it was a surprise to me.

"I heard about the meeting last night," he whispered, stepping closer. I was aghast. "Yeah, you and Jake — Jake — what's-his-name. I heard from Wanda you guys totally know your shit. Praxis, right? Half the time, I don't know which way to take a piss. 'Do I dare?' You know what I'm saying? J. Alfred Prufrock and shit, right?"

"I don't know if he was there."

Tommy laughed and slapped me on the shoulder. "Listen," he said, "I'm up shit's creek in Clock's class. Do you think you or Jake could, maybe, tutor me or something?"

"Jake went home. His mom died."

"Oh, dude, I'm really sorry about that. How 'bout you? Could you help a brother out?"

"Ah, sure," I lied, hoping he'd let me go.

"Excellent! I'm glad you're here, you know — that you came out to this." He gestured at the crowd around us. A voice was bellowing through a bullhorn.

"Yeah," I muttered, "you know how it is."

"Well, I just wasn't sure, you know? Obviously, I think Holocaust Deniers are scum of the Earth. When I heard the *Daily* was planning to publish one of their ads, I about lost it. But like I said, I wasn't totally sure — "

"About what?"

"I mean, I don't think this has jack to do with the First Amendment," Tommy fumed. "If the *Daily* is going to accept ads from the Institute of Historical *Bullshit*, then they should publish any trash whatsoever, right? That's all I'm saying. It's the hypocrisy. I heard someone from the ADL on the radio this morning — he really kicked ass — asking the editor if he could publish an ad from his Institute that reveals the shocking truth that slavery is a hoax created and perpetrated by Black academics to provide African Americans with free access to the hard earned capital of white Americans though programs like Affirmative Action. The dumbass editor started stuttering all over the place, and then they went to a commercial. Censorship my Black ass."

I nodded like an imbecile in the face of Tommy's outrage.

"Sorry, dude," he finally said, catching his breath. "Like I said, I'm glad you're here too because of this whole thing with Clock. I mean, don't get me wrong, I get a kick out of deconstructing texts and all that."

"Yeah, totally."

"This whole thing here pisses me off, but if everything in the newspaper is just a conglomeration of empty signs and symbols, what's the point of getting all riled up about it, right?"

"Exactly! I've been thinking the same thing!"

"That's why I'm glad to see you here. I feel a lot better. That kind of trash may not have actually gotten into the paper this time, but someday it will. One year there won't be a Jewish kid on the *Daily* staff to go screaming to the president."

"Are you Jewish?" I asked, figuring it was possible, if unlikely, given that Tommy was African-American.

"No, why?" he asked.

"No reason."

"Listen, man," Tommy said. "I'm here because someday someone *is* going to lay that bullshit about slavery being a hoax. We all need to be out here when shit like this goes down. This university is racist as hell as it is."

"U of M is racist?"

Tommy threw his head back and smiled broadly, then slapped me on the shoulder again. "U of M is racist?" he repeated, imitating me. "That's a good one!" he laughed. "Classic."

"Listen," I said, "I'm really glad you came out, but I just remembered I'm supposed to meet a friend somewhere. I really gotta go, but we'll get together to study, okay?"

"No problem," Tommy said. "Thanks a million." Then he turned and walked into the crowd. He started yelling, but his voice blended immediately with all the other angry cries.

Feeling ill, I walked swiftly away until I found myself veering into the Law Quad, where I collapsed on the lawn. I stayed there for a while, supine yet again, gazing blankly at the elaborate, ivy-laden facade of the main building. Brightly colored Frisbees sailed over and around me. I thought about my night with the Foucauldians and didn't know what to make of it, and I couldn't understand why Clock's ideas were so inspiring in class but seemed so absurd in real life. His grand point, I gathered, was simply that there was no such thing as Truth. But wouldn't that have to be true to be right?

I knew I couldn't face Clock's class anymore, not with Wanda telling everyone about last night and Tommy expecting me to tutor him. I decided to go sign up for Love Notes again, which reminded me I hadn't picked up the outlines for my other classes in a while.

Which reminded me that my Business Marketing proposal was due.

Tomorrow.

I leapt to my feet. Could I claim to have been sick? Throwing up blood? Dead grandfather? Family Crisis?

Panicked, I started sprinting home, but when I saw the copy store, I stopped.

It was worth a shot.

I have no idea why I felt the need to lie to the guy running Love Notes, but I did. I told him I'd been totally out of touch with my courses because my grandmother had come down with Alzheimer's, and I was taking care of her. I wondered aloud if, since the business came out of Deadmarsh's class, there might be something in the way of spare proposals lying around.

The guy gave me a very disapproving look, which I thought was fairly inappropriate given the nature of his enterprise, but I was in no position to complain. Fortunately, after thinking it over, he offered to write me a guaranteed winner for a hundred bucks.

We agreed that I'd pick up two copies first thing in the

morning, so that's exactly what I did. I slipped into class just as it was ending and handed one in with everyone else.

When I got home I dropped all my things on the floor, then went to my room to sleep.

I dreamt about Darby, Sandy Sikofski, Janice Walker, the Depeche Mode girl, and Cherry. They were all students in Clock's class taking copious notes, but I was the professor and I was showing movies about the Holocaust. And of course I was naked.

Around one, I heard Milo snorting loudly, so I hauled myself out of bed to find him at the kitchen table reading the second copy of my proposal. "Oh, man, this is good," he said when he saw me. "I'm laughing my ass off over here."

I saw a sticky note with the Love Notes logo on the floor by my backpack, so I went over and picked it up.

It said: "*My* grandmother has Alzheimer's, dickface!"

My knees went weak.

"I wouldn't have been so p. o.'ed if I'd known you changed your schedule," Milo said.

"What?"

"I wouldn't have been so pissed that you weren't coming to Anatomy if I'd known you dropped it. What is this? Did you sign up for that class on satire? It's like that Gulliver's Travels guy's thing we read that one time, the one about eating homeless people."

"It's for Business Marketing."

"That's a good one," Milo laughed. "Business Marketing. Now *that* would be funny."

It seemed I wrote a plan for a video rental business catering to people with Alzheimer's. The business (unnamed—my nod to demography) required only a hallway with doors at either end. I'd outlined what I imagined would be a typical exchange with the target clientele. An Alzheimer's patient ("patron") would enter one end of the establishment and meet a clerk under a sign reading, "Check-outs." Regardless of her request, she would be handed the store's video (one tape being the entire inventory) at the bargain cost of one dollar. The patron would then walk down the comparatively long hallway toward the exit (slowly—another distinguishing trait of the target market). The clerk, minimally semi-able-bodied by job description, would make haste to the counter there and wait under a sign reading, "Returns." When the patron arrived, the clerk would cheerfully say, "Thanks for coming back. You can return the tape here. I'm so glad you enjoyed it."

I forecasted astounding profits and even speculated that a physical therapy program could be arranged for a branch actually located in the university hospital, allowing patients to circle in and out of the store doing fortifying laps while paying meager sums for can't-miss entertainment.

"What was the assignment?" Milo asked. "To make up the most offensive business in the history of the universe?"

"Not exactly." I was standing there, paralyzed, trying not to throw up.

Milo scrutinized me for a moment, then seemed to comprehend the situation. "Jon, you could get in deep shit for this," he said. "This is the most un-*PC* thing you could write, and this is the most *PC* school on Earth!"

I'd never cheated on anything before in my entire life. Before I could decide what to say, the phone rang.

Milo was still eyeing me when he picked it up.

"Hey, *Jake!*" he exclaimed. But then his face went grave as he listened in silence for a minute or so. "Ah, shit, man," he finally said. "Really? For how long? The rest of the term?"

"What?" I asked.

Milo put the phone beside his chin and muttered, "Jake's not coming back to school. He's going to stay at home and do some therapy program with his brother. He already got an okay to withdraw for the term." Milo listened to Jake for a minute or so more, then handed me the phone.

"Jon?"

"Yeah, Jake?"

"I'm just a little messed up right now. I'll be back in January, but I can still pay my part of the rent."

"That's cool, Jake. Don't worry about it."

"The funeral was creepy."

"I'll see you soon, Jake."

"What?"

"I feel like crap right now. I'll talk to you soon, okay?"

"Wait, one sec, Jon."

"What?"

"I'm sorry."

"For what?"

"Just—well—I'm just sorry."

"Cool. I'll call you later."

"Okay."

I didn't attend any of my classes that week or the next, and I missed my exam in Clock's class. I didn't go out at all, partly because I was hiding from Tommy Davis, but mostly because I was simply waiting to be devoured by whatever monster I'd summoned. I just stayed home watching Sports Center and ignoring Milo.

Eventually, it was I who was summoned.

"Some TA called," Milo said when I woke up at noon on Thursday. "And not the good kind. He said you have to go meet Deadmarsh in his office today, at one. Dude, you're screwed."

Deadmarsh was in his office, leaning back in a padded leather chair, looking at my proposal when I arrived. I shuffled in and stood uncomfortably surveying the impressive looking books lining his walls. The professor pointed to a rolling swivel chair, so I sat down.

He turned the proposal over a few times, regarding it like a perplexing trinket in a curiosity shop. Then he handed it to me. "I'm not sure just what to say about this piece of work, Mr. Schwartz," he said, fixing me with his beady eyes. I made no response, but rather sat there staring at him stupidly, ready to tell him I didn't know why I'd done it. "Of course," he continued, "I can't accept it for the purposes of the class—but I'm—let's say—"

Here we go, I thought.

"—*intrigued.*"

My eyes went wide.

"That *has* something," Deadmarsh mused. "It shows someone capable of—Well, let's just say the growing tendency of young Americans to shy away from, let's say, *nuanced* opportunity, distresses me." Then he looked at me, pursed his lips, and spoke his mind. "Let's face it, Jon, we're raising pussies, here. These kids have no idea what it is to go out and fight and sweat and bleed for a living. They think money grows on trees and having too much of it is a disease. People like that—no guts, no balls!—Jesus, it's a cut-throat world out there—With no rules! Eat or be eaten. We're breeding our own demise!"

My eyes couldn't open any wider. My professor just said 'pussies.'

"I have some associates who operate what you might call a— *think tank,*" Deadmarsh continued, "only what they think about is creative ways to, ahh, raise cap—"

There was a knock on the door, which then opened to reveal an elderly man wearing a red V-neck sweater over a maize and blue striped tie. "Excuse me," he wheezed, sticking his head over the threshold. "I don't mean to interrupt—"

Deadmarsh rose swiftly. "Come in, Dean—no interruption at all."

The old man took a seat next to me. He attempted to clear a

throat full of phlegm while regarding me with an appraising smile. I smiled back. Then he turned to Deadmarsh, who seemed confused about the visit. "That article," he said. "For Philip Morris?"

"Right!" Deadmarsh cried. "It's ready! In the copy room—it should be on the printer." He rushed out to get it.

"Hello there, Mr. —?"

"Schwartz."

"My name is Dean," he said, shaking my hand. "I'm the Dean of the Business School."

"Dean Dean?"

"That's what they call me."

A flash of recognition crossed the Dean's wrinkled face. "Michael Schwartz's boy!" he declared. "And the *You Scream* kid!"

I nodded.

"Your father was a national treasure! And in for extra support! Well done, young man."

"Thank you," I croaked. I was still holding my proposal, which felt like it was on fire. I wished it would spontaneously combust.

"I'll bet you're a great writer, too."

The following words then came out of my mouth entirely of their own accord: "Would you like to have a look?"

"I'd be delighted."

Deadmarsh came back in with a stack of papers and saw the Dean reading my proposal. He looked at me, alarmed.

When the Dean finished, he looked at my professor and said, "You did the right thing, Steve."

Deadmarsh didn't reply, but he didn't have to.

The Dean wheeled around on me and tried to speak, but his voice caught in his throat. I didn't know whether it was mucus or rage that snagged it. His face went twitchy, and then he started shaking all over. Finally, in a high, crackling voice, he went off.

"That was the most perverse—the most twisted, disgusting, abhorrent, detestable, obscene, depraved piece of—of—*fecal matter* to which I have ever had the displeasure of being subjected!" A vein in his neck and another at his throbbing temple threatened to rupture. "MY BROTHER HAS ALZHEIMER'S, YOU SORRY LITTLE SHIT!"

"I'll just go."

"No you will not! You will listen to me for one more minute, young man!"

I knew what was coming, but I felt strangely calm about it.

"I do not give a damn who your father was," the Dean spat. "I am certain he's turning over in his grave right now, especially if he sees how dispassionately you sit confronted by the product of your lowest, most menial and depraved instincts. I am leaving this office right now to fax a copy of your little "joke" to the *You Scream Ice Cream* corporate office. Expect your scholarship to be revoked before the last foul page slithers out of the machine. Consider your acceptance at this university in jeopardy as well! Now, GET THE BLOODY HELL OUT OF HERE!"

I squeezed sideways past Deadmarsh to get out of the office. He hadn't moved a muscle.

I'd only just stepped foot back in the apartment when Milo announced that some guy from "Creamy Jeans" called. "You need to call them right away," he said. "You're royally fucked, aren't you?"

"I'm going home."

"I don't *believe* this! You *wanted* to get kicked out, didn't you!"

"I don't know what I want, Milo."

"Is it 'cause you don't want Jake to be the only one to drop out, or 'cause you couldn't stand to live with me alone? Maybe I'll jump your bones in the middle of the night—is that it?"

"Milo," I sighed.

"*Why, then?*" he demanded. Tears were coming again.

In an effort to fabricate something that would appease, I found something like the truth. "I'm just not ready."

"Oh," Milo said. "You're coming back, though, aren't you?"

"I don't know."

"They aren't kicking you out, are they? It's just *You Cream*, right? So your mom can pay?"

"It doesn't look good. But we'll see."

"Sure," Milo muttered. "Meantime, I'll just hang out here picking my dingleberries until you guys come back."

"You'll be fine," I told him. "You're the one with all the new friends. I wish I spent some more time actually meeting people."

"Whatever."

"What do you mean?" As soon as I asked that, I knew I'd be sorry.

"I mean that I don't have any new friends, genius."

"They're mad at you?"

Milo gritted his teeth. "No, you friggin' idiot! I never had any new friends!"

"But—"

"I've been walking around campus alone all the time. That's why I know my way around so well! There, you got me to admit it! Are you happy now?"

"Look, Milo," I said, "I'm going to take off for home tomorrow. Will you call Olivia and tell her what happened? Say there's been a big misunderstanding—about everything. She'll tell my mom and Nadia. Call Jake, too."

"Olivia and Nadia already know—probably everyone else, too."

"What are you talking about?"

"Well—" Milo looked for a moment like he was casting about for a lie, but then seemed to reconsider. "I told Jake about your paper when he called. He also called right after the ice cream people."

"So?"

"*So*…Ah, screw it—I'm sure he called Nadia right away."

"*Why the hell would he do that?*"

"Boy, you're an idiot. I'm starting to wonder about you, you know. You don't know half of what you pretend to know."

"What are you saying, Milo?"

"Fuck it—Jake's been spying on you for—since forever." Olivia promised to *do* him during winter break if he narked on you to Nadia."

"You're so full of shit!" The walls were closing in around me, but I finally understood Nadia's clairvoyant powers. I hated her. And of course I knew exactly when Olivia had procured Jake's participation. There was no furniture moving in the garret that day, only the moving of an eminently movable will. And he must have called Nadia from his own party when I was with Darby! I was going to kill him. I hated him, too.

"I'm just telling you what Jake told me," Milo explained. "He's pissed off 'cause Olivia reneged—said he came back before break so the deal is off. He's flipping out because he feels like the pathetic loser he is, and a traitor, which he is, too. That's why he told me, and because he thought one of them would try to suck me in now that he's gone. And you know what else?"

"Of course not."

"I'd bet my left nut that little deal was the only reason Jake didn't go to Ithaca."

I lingered around our apartment the next morning, packing listlessly. Milo cleared out to let me have the place to myself for a while, or so I thought until he didn't come back to say goodbye.

No one would rent a car to me, but I found a bus departing for Pittsburgh at two. I can't remember thinking a single thought the entire way home.

PART IV

I had a cab drop me off a few blocks away from our house and sneaked around back, hoping to talk to Olivia before doing anything else. The garret was unlocked. I peeked in and could see she wasn't there. The place looked recently cleaned. Four matching pink suitcases sat by the door.

"Jonson!" someone called, startling me. It was Myna, out on the back porch. She looked older and skinnier than she had when I left for school. Her cheeks were sunken, and she was a bit stooped. I'd never looked at her and had the word 'elderly' cross my mind before.

I realized I hadn't called her even once.

"Grandma!" I rushed down the path and up onto the porch, where I gave her a hug that I instinctually softened for fear of hurting her.

"You are smart to come early tonight," Myna said. "No rushing for you this way in the morning." I had no idea what she meant by that, but didn't get the chance to ask. "Come inside and sit down, Jonson," she insisted. "Your grandmother is lonely."

We went into the kitchen and sat down at the table. "Where's Olivia?" I asked.

"Celebrating, of course!" Myna said. "Her plane leaves very late tomorrow in the night. She'll be sorry she went out before you could paint towns with her."

I was even more confused now. "Is it—ah—a *direct* flight?" I ventured, fishing.

"Of course!" Myna said again. "They are flying her in the First Class! It's a very small part, but movies these days! The meshugenah money they spend! Susan Sarandon! I like her very much."

It seemed Olivia was going to Hollywood after all. And she didn't take off with her tuition money like I'd half expected her to have done by then.

"Wow," I said. "What does Mom think?"

"Jonson. Your mother—"

"What? What's wrong, Grandma? Is she sick?"

"Yes, with this drinking."

"Where is she?"

"Nadia told Olivia, a few weeks ago, to take her to one of those programs at the hospital."

"Why didn't anyone tell me?"

"Your mother wouldn't allow it. She especially ordered that we can't tell you because she planned to return home quickly. This was silly. You handle everything so well."

"Grandma," I said, wanting more than anything to tell her—and everyone else on the face the Earth—that I didn't know how to handle anything at all. Instead, I asked, "Does Nadia think Mom will be okay?"

"Oy. Your sister is very busy. I can't follow, of course, but she's on this team of research and that special project. They've already accepted her for a double doctor program for when she finishes her degree—at the University of Pennsylvania, no less."

"What's going on, Grandma?" I pleaded. "Why won't Mom stop blaming herself for what happened to Dad?"

"I have failed to make her see, Jonson. But I will tell her tomorrow."

"Tell her what?"

"This is my punishment, Jonathan — to lose my husband, my son, my family. And so much worse because it is your mother's too, and all you children suffer. I thought I can hide forever. I hide so long I forget I am hiding. Leon was never this way. Never for a moment could he forget the farm."

"What are you saying, Grandma? I don't understand."

"Jonson," Myna said, "when we came to America, my family and me—"

She paused, and I tried not to look annoyed. This was hardly the time for another rendition of her absurd non-story. "I know, Grandma. You escaped *Adolf*."

"My family," she whispered, oblivious of me then. "They wouldn't look on me from the moment we are off the boat — because they know."

"What happened, Grandma? I thought you applied for visas and were lucky to get them because things were all messed up at that time. I thought getting out was easy."

"Easy, yes," she confirmed, but woefully. Her eyes were elsewhere. "A big bribe was needed for everything then, Jonathan. Everything was easy with the bribe, but only maybe. Asking was not safe if who you asked was in a bad mood or didn't need money that day. But everyone needs money every day. We have only a small amount of money, enough maybe to start a life if we get away. And we don't want to leave without family. We are nine people."

"But you did have enough for a bribe, right?"

"Enough money?" Myna said. "No."

"But, you told my class—"

"There are other currencies, Jonson—"

"I don't—"

"I was very beautiful," Myna said. "A disastrous beauty, a man once called me."

To this, I didn't respond.

"The men, these officials," Myna continued, "they make me pay for our visas. I pay them for months, until they are bored."

It took another long second, but I finally understood. "But you saved their lives!" I cried. "Anyone would've done what you did, Grandma — if they could. You *sacrificed* yourself for them!"

"Thank you, Jonson. Maybe this is true. But I sacrifice much more. Nathan, he got the cancer, and now your parents pay the bills. But you kids — you are okay. You are happy. Especially you, Jon. Your happiness means the worlds to me."

"But, Grandma," I said, wanting to scream that I was anything but happy, "you believe in fate. It was your fate to sacrifice yourself — your *fate,* not your fault."

"Fate, *shmate,*" Myna said. "This is nothing but a big excuse."

Now I wanted her to believe in it. But I didn't know what I could say to make her.

"Your mother will be here in the morning," Myna said. "The wedding is at noon. I will tell her this perhaps after, and she will understand not to blame herself any more."

"The wedding —" I said as neutrally as I could.

"So wonderful, a nice wedding," was all Myna replied. "The most wonderful thing in the world."

"Mom's coming, right — to the wedding?"

"Of course! She's known Corrine for so long."

"Corrine — *Minor?*"

"Who else?"

"Did something happen to Cory's dad?"

"Don't be silly," Myna said. "God forbid, just before his son marries."

"*Cory!*"

Myna patted my hand. "I need to get some rest," she said. "I think maybe you do, too."

"Okay, Grandma. You're right. I do."

"Come here and give your old granny a kiss."

Rage coursed through me as I lay in bed, directed at practically everyone in my life. My parents, Nadia, Olivia, Jake, Milo—and now Cory! We'd all talked with him at least once a week, and he'd never said a word! I wanted to commit violence on a grand scale. Eventually, I fell asleep anyway and dreamt about the golem getting married to the dybbuk. I was the rabbi, but I attempted to strangle them both.

I woke up at eleven the next morning and wandered downstairs in my pajamas, just the way I had my entire life. Everyone was in the kitchen eating breakfast.

"*Jonson!*" my mother yelped, jumping up. She enveloped me in an enthusiastic hug. She looked good. "Why aren't you dressed?" she asked. "We need to leave in half an hour."

I looked at Olivia, who was giving nothing away.

Nadia was there, too, but I wasn't going to look surprised. "Quite the catch, that Glickman chick," she said. "And I heard she has a hell of a defensive line."

I sprinted back upstairs.

Sarah Glickman!

The world had utterly and completely stopped making sense.

While I was getting into an old pair of slacks I found still hanging in my closet, Nadia walked into my room. I looked at her, and she looked at me—we stared each other down like a couple of old-west gunslingers, except I had only one leg in my pants. I pulled them on properly while trying to maintain my glare, which was difficult.

"What do you want, Nadia?"

"You don't believe that crap about Susan Sarandon, do you? She'll be back in six weeks with her tail between her legs. Unless she finally gives it away, of course."

"No, she won't be back, Nadia. And it's her business. Why don't you mind your own goddamn business for once?"

"Oh, my!" Nadia said, grinning. "What have we here?"

"Why are you coming to the wedding? You're not going to do anything, are you?"

"What do you mean?" Nadia asked, feigning hurt. "We were all invited. And as a matter of fact," she added, "I'm quite sure I am responsible for this wedding. I think the big gorky fool knows it, too."

"Yeah, right. Whatever."

"Notice how he didn't turn into a male whore like everyone else on his team?"

"That's cause he stank, Nadia."

"No, it's because of what I had Olivia do to him. He was too afraid he'd embarrass himself. Cheerleaders need a lot more than five seconds of attention."

I had to think a second before I realized she was talking about the No-touch night, which I tried to forget again. It wasn't entirely out of the realm of possibility.

"Notice also," Nadia said, looking increasingly pleased with herself, "how he didn't become your typical drunken jock loser, either. Take a look at this, since we're on the subject." Nadia walked over to my bed, knelt down, and reached under the box spring. I heard a tearing sound, after which she pulled free an envelope with masking tape clinging to it.

"What the hell is that?"

My sister pulled a Polaroid out of the envelope and handed it to me. At first, I thought it was a picture of a clown, but it was obviously Cory. He was lying back on a couch with the whites of his eyes showing through half-closed lids. His face was powdered white, and across his forehead and cheeks, written in what appeared to be red lipstick, were the words, "Typical Drunken Jock Loser."

I realized where the picture was taken: Jake's basement. I could see Jake's shoulder slumping out of the frame. "You came back!" I cried. "This is how you're going to ruin the wedding!"

"Keep your shorts on, Jonson. He's already seen it."

"*What?* You didn't!"

"Numskull, he saw it a few days after I took it. He couldn't believe he was that out of it."

"I don't understand. What did you make Cory do?"

"Nothing. Just asked him to keep an eye on you—which he refused to do, actually. I let it go, though. This was just a little joke between the two of us. He wasn't mad at me, either. He was mad at himself. He couldn't believe he put himself in a situation where something like that could happen. *He thanked me.* I just put the picture under your bed and bet myself you'd never find it. As usual, I was right."

My mind was temporarily whisked away by thoughts of Cory. It was after our inaugural shotgun party that he really started distancing himself from us and refusing to drink—but he always said it was because of his workouts!

"Why, Nadia? Why can't you mind your own business? Why are you obsessed with mine?"

"What a little diva!" Nadia laughed. "It's not all about you. And by the by," she added, "did you know it was me who used to send those flyers to your other idiot friend's parents?"

"Milo's?"

"That's the one."

"What are you really doing here, Nadia?"

"I came to talk to Mom."

"What do you mean—to push her over the edge?"

"I'll leave that for you to decide. I came to tell her that Dad really was doing research. He never considered joining those lunatics for a second. The mere idea is absurd."

I lost whatever fragile thread I was still clinging to and reverted to the helpless child I'd always been in Nadia's presence.

Mom's voice came over the intercom. "Almost ready?"

Nadia walked over, depressed the talk button and said, "Almost. Jon's just looking for his manhood — I mean his blazer."

"Nadia, is it true?"

"Does it matter?" she said. "Maybe he managed to call me because he knew he was going to have to do some dangerous shit that night and wanted to make sure someone knew the details in case all hell broke-loose. Maybe I told him that if he didn't leave those freaks that instant and get the fuck home, I'd hang up and call the news to tell them he got killed. And maybe he said he had to do what he had to do, so maybe I did what I had to do — but then maybe he got killed anyway."

I had nothing to say to this. I didn't know if it was true or not true or whether it was good or bad news. Good, I supposed, for my mother.

"Jonson," Nadia said, "don't *reel*, for God's sake. Don't believe a word I say. I'm a pathological liar — Oops, I'm lying again."

"I don't understand you, Nadia."

"That's the difference between you and me, Jonson. I understand everyone."

The intercom went off again. "Let's go, kids!" Mom insisted. "We're just going to be on time now!"

"Coming!" Nadia answered, and then she casually walked out of the room, forcing me to follow after I grabbed a random blazer. "By the way," my sister said over her shoulder, "some woman from the ice cream company called. They want to talk to you immediately. I hope there's been no trouble."

"Have fun, darlings!" Myna called as we all rushed out the front door.

Hanging up my jacket in the shul, I noticed Jake and Milo standing in front of the main sanctuary, both looking hangdog and haggard. Jake saw me, but I turned away, and when I looked back, he was gone. Milo was still there, so I dashed toward him.

"What the hell is going on?" I demanded.

"I called Jake after you left," Milo told me. "He found out from Olivia. I made him come get me in Daniel's car."

"When did this happen?" I demanded, waving a hand at the arriving guests.

Milo raised an eyebrow to indicate the turn of events was bizarre to him as well, which made me feel much better. "Dude, he didn't tell anyone," he said, amazed. "He has no freakin' groomsmen! His dad is his best man. I think he purposely lost our invitations before he mailed them. You shoulda seen his face when we came in. And did you know he freakin' *converted?*"

In the main sanctuary, violin music issued from speakers suspended above the chupah. Standing at the pulpit was Rabbi Glickman. It seemed like years since I'd seen him, though he looked the same as ever. He beamed as the honored guests marched down the aisle.

Cory came in through the double doors in a huge but snappy tuxedo and walked right by us with his parents. He either didn't see us or didn't look while I was looking at him. Sarah swished past a few minutes later. She looked stunning in a long-sleeved beaded gown. She was a woman, for sure.

"Wowza," was Milo's reaction.

When everyone was in place and the cantor finished chanting, Rabbi Glickman began speaking in his inimitable style. "I am almost unable — to express my feeling on this occasion," he began. "As a rabbi — there are two events that gratify more than any — other. The first is welcoming a person into the arms of the Jewish people — into the heart of a — tradition 5,000 years in the making — to welcome a new soul committed to living an ethical life according to the laws — of our people. This extraordinary young man, Cory Minor, has more than fulfilled the necessary requirements to — embrace the Jewish people, who have embraced him in return. I have never seen a young man like him, so dedicated, forthright and committed — to learning and understanding the principals upon which—our people have sustained themselves through—a history too much marred by pain and suffering. He and I met weekly for the—last year and a half—"

Milo and I turned to each other, mouths agape.

"The second event I cherish taking part in," the Rabbi continued, "is—the joining of two souls in this beautiful ceremony, to preside at that sacred moment when two individuals give—up their beings as they were to enter a new state, a state—in which they are one as much as they are two. The fact that I have the opportunity to perform the ceremony for—my own daughter—I am beside myself with joy. If only her mother could be here today, though I know she is—in some way."

I didn't hear anything more and missed the entire ceremony, lost in inarticulate thought about Cory's secret life. I didn't even hear the glass break when he stomped on it. Milo elbowed me when everyone stood to clap for the happy couple jogging back down the aisle.

"Chow time," Milo said. "I guess I'll find an empty seat somewhere. The high and mighty Schwartz clan has the honor of sitting at the main table. Isn't that special?"

At the long table in the front of the hall, I found place cards for four Schwartzes. (Unaware of Cory's subterfuge, Mom had RSVP'ed for all of us.) There were also cards for two newlyweds, the Minors, the Rabbi, and three grandparents. I made absolutely sure to sit next to Nadia, who didn't seem to have dropped any bombs. I had no idea whether I wanted her to or not. I saw that she was scrutinizing Mom, who was half-heartedly reminiscing about being little girls and playing "marriage" with Mrs. Minor. Mostly, she was just shifting silverware and glasses around on the table in front of her.

"I need to talk to you, Nadia," I whispered out of the side of my mouth.

"Why, Jonson?" she asked, loudly. "Are you feeling anxious

about something?"

Just then music came to life from a three-piece band. The singer began the first song, *What a Wonderful World*. Part way through, she paused and announced, "Mr. and Mrs. Cory Minor!"

The couple made their entrance on cue, and the room burst into applause.

The newlyweds danced, then came to our table to hug everyone. When I hugged Sarah, she whispered, "Give him some time." I apologized for hitting her in the neck with the penny and she laughed. Cory was right behind her, so I put my hand out to him. He took it awkwardly and held it. "All this wasn't—it wasn't all for—" he stuttered. "I mean, at first—I did meet with him to see her, I admit it, but then it all changed. I—"

"The food *is* better, isn't it?" I whispered. "I never told you that."

Cory beamed. "Unbelievable," he said.

When we were all seated, Mr. and Mrs. Minor walked over to a podium set up in front of the band and both said a few words. Mrs. Minor talked about how much they loved Sarah already and what a welcome addition she was to their family. She went on at great length about how much love and acceptance they'd been shown by the synagogue and the Jewish community in general. Then she broke down crying and called Cory her big baby. Sarah's hand, half the size of Cory's, was on top of his. It shook as his trembled on the table underneath. I supposed it was natural to be nervous at such a time, but I'd never seen his ears turn that intensely purple before.

Turns out he was terrified of what his father was going to say.

"My son is the most impressive person I have ever known," Mr. Minor declared in his deep, resonating voice. He was robust and had an air of professional power that made him seem like a high-ranking official, and he emanated the same air whether he wore a tuxedo or a jogging suit. The way he spoke this one sentence commanded the absolute attention of everyone in the room. I caught Milo's eye at his table. He was sitting next to Jake, who didn't look in my direction. "To put in the intense hours of conditioning the way he did for four years in high school," Mr. Minor continued, getting teary, "and to never play more than a few downs a game—"

I glanced over at Cory, who looked about ready to fall out of his chair. He pulled his hand out from under Sarah's and put it over his face.

"My son had these two quotes he believed in," Mr. Minor said. "Okay, he had more than two." There was good-natured chuckling from Cory's relatives at this. "But two I took to heart. The first was from our own Chuck Noll, who said—"

A burst of clapping from a table in the rear met the mere mention of the Steelers' famous coach.

Mr. Minor smiled and continued. "Coach Noll once said, 'The most important thing about this sport is the activity of preparation—any aspect of preparation for the games. The thrill isn't in the winning, it's in the doing.' It's a rare person who believes words like these." Mr. Minor swallowed a lump in his throat, then went on. "The other one Cory said to me during his senior season, when the team was losing every game. He looked at me one day when I was foolishly trying to tell him that things would look up and said, 'Dad, you can learn a line from a win, but you can learn a book from a defeat.' I think that one was Paul Brown." (At this, a boo from the same rear table.) Mr. Minor chuckled, but had to put a handkerchief to his eyes anyway. Everyone was getting teary at his emotional display. After a few dabs, he looked back up and said, "Never try to give advice to a kid who can solve that damned Rubik's Cube faster than any engineer at Westinghouse! So much for highly skilled workers!" This drew raucous laughter.

"I challenged him on that one," Mr. Minor added, "but the truth is that Cory challenges himself. On top of his unswerving commitment to be the best he could be physically, he never let me stop challenging him with his studies in math. He insisted – *he demanded* – that I keep pushing him. His friends here can tell you how many fun times he missed: parties, get-togethers, movies – all because he was dedicated to improving his body and mind every day. At first I thought Cory was cheating himself out of some of his childhood, but look at him now, the top undergraduate math student in State College and now married to the most wonderful young woman in the world."

At that point, Mr. Minor broke down entirely and hugged his wife. Most of the guests were wiping tears, but I was looking at Milo, who was looking back at me, again with an identical expression of disbelief. Cory still had his hand over his face and was leaning so far forward that his head practically rested on his plate. Sarah was trying to straighten him up, but that was like a chipmunk trying to lift a fallen tree. Cory finally sat up when the Minors got back to the table, but he wouldn't make eye contact with me.

I would've lost our invitations, too.

Some time later, I found myself watching everyone dance the Hora. Cory and Sarah bobbed in the center of the madly spinning ring, held aloft in chairs – though the groom's chair was decidedly lower than his bride's. I had no idea where my mind kept going. I realized I couldn't see my mother anywhere, which made me panic. But Nadia was there, sitting next to me. She was watching the dancing, too.

Jake ventured near twice, but veered away at the last second both times.

I scanned the room and found Mom. She was sitting with the Rabbi at an otherwise empty table. He was patting her hand sympathetically. She broke into heaving sobs, so he leaned over and hugged her.

"How did you get Olivia to use Jake like that?" I asked.

"Easy," Nadia said. "Way back when — the night Dad went off the rails, actually — when you rushed off to your precious football game, I promised I'd leave her in peace if she did me a favor every once in a while."

"Oh."

Someone put her hands on my shoulders. Startled, I turned around, realizing I was alone at the table. It was my mother. "Honey," she sniffed, "I'm going home a little early. Rabbi Glickman offered to take you three home whenever you want."

"Can I just go with you now?" I pleaded. "I'm really not feeling well."

"Of course. I'll see you up at the coat rack in a few minutes. I need to go to the powder room first."

"Okay."

Cory approached me, cautiously.

"Congratulations," I said.

"Thanks."

"Sounds like things are going great so far this year."

"Yeah. I haven't been working out so much, though."

"Seems like you've been busy. That's great. Sarah's great. I always thought so."

"Really?"

"Listen, Cory — about your dad's speech —"

"Yeah?" he said, flinching.

"We all knew," I lied. "It's cool. We knew you didn't want people to know about Sarah. We just liked to give you a hard time 'cause you're a math genius. Same with the rabbi stuff."

"You're shitting me," Cory said.

"I kid you not, man. Don't sweat it, okay?"

He suddenly started crying. He was beaming, but crying, and he hugged me hard enough to snap my spine.

"And don't let Milo break your balls about it either," I said when he let me go. "Same goes with Nadia and that picture. It's no big deal. She probably did you a favor."

"Thanks, Jon," Cory said, wiping tears. "Sarah and I used to talk on the phone every night in secret, so her dad wouldn't know. I wanted to tell you about it, but—Milo—I thought you'd understand."

"I'd've done the same thing," I assured him. I suddenly had the to urge to talk to Cory more, much more, about Sarah and his conversion, but my other concerns came back to mind. "Well," I said, "my mom isn't feeling too good, so I'm gonna take off with her."

"Okay, Jon." We shook hands. "Thanks again."

I walked away feeling a sense of elation mixed with sorrow. It felt like nostalgia for something between us that it seemed Cory and I never actually had.

I was nearly through the door when Jake intercepted me. "Hey," he ventured.

"Hey," I replied. Then we just looked at each other for a long second. I spotted Milo spying on us from across the room.

"Look, Jon—"

"Don't worry about it."

Jake looked down at the interlocking geometric patterns on the carpet and shook his head. "I know I'm an asshole," he said, "but even more asshole'ish than that."

"She does that to people."

"Um—I'll be going to Cornell in January."

"Where you should've gone in the first place."

Jake looked at me and nodded, but then looked down again. "One more thing," he said.

"What's that?"

"I never touched Olivia."

"Too bad for you."

Jake smiled ruefully, but then shook his head as if to cast off unhelpful thoughts. "I need to tell you something," he said.

"Don't even try to tell me she touched you."

"I'm going to say this fast and then maybe never again, I don't know. But I owe it to you."

"Jake, you don't owe me—"

"I'm gay."

Silence.

More silence.

"But—but," I finally managed, "Olivia, and all your—"

"Jon, I've been looking for someone to fix me. Olivia—if anyone—I always knew she'd be the—"

"I understand."

"I'm an idiot, I know. Just don't tell anyone yet, especially—"

Milo was suddenly standing next to us looking wretched, but he hadn't heard. "My parents just showed up," he muttered, "and I think they're wearing hemp underwear."

Mom slumped over the steering wheel and started sobbing. She hadn't even started the car. "I'm so sorry, Jon," she choked. "I'm so, so sorry. I know what it's like to realize your parents don't know what the hell they're doing in life. It's horrible. _Believe me_, I know."

"It's okay, Mom. Really."

"Oh, God, how I miss your father." Mom was shaking. "I'm scared because you're all leaving. I'm going to be alone."

"Well, about that—"

"What? What's wrong?"

"I have something to tell you, Mom, and I don't want you to be upset. It's about school. I—I haven't done very well this first quarter. I—"

"I knew it! I was so worried something like this would happen. I have an apology to make to you."

"Really, Mom, you don't—"

"All I ever wanted was a life for you as far removed as possible from my father's experiences, and from mine being raised by him. Your father felt exactly the same way."

"Mom, really —"

"I've been very selfish, pushing you the way I have. The Rabbi made me face that. I've felt guilty for many years about giving up being Jewish, *living* Jewish — never mind who my mother was — I've never been able to justify tossing away something millions of people were murdered for. But I never felt comfortable with it, either. I tried to force it on you, Jonson. It was a terrible thing to do. If it's going to be for me, then I'll take hold of it myself."

"That's okay, Mom. No big deal. I like being Jewish."

"You handle things so well," Mom sniffed. "I really admire you. And that's why you can't sabotage yourself."

"I want to go into Creative Writing," I announced, suddenly deciding it was true. "I'm thinking about Pitt so I can be closer to home. I'll move into the garret if that's okay."

Mom nodded and started the car. "That would be just fine," she said. "It would be wonderful. Remodeling that room was one of Nadia's best ideas, ever."

The moment we got home, I ran upstairs to tell Myna I was moving home. Her door was ajar, so I quietly pushed it open to find her napping in her rocking chair. There was simply no possibility of my waiting for her to wake up on her own, so I went over and touched her arm. Then I touched her cheek.

She was dead.

Mom called 911.

We listened to the sirens approach together.

The soundtrack of our lives.

Half an hour later Olivia and Nadia got home. They'd panicked at the sight of the ambulance, but Mom was waiting at her usual station by the window, watching for them. The Rabbi stayed outside with her when they came in.

She wanted us to have some time alone with the body.

I went into Myna's room first. She'd been laid out on the bed. She looked, frankly, amused. I hoped she was telling offensive jokes again, wherever she was.

Nadia came in a few minutes later. "You didn't spill the beans about Dad," she said, looking pained at the sight of our dead grandmother.

"I'm not your puppet," I told her.

"If you say so. By the way, the Rabbi confessed to Mom that he used your little Hebrew School episode as an excuse to come here to meet Dad. It's been eating him up ever since."

"You're kidding."

"Mom's going to start meeting him for conversion classes. She blabbed everything about her real mother."

"You told Myna to cause that scene at the airport, didn't you? She called you that night after I talked to her."

Nadia shrugged. "You'll probably stay at home now, huh?"

"Yes."

"Good idea."

Olivia came in. "Oh, my God," she gasped, covering her mouth. She stared at Myna for a while, then turned away.

None of us spoke for a minute or two. Then Nadia said, "So why such a small part? You tell Peperchuck he had small parts?"

Olivia smiled. "No," she said, "I just wouldn't have sex with him."

Nadia nodded.

"I'm still a virgin," Olivia announced. "You may as well admit you were wrong for once in your life."

"What?" I asked.

"Nadia bet me I couldn't make it to Hollywood without sleeping my way there."

"You're not there yet," Nadia pointed out. Then she said, "Did you know Jonson here is thinking about writing screenplays? You should collaborate."

"Over my dead body," Olivia said before I could object.

Now we all gasped.

Then we burst out laughing.

"Why do my children find the death of their grandparents funny?" Mom had come into the room. I guess we all found that funny, because all four of us cracked up.

Mom and the Rabbi left with Myna and the paramedics.

And that's when the fun and games ended once and for all.

While hanging up my blazer in the entry hall closet, I discovered an old copy of the Purity Test in one of its pockets. I'd just unfolded it when the doorbell rang.

As per my years of conditioning, I instinctually headed for the steps. I'd actually taken two before I realized what I was doing.

Nadia and Olivia were both upstairs, so I went and opened the door.

"Wheeere's *Livy?*" a man sang, shoving something — a box — directly into my face. When it moved I found myself confronted by two drunk men wearing mullets and black Metallica T-shirts. Without warning, the bigger one punched me directly in the eye, which seemed to detonate inside my skull. My knees went to jelly and I crumpled. One of them pushed me down on my back, then both stepped on my chest as they came inside. I heard the door shut and lock. Then I was yanked to my feet and dragged toward the steps.

"Yoo-hoo! *Liiiivy!*" the men called, hauling me upstairs. Music was coming from the third floor, Madonna's *Holiday*. When we reached the second floor, I managed to say, "There's no Liv —" but I was dropped on my face. A boot stomped my back, crushing the wind out of me. Then I was hauled up again by my belt and dragged to the third floor.

The bigger man kicked the pink door open. Olivia, sitting on her bed looking at photo albums, jolted, spilling them on the floor. She'd been crying.

"Liv!" the smaller man cried, waving the box he'd shoved in my face. He tossed it at Olivia, who didn't react. The box hit her and fell to the floor. It was a video sleeve. My sister was on the cover, a topless genie rubbing a penis-shaped lamp.

Olivia looked terrified at the sight of me, but she spoke. "You're the porn guys," she said. "You're the ones who always —"

"Worked on all them other bitches," the larger man spat. He stepped forward and backhanded Olivia across the face, knocking her right off the bed. She didn't even try to get up. I was still in agony — flashes of light were bursting in my eye — but the shock of seeing my sister struck was profound.

"What the fuck is going on in here?"

Nadia was there. We were going to be okay.

There was a brief moment during which the men seemed too surprised to speak. My uninjured eye was open, and I could see Nadia lacing them with a wicked look of condescension. "Oh, *please*," she sneered. "You two limpdicks can't afford the price of a video, is that it? Or did you short out your Betamax jacking off into it?"

The men looked at each other. The agony in my eye subsided a moment as I waited for them to skulk away.

But that's not what happened.

Without a word, the smaller man grabbed Nadia by the hair, bent her over, and kneed her in the stomach. I heard her gasp as the air went out of her. She fell in a heap.

No one had hold of me, and I was on my feet, but I couldn't move. I told my body to attack, but it wouldn't obey.

"Get rid of him," the bigger man said.

This time I was punched in the nose. Bones broke and seemed to impale my brain. I dropped like dead weight and was shoved into the closet. I heard Olivia's dresser moved in front of the door.

"You boys really are my biggest fans, aren't you?" I heard Olivia say. The closet door was thin and slatted. Her voice cracked, but it had some of *Olivia* in it. "I guess you fellas deserve a backstage pass."

"That's what I'm talkin' about! Told you, she'd come around if we showed her who was boss! Told you!"

I somehow got to my feet and found my voice, but all I could do was scream, "Nooo!" while blood poured out of my mouth. I pounded on the door so hard I felt bones snap in my hand.

"Shut up!" one of them shouted, kicking the dresser into the door.

I stopped pounding.

"Dude! Look! Strip show!"

"Told you, motherfucker!"

I pressed my head into the slats. I could feel Olivia's clothes and hangers against my back. Madonna was still singing. The men cheered.

I knew everyone was going to be okay. I could handle this. Everyone always said I could handle anything.

But they'd always been wrong.

The song ended.

"I'll take the other one," one of them said.

"No!" This was Olivia, her voice firm now. "I want you both," she said. "I don't share."

"Holy," both men said.

I heard the springs on the bed creak.

I banged my head on the door.

"No!" I screamed, banging my head. "No! No! No!"

"Shut the fuck up!"

I banged my head, banged my head, banged my head—but the door wouldn't break.

Instead, I blacked out.

I came to on the floor looking at the space where the door didn't quite meet the carpet. I put my lips to it. "Nadia," I hissed. There was no response. My hand hurt too much to knock on the door, but I twisted the knob. The door actually opened a bit before hitting the dresser. I could see into the room.

Six feet on the bed. Noises I would not hear.

Nadia in the fetal position on the floor. Her unblinking eyes staring right at me.

"Nadia," I whispered. "Stand up. Right now. Stand up."

She obeyed.

"Push the dresser out of the way. Do it right now."

Nadia tried to push the dresser away, but the carpet made it hard to move. My vision was nearly gone, but I could see she had no expression on her face. None at all. She didn't look over at Olivia even once.

The dresser finally moved. The door opened enough for me to slide out.

It sounded like the world was under water.

I wasn't in a hurry, but I walked swiftly to my room. Blood was still running freely down my chin.

I dragged the broadsword out of my closet and carried it back to Olivia's room.

Nadia wasn't there anymore.

I walked to the bed and raised the sword above my head.

The men with my sister had their eyes closed. Olivia's eyes were open. She stopped her act for just an instant and looked into my eyes.

PART V

I opened an eye on a blurry hospital room. I was in the bed. It hurt to see, to think, to breathe. My nose was packed. My hand was throbbing. My eye was patched, and my ears were ringing. It was nearly forty-eight hours later.

Mom was there. Her eyes were red and puffy from sobbing, but now she cried from joy. Olivia was there too, sitting in a visitor's chair with her legs tucked up under her. She was wearing her favorite ripped jeans and a long sweater, looking exactly like she always did: radiant. Silent tears rolled down her face when she saw my open eye.

Two cops came in. They asked me to describe what happened a dozen times, making me repeat what I remembered over and over. They seemed fixated on Nadia, what she'd done, not done, and where I thought she might have gone when I went to get the sword. I had no idea.

They said in all likelihood there weren't going to be any kind of manslaughter charges.

Evidently, it was important that I'd swung the sword only twice.

After Olivia shoved the dead men off of her, she dialed our family's favorite three-digit phone number. I was on the floor, unconscious.

I don't know how to write what comes next.

Nadia is dead.

When I went for the sword, she went down to my parents' bathroom and took a month's worth of Mom's Valium. They eventually found her in her closet.

I had no idea Mom was taking Valium.

It turns out Nadia was never admitted to Swarthmore. She'd paid a girl with an apartment there to pretend they were roommates and to call her if any of us phoned.

Nadia used the money Mom gave her for school to rent the Murphy's house. She'd been living right across the street from us the whole time. I mooned her the night I was almost with Darby.

Who, Olivia told me, has since been diagnosed with that new and horrible disease, AIDS. Olivia also told me that Nadia knew Darby's reputation. She may have saved my life that night.

Which got me thinking.

The night of the No-Touch affair, Nadia left me alone in her room for a few minutes, evidently to intercept Cory in the hall. She knew it was Olivia's turn, and she had the ponytail holder in her pocket. Here's what I think: her original plan wasn't to "implant a lifelong sexual inferiority complex" in Sandy Sikofski, but rather in Olivia.

And here's what else I think: she was trying to save our disastrous beauty of a sister from herself. The bet they had about Olivia's virginity tells me she never stopped trying.

I now suspect that Nadia only really started working on her high school diploma after Olivia made that fuss about not being able to live with her anymore, the night Dad "went off the rails" — the night she promised to leave Olivia alone in exchange for favors.

I think the only reason Nadia left the house was to keep Olivia in it.

Like Mom, Nadia didn't want any of us to leave home. Unlike

Mom, she tried to keep us there. She got Myna to move in, maybe to supervise us in her stead. She arranged it so that Olivia didn't move out for college, and when I managed to leave, she essentially suggested me into failing my way back.

I only wish she'd done a better job with Dad. I asked my Mom to bring me copies of his books. She's going to read them to me when I'm not writing.

I think Nadia never could live in this world. I think she knew we could, though, however imperfectly. And I think she might have hated us for that.

I have a theory: my sister could not separate love and hate.

When there was nothing more to tell me, Mom asked why I had a Hebrew word tattooed on my head.

Of course, I scoffed at the very idea, but she brought over the little magnifying mirror she kept in her purse and held it just above my forehead. Some hair had been shaved for the stitches they put in.

There were tiny Hebrew letters there. I was speechless.

"*Emet*," Mom said. "Rabbi Glickman told me it means 'truth.' Do you want to talk about this?"

Cory wasn't Nadia's only art project that day in Jake's basement. She must have seen Daniel's tattooing paraphernalia in the kitchen. That's why I thought I'd cut my scalp the next morning.

"They can remove it when you're all healed up," Mom said. "If you want. But it's not like anyone can see it, thank goodness."

"I think I'll keep it."

A golem is animated when the word *emet* is written upon its forehead. It can only be stopped when the first letter is removed, creating the word, *met,* which means 'dead.'

I don't think I'll take any chances, not where Nadia is concerned.

I was my sister's puppet, but that was just as well because I couldn't think for myself. I want her back. I want to tell her that I love her and that now she's not the only person in the world who can understand people better than they understand themselves. I want to tell her that even though the world and everyone in it might be insane — every last Schwartz included — we will be okay because we are a family.

She left a note.

It said she'd followed Olivia to one of her tapings and found the two scumbags who'd been trying to lure her to their phony porno shoot. She'd threatened them a thousand ways to keep away from her, but she didn't know they hadn't known Olivia's real name.

Which she'd used.

That's all it said.

Leon. Myna. My father. And now my sister. I've lost more of my immediate family in 1980's Pittsburgh than my grandparents lost during the Holocaust.

What does that mean?

AFTERWORD

"Hallo?" said a man in black, sticking his head into the room. "I saw the Rabbi leaving from down the hall."

It was after lunch the next day. An hour earlier, Rabbi Glickman had found Olivia and me sitting silently in my room. We hadn't said a single word to each other all morning, but she'd stayed with me all night and didn't appear to have plans to leave any time soon. The Rabbi talked to us awhile about grief and the inevitability of loss. I'm sure it was valuable, but neither of us listened. The speech ended when my mother came in because they left to talk privately. We'd just watched him steady Mom with an arm on their way out.

Olivia predicted they'd be married in less than a year. I said I thought that would be good. Then she said Mom told her I was moving into the garret, which was cool with her. She admitted there was no movie offer and said she was going to take over Nadia's lease at the Murphys with a few girlfriends—not video girlfriends, she promised. I said I thought that would be good, too.

The man in black was Rabbi Emanuel Speigleman. "It was I who arranged your father's travel to Hebron," he said. "I tried many times to speak with your mother."

This is what he told us:

Dad's decision to go to Israel was the result of our meeting with Rabbi Glickman, but it had nothing at all to do with my mother's falsely related phone calls or divine intervention for my grandmother's supposed moral failings.

It had to do with the story Myna told Rabbi Glickman about her defeating that anti-Semite who invaded their store to throw pennies at them. Dad told Rabbi Speigleman that he had absolutely no memory of the endless harassing he'd endured throughout his childhood.

Upon recalling the incident, Dad realized, with a clarity of mind he'd never experienced before, that his entire life—every word he'd ever committed to paper—was motivated by a need to prove to the world and to himself that he wasn't a greedy Jew.

One way to do this, of course, was not to be a Jew.

But my father was far more ambitious than that. There would be no religion at all, for anyone.

Dad admitted to Rabbi Speigleman that a single stalk of fear had secretly governed his life, a marrow-deep certainty that at the end of the long, hot day, his family would be crammed into the boxcar when the boxcars were once again crammed.

When the bad guys threw pennies, Dad wanted someone to throw quarters back. He went to live with the Halacha because they weren't afraid to defend themselves. He wanted to learn what that meant.

But Nadia was right: he never planned for a moment to leave his family, whom he loved with all his heart.

When we asked what came of Myna writing to the group about Dad's real identity and Mom's true lineage, Rabbi Speigleman told us it made no difference. He said they'd somehow known who my father was all along. They'd pretended to be fooled because they thought they could convert him—a big prize—after which they'd worry about the rest of his family.

We said we'd tell our mother right away.

When Rabbi Speigleman left, I turned to Olivia. "He was scared and confused," I said. "He was only scared and confused."

Suddenly, I understood why in the garret the night my father died I was so certain I could never throw over everything I believed.

I'm happy to say that now I think such a thing might someday be possible.